VOLUME FOUR

AIRSHIP 27 PRODUCTIONS

The Purple Scar Volume Four

"Seven Swans a' Swimming" ©2023 Gene Moyers
"The Scar's Close Shave" ©2023 Felix Cruz
"Golem Clay" ©2023 Michael Housel
"The Blackmail Heist" ©2023 Fred Adams Jr.

Published by Airship 27 Productions
www.airship27.com
www.airship27hangar.com

Interior illustrations ©2023 Chuck Bordell
Cover illustration ©2023 Adam Shaw

Editor: Ron Fortier
Associate Editor: Jonathan Sweet
Marketing and Promotions Manager: Michael Vance
Production Designer: Rob Davis.

ISBN: 978-1-953589-44-6

Printed in the United States of America

1 2 3 4 5 6 7 8 9 0

THE PURPLE SCAR

VOLUME FOUR
CONTENTS

What is so valuable about seven small ceramic swans that a mysterious gunmen would kill to possess them all? The Purple Scar hunts for both the answer and the savage killer.

When a gang of young hoods start a crime spree, the Purple Scar intervenes only to discover a greater evil has been unleashed on his city.

The Purple Scar battles one of the most hideous villains he has ever encountered. A soulless monster in clay.

When a friend of Doc Murdock is framed for thievery, it is up to the Purple Scar to prove him innocent.

SEVEN SWANS A' SWIMMING

GENE MOYERS

The sign painted on the window glass read *Hansen's Fine Art and Furnishings*. As Dale Jordan pushed open the door a bell connected to it tinkled pleasantly. Inside, the store was filled with displays of ceramic pottery, vases and small statues. Paintings adorned the walls. There were items of decorative furniture scattered about such as standing Grandfather clocks and glass fronted collectible cabinets. There was even a full sized suit of armor which a portly gentleman was standing in front of. He was speaking to a well-dressed man who nodded and moved off to look at some vases.

The portly man smiled at Dale as he crossed the room toward her, "Good day. May I help you find something?"

The tall, graceful woman stepped forward her hand outstretched, her green eyes sparkling, "Hello, I'm Dale Jordan, I'm redecorating my apartment and I've heard good things about your shop so I thought I'd drop by and see what kind of things you have."

The portly man shook her hand lightly and said, "Miss Jordan, I'm Frances Hansen the owner. It's a pleasure to meet you." He gestured with his hand, "Please feel free to look around. We have some very nice pieces in stock. I have been importing many new items from Europe lately."

Dale pushed a lock of her luscious Reddish-brown hair back from her face and smiled again, "Thank you Mr. Hansen, I will." At that moment the door opened with a tinkle and a uniformed delivery man entered. Consulting a clipboard he called out, "Delivery for Hansen?"

Hansen hustled forward, "That's me." He signed the paperwork while the delivery man returned pushing a large wooden crate on a portable hand truck. He pushed it toward the back of the store where Hansen helped him set it on a work table near a curtained door to a back room. The delivery man wheeled out his truck, tipping his hat to Dale as he left.

Dale gravitated to a table of ceramic bowls and vases. Toward the back Hansen had produced a small crow bar and began to open the newly delivered crate. Dale examined several of the vases but decided they weren't what she was looking for. She moved toward a display of mantle clocks, some of marble and some of beautifully carved wood. She was looking one over closely when she glanced toward the rear of the store.

Hansen had the top of the crate open and was lifting something from the interior. He brushed off the clinging excelsior and exposed a delicately sculpted ceramic swan. Dale found herself drawn closer. The swan was beautifully painted in realistic colors. Hansen placed it on the table next to the crate and once again reached inside. Dale watched with interest. To her surprise, he pulled out another gracefully molded swan. The pose was different from the first but it had obviously been sculpted by the some person. Dale exclaimed, "Oh, A set."

Hansen looked at her and nodded, "Yes, that's what I ordered."

"They're beautiful. May I see one?"

"Of course," he handed her the statue and returned to the crate. Dale examined the statue closely. It was delicate and quite beautiful. She decided that she had to have one…maybe both of them. She was surprised when Hansen remarked, "Well, what's this?" Dale turned to find him brushing excelsior from a third swan. Wonderingly Dale asked, "How many are there?"

Hansen frowned, "I don't know. I was only expecting two birds in the set I ordered." He set the bird down and dug once more into the crate. Minutes later the crate was empty and seven swans sat on the table. Dale marveled at them. They were all very similar but each was carved in slightly different poses. Together the set was quite impressive. Hansen scratched his head, "What am I going to do with all these swans? I ordered two matched swans…not seven."

Dale spoke up quickly, "First, you can sell two of them to me. And these are so beautiful I don't think you're going to have any trouble selling the rest." Hansen was pleasantly surprised. They quickly came to terms with Dale paying what she considered a reasonable price. As she left the store fifteen minutes later marveling at her good fortune, she met a prosperous looking couple just coming in. The man tipped his hat as he held the door for Dale. Once outside she smiled thinking how wonderful the swans would look in her living room.

+++

Back at the Swank Street clinic of famous plastic surgeon Dr. Miles Murdock, Dale changed back into her starched nurse's uniform and prepared the surgery for work. When the room was prepared, his instruments laid out in order, she knocked at his office door and entered.

Dr. Miles Murdock looked up from a patient's chart he was going over. His handsome features lit up with a smile and his black eyes sparkled when saw his attractive nurse, "Dale, is everything ready?"

"Ready doctor. It's almost time for the finest plastic surgeon in America to perform another miracle."

Doc laughed briefly as he ran a hand through his curly black hair, "I wish I were that good Dale. But I do what I can."

Gazing fondly at the man she loved Dale replied, "We'll ask the parents of this little girl what they think when you're finished."

Doc stood up and walked around the desk carrying the chart. He reached his other hand out to guide his fiancé toward the door, "We'd better go then. The Drapers should be here any minute."

Minutes later Doc was greeting the Drapers and their little girl. He had examined the girl and previously consulted with them several times. They were more than ready for the surgery. Their daughter Sally had been born with a cleft palate. They were well off financially and had searched the country for the best doctor to treat their daughter. Their search had brought them to Akelton and Dr. Murdock.

Doc for his part was more than happy to help them. He would not even have charged them if they could not afford the treatment but since they could, he would gratefully accept payment. It was payment from wealthy clients that financed his work with the poor at his Down Street clinic in a poorer part of the city.

Soon they were in the surgery and ready to begin. Dale administered the ether while Doc held Sally's hand and reassured her. When the child was unconscious Doc, took a breath and held out his hand. Dale placed an instrument in it and Doc leaned over to begin the surgery.

Hours later, the surgery over, Doc was washing up. Dale commented, "That was wonderful work you did, Miles. You're going to change that girl's life."

Doc nodded, "I hope so. Not to mention the people we can help with the fee."

Dale agreed. They made small talk and it was then Dale told him of her purchase of the swans. Doc offered to take her home so he could see them. Soon both Dale and Doc were dressed in street clothes and closing up the clinic. Doc then piloted his roadster across town to one of their favorite restaurants. After a leisurely dinner he drove her and the swans' home. Once inside her apartment, Dale unwrapped them. Doc's comment was, "You're right, they are beautiful. Where are you going to put them?"

Dale frowned and moved toward a side table "Maybe, one here" she said thoughtfully. Meanwhile Doc was examining one swan closely, "How many of these things did you say there were?"

Dale answered, "Seven, Why?"

Doc smiled and whistled a few notes a popular Christmas song about gifts, "It just reminded me."

Dale gave him an old fashioned look, "Very funny. Besides, Christmas is nearly three months away."

"Just trying to get in the mood," Doc replied with a grin. He stayed long enough to help get her new purchases arranged then headed home himself.

Doc lived on the top floor of his Swank Street clinic. He had converted the whole floor into a comfortable space for himself and his work. As well as his private quarters, it also contained a well-equipped gym and a complete studio in which he sculpted the faces of those he worked on. As he poured himself a drink, a figure clumped up the stairs leading to the alley behind Swank Street.

A thin, middle-aged man entered the room. He took off his cap and ran his hand through his thinning hair. Seeing Doc, glass in hand he spoke, "I could sure use one of those Doc, seein' as how you're pouring." Doc obligingly poured a drink for the little man. Taking the glass Tommy Pedlar sipped gratefully. Doc waited a moment before asking, "How are things on the streets?"

Tommy replied, "I've talked to every fence, stoolie and low life I can think of and nobody's got a line on this new cat burglar. There's a lot of talk about him but nobody knows nothin." He paused and sipped, "He must be from outta town. And he must be sitting on his loot because he isn't using any local fences we know."

Doc nodded, "So we're looking for somebody new in town. Maybe we ought to start checking hotels. Keep on it, Tommy. I want to know more about this guy, whoever he is."

Tommy stood up, "Right Doc." He turned to leave but stopped, "All the joints this guy has been hittin' are high class. How does he know who to rob if he's new in town?"

Doc stroked his chin, "That's a good question Tommy. I need to think about that." Tommy nodded and trotted down the back stairs. Doc prepared for bed his mind wide awake with questions.

Two days later Dale left the Down Street clinic and headed home. It was nearly seven o'clock. Doc had seen more than the usual number of patients at the clinic today and she was tired. Reaching home she made herself a simple dinner while listening to the radio. She tried reading the new issue of *Argosy* that had just arrived but found she couldn't keep her eyes open. She soon gave up and after making sure the door was locked, went to bed.

Much later Dale woke up. It was dark in her room. The only light came through her drawn drapes. She wondered what time it was and then wondered why she had woken up. She closed her eyes to get back to sleep but they immediately flew open as she heard a noise from somewhere in the apartment. Dale sat up and listened for a moment then reached for her robe lying across the foot of the bed. She slipped it around her shoulders and silently slid open the small drawer in the nightstand next her bed. She pulled out a hammerless .32 automatic and crept toward the door to her bedroom.

Listening at the door she heard nothing. She eased it further open and slid into the hallway. As she moved forward she again heard a slight rustling from the darkened living room. There, the light from a wide open window revealed a black clad figure moving across the room. Reaching blindly to her left she found a light switch and pressed it 'on.' Light flooded the room and she squinted against the glare. A thin figure dressed completely in black, including gloves and a black mask covering his lower face, stood reaching for one of her swans on a side table. A bulging, cloth knapsack was on his back. Both the intruder and Dale froze for a split second. Then Dale raised her pistol and the black clad intruder turned and dove over her sofa to the floor behind it. Shocked Dale called out, "Don't move," and edged toward the telephone on a table against the wall.

Her intruder did not co-operate. Instead he sprang for the open window. Dale threw up her gun but held her fire. The intruder seemed to be committing suicide as he disappeared through the sheer curtains. Dale waited for the scream but heard nothing. She moved cautiously to the window and stuck her head out through the wavering curtains. Looking down three floors all she saw was empty sidewalk illuminated by a nearby street light. Nonplussed she looked to her right and there, edging along a narrow ledge, face to the wall was the intruder. She watched in amazement as he sidestepped along the ledge, arms spread and chest pressed to the stone work. He came to the corner edged carefully around it and disappeared from view.

Dale pulled her head back in to the apartment and turned toward the phone. She set down her gun and picked up the receiver in one hand and the candlestick base in the other. She was about to call the operator and ask for the police when she thought better of it. Instead she dialed a familiar number. When Doc answered in a sleepy voice Dale spoke calmly, "Miles, I just surprised a cat burglar in my apartment. Can you come over right away?" Doc answered in the affirmative and Dale hung up.

Fifteen minutes later Dale opened the door and Doc rushed in. Grabbing her shoulders he looked concerned and asked, "Are you all right?"

Dale nodded, "I'm fine, just a little shook up." Doc led her to the sofa and sat next to her as she related all that had happened since she had gone to bed. When she had finished her tale Doc looked thoughtful, "And he took nothing else?"

"The only thing missing is one of my new swans." She pointed to where it had been. Doc stood up and went to the window and looked out. He then turned shaking his head. Next he moved to across to the remaining swan. He hefted it and then turned it in his hands examining it carefully. Finally he looked at Dale, "I think the man who burglarized your place tonight is the mysterious new cat burglar that has been operating in town lately. Tommy and I have been trying to find him but he is elusive and smart." He thought for a moment, "I wonder why he wanted these?" He handed the swan back to Dale and said, "Tell me more about this shop where you bought these swans."

Dale quickly related the story with Doc interrupting to ask questions. When she was finished he praised her level headedness then glanced at his watch, "It's nearly four o'clock. I want you to pack enough clothes for a few days. Also gather up anything else you may need. You can't stay here alone. And don't forget the swan. He'll be back for it."

+++

Just before noon the next day Doc left the Down Street clinic and drove across town. Dale had returned and spent the rest of the night at Swank Street. Tonight she would stay inside the clinic in one of his patient rooms. Doc would feel better if she and the swan were safely at Swank Street where he could keep an eye on them. Now he was on the way to Hansen's art store. He needed to find out more about these swans.

As he pulled to a stop near the shop he could see a police cruiser just pulling away. Doc frowned as he parked and walked to the shop. There was a closed sign hanging in the door window and it was locked. This was not a good sign Doc thought as he knocked. He was afraid their friend the talented thief had already been here looking for the other swans. Finally the door was opened by a thin, stoop shouldered man in a black suit. He only opened the door half way and said, "Sorry, the store is closed."

Doc replied, "Yes, I understand but it is very important that I speak to Mr. Hansen."

The man looked surprised, "Then you haven't heard?"

Doc felt his heart sink, "Heard what?"

"Why, Mr. Hansen has been killed."

"When did this happen?"

"Almost three days ago now."

Doc had a bad feeling. That was the day Dale had bought the swans from Hansen. He spoke again, "I may have some information regarding this terrible event. May I come in?"

The man hesitated and then swung the door open. Doc entered and asked the man's name. It turned out his name was Walker. He had worked for Hansen for years. Now he was taking inventory to see what was missing since the police thought the murder was committed during a robbery that Hansen had come upon. Doc listened carefully then posed some questions, "What time did this take place?"

"The police aren't sure, but they think sometime between closing at six and nine o'clock when his wife came looking and found him." Doc winced slightly at that unpleasant thought, "Have you discovered anything missing?"

"Not yet. I was just finishing up. There is no money missing and the entire inventory seems to be accounted for, as far as I can tell." This surprised the surgeon. He was sure the swans must have been the reason for the break in and murder. His train of thought was interrupted by the employee continuing, "In fact the only thing I have found missing is the sales ledger. And who would steal something like that?"

Doc could easily imagine who. He asked politely, "That is some kind of list of all your sales?"

The man held his hands more than a foot apart, "Yes, it is a large, leather bound book in which we write down every sale." He frowned, "But you said you knew something about why Mr. Hansen was killed."

Doc smiled disarmingly, "Yes. I may very well have a motive for all this and I will be speaking to the police very soon. Of that you can be reassured. But tell me, where are the swans that Mr. Hansen received three days ago?"

Surprised, the clerk had to shift mental gears, "Swans? Why do you want to know about the swans?"

Doc replied carefully, "I believe someone may have been looking for them."

The clerk looked confused, "But they're not here. They all sold the same day they arrived. Mr. Hansen was quite surprised."

Doc nodded, that was what he had been afraid of. He then asked, "Is that the only record you had of the sales?"

"Well…no, there are the sales receipts. They need to be sorted but we still have them." Doc asked eagerly, "May I see those, please?"

The clerk was getting suspicious at Doc's questions, "I don't think so. I think you need to talk to the police."

Realizing he had played out this hand Doc decided another method needed to be tried. He turned to leave the store thanking the clerk for his co-operation. The clerk pursued him out to the sidewalk and called out, "What did you say your name was?"

Doc just waved as he hopped in his roadster, made a U-turn and sped away.

Back at the Swank Street clinic Doc was examining Dale's swan with a magnifying glass when she walked in, "What did you find out from Mr. Hansen?"

Doc looked at her soberly, "I'm afraid Mr. Hansen is dead, Dale. And, all the swans are gone as well as the sales ledger."

Dale's hand flew to her mouth, "That's terrible. He was such a nice man." Doc agreed, "Yes, it is terrible. It also means that your burglar was somehow involved with Hansen's murder. He is more dangerous than I thought."

"What are we going to do?"

"We are going to find out what is so special about this swan." He walked to the X-ray machine. Dale understood his intention and moved to help. A half hour later the two stood in front of the illuminated X-ray. Dale sighed,

"I don't see anything."

"No. There's nothing inside," Doc agreed.

"But Miles, if there's nothing inside the swan why would the thief want it?"

Doc was silent for a moment, "Just because there's nothing inside this one doesn't mean there isn't something inside one of the others... something important." He looked at his watch, "Right now we've got to get back to work. But this is getting serious." As they both headed back to the front of the clinic Doc added, "I have to talk to Tommy."

The afternoon passed quickly. Doc had Dale cancel his last patient. As they closed up just before five that evening he told Dale to stay inside and be careful. He then walked upstairs to his private quarters. There he changed into a dark suit. Going to a wall safe he spun the dial and pulled out a .38 revolver. He checked the load and put in a holster that he strapped to his right hip under his jacket. He added a set of master keys and a pencil flashlight to his pockets. Lastly he pulled what appeared to be a limp rubber mask from the safe and stashed it in a hidden pocket inside his jacket.

As he completed his preparations Tommy strolled in. Doc turned, "Just the man I'm looking for."

"What's going on Doc?"

Doc brought his confidant and right hand man up to date and finished with, "So, it's more important to find our burglar than ever. And put out the word about the stolen swans. Someone on the street must know something." Tommy nodded, "What about you, Boss?"

"I'm going back to Hansen's shop. The clerk may be a little more forthcoming if he's paid a visit by the Purple Scar." Tommy nodded and left via the back stairway. Doc followed and quickly made his way to his roadster. Minutes later he was pulling up near the mouth of an alley. He parked and seeing no one taking any interest in him he slipped inside. He made his way through alley and reached a side street at the other side. He crossed the street and entered the alley that ran behind Hansen's shop. In the shadows he pulled the rubber mask from its pocket and pulled it over his face. Miles Murdock had vanished. Instead the figure standing in the alley wore the horribly scarred face of the Purple Scar.

The Scar moved silently down the alley until he found the rear door of the art shop. Using his master keys he tried to open the lock. It turned on the third key he tried. He pocketed his keys and drew his revolver. Opening the door he quickly slipped inside closing the door quietly behind him.

"No. There's nothing inside."

He made his way carefully past shelves full of merchandise and empty shipping crates. Eventually he could see a curtained doorway leading to the front of the store. Barely parting the curtain the Scar peered through and saw the back of Walker the clerk. He appeared to be writing a note on a pad of paper.

Walker was an apparent innocent so the Scar had some reservations about what he was about to do but saw the necessity of it. Other innocent people might be hurt if he didn't get a grasp on what was going on. He stepped forward and pressed the un-cocked revolver against the Walker's back, simultaneously he grated out in his fearsome tone, "Don't cry out. Just step back through the curtain." Walker stiffened then stepped slowly back three steps. Once through the curtain the Scar grabbed Walker's shoulder and spun him around.

He quickly holstered his weapon. He then leaned toward the clerk and whispered hoarsely, "Do you know who I am?"

He could see the clerk's face go pale even in the dim light of the back room. He licked his lips and nodded. The Scar hissed, "Good. Then you know I mean business. I need to see the sales receipts for the day that Hansen was killed. Now!"

Walker nodded wordlessly and pointed to a desk file that sat on a table used as a desk. The Scar gestured. Walker walked shakily to the table and turned on a goose neck light that illuminated the table. He winced away from the Purple Scar's horrific visage as he asked in a quavering voice, "What do you want?"

"I want the sales receipts for all seven swans that were sold the day of Hansen's death."

Walker turned back to the file and sorted through the file of receipts. It took a couple of minutes because his hands were shaking but he finally came up with a handful of yellow copies. He reached them out to the frightening figure. Scar took the receipts and asked, "Is this all of them?"

Walker nodded and asked shakily, "What's so important about them?"

The Scar shoved the receipts into a side pocket of his jacket, "That's not important for you to know but they might just save someone's life. Now just sit there and wait until I'm gone." Walker nodded and the Scar faded toward the rear of the store. He let himself out into the alley and dashed to the far end where he had entered. He pulled off his mask and stuffed it back into its hidden pocket. He then walked calmly across the side street and entered the alley opposite. He then ran down it toward his car. Minutes later he was driving casually back to Swank Street.

Late that evening as Doc gobbled a hastily made sandwich in his kitchen he examined the receipts. There were five of them. Dale's purchase was the first. Then followed three individual purchases. Lastly one person had purchased the final two swans. Doc sat back and thought to himself. All seven swans had been purchased the day they had arrived. Certainly Dale's purchase had been coincidental. She had been shopping when they were delivered. But it was unlikely that all the rest of the purchases had been just as casual.

Glancing at his watch Doc decided there was still time to pay a visit to some of the swan buyers this evening. Pocketing the receipts he grabbed his hat and headed for the back steps.

He located the first address easily. It was a large house in one of the nicer residential areas of Akelton. Lights illuminated the house. Regretting how he had frightened Walker, Doc decided on an open approach at first. He walked boldly up to the front door and knocked firmly. A moment later the door was opened by a well-dressed man, his jacket off. Doc inquired politely, "Mr. Doakes?"

The man nodded. Doc continued, "I'm interested in locating a certain object that was purchased a few days ago at Hansen's art shop. Do you have in your possession a ceramic swan?"

Doake's face had been rather bored but half through Doc's speech it stiffened and grew hard with interest. When Doc had finished he spoke brusquely, "You aren't with the police. Who are you?"

Doc hesitated, then a thought came to him, "I also purchased a swan. Has anyone approached you about your statuette?"

Doakes looked annoyed, "You mean other than you? Does the guy who broke into the house and stole it last night count?"

Doc kept his face neutral at this news, "You're swan was stolen? Was anything else taken?"

"No, that's the annoying part. I paid a good price for it but there are lots more valuable things in the house. It was a gift for my wife."

"What do the police say about it?"

"What else can they say? They'll do their best but they can't promise anything." He made the last statement in a clearly disgusted voice. When Doc looked expectantly at him he added, "They said it was a professional job, if that's what you're looking for." Doc nodded and thanked the homeowner for his help. As he turned away, Doakes asked him, "Who did you say you worked for?" Doc just waved as he headed back to his car.

On the way to the next name on the list Doc was pessimistic. He felt he was playing catch up. Perhaps the thief already had the rest of the swans. Still he had to try. It was nearly nine o'clock when he pulled up in front of the next name's address. It was a four story apartment building. The door was locked but he found J. Simpson's name next to a buzzer marked 3A. He took a step back and looked up the front the building. There was still one light on the third floor so someone was still up. He pressed the buzzer and waited. Soon a sleepy sounding voice replied, "Who is it?" Doc replied confidently, "Police, Mr. Simpson. We need to speak to you."

The voice came back much more alert, "Uh, sure. I'll buzz you in." The door buzzed and Doc pushed through into the lobby. Ignoring the elevator he took the stairs. Deciding he had been showing his true face around a little too much he tugged out the hideous mask as he climbed. Reaching the third floor he pulled on his mask and gloves and knocked at the door marked 3A. His revolver remained in its holster.

The door opened and a man in shirt sleeves, slippers and a sweater opened the door. Before he had a chance to speak the Scar pushed him back into the apartment and shoved the door closed behind them. The man's face showed his shock. The Purple Scar held up a reassuring hand. Softening his grating tone somewhat he spoke, "I'm not here to hurt you. I just need some information." The man closed his mouth, halting the shout for help he had been about to give. The Scar continued, "Do you know who I am?"

Simpson nodded.

"Then you know I do not harm the innocent. I came here only to find out about the swan statuette you bought recently. Do you still have it?"

Simpson seemed surprised for a moment then nodded, "Yes, but why . . ."

"Why am I interested in it? Other swans sold from that lot are being stolen and the man who sold them is dead. As long as you have that swan, you are in danger."

Getting over his shock Simpson replied, "But it's just a ceramic statue. I paid twelve dollars for it but that's not worth killing for."

"Perhaps not but you are still in danger. Where is the swan?"

"In the living room."

"Get it, please." Simpson turned and entered an arched doorway. By the time he returned holding the swan the Scar had reached in his pocket and peeled off two ten dollar bills. Scar reached out and plucked the swan from Simpson's hands and in return handed him the money, "Take this. I will return the swan when this is all over. Meanwhile you should pack a bag and leave town for a few days."

"Leave town . . .?"

"Immediately. Someone else will come looking for this very soon. You should be gone before he finds out where you are."

The Scar turned and opened the hall door. As he did he heard Simpson say, "You're not who the papers say you are."

Turning back the Scar grated out harshly, "Pack that bag and get out of town…for your own good!" Two minutes later the Scar exited the building and faded into the shadows as he made his way back to the roadster. He had met no one else in the building. He wrapped the swan in a blanket and placed it in the trunk. Pulling off his mask he then motored quietly away.

Locating a late night drug store Doc parked in front and went inside. The clerk looked up from a newspaper he was reading but Doc just held a hand to his head and said, "Telephone?"

The clerk pointed to a far corner, "In the back."

Inside the wooden booth Doc closed the folding door. He put a nickel in the machine and dialed a number. Soon Tommy Pedlar's familiar voice answered. Doc spoke quietly, "Tommy. The swans are being stolen, probably by our cat burglar friend. I have one of the birds. You need to get over to the last name on the list. If no one's there, look around for signs of a break in. If the owner is present, stay there and cover the house. Watch for our burglar. I'll come by and get you in the morning." He quickly gave Tommy the address of Mr. Samuel Jones, the last name on the list of purchasers. Tommy quickly affirmed his orders and hung up. Doc did the same and left the drug store.

Back in his roadster Doc drove to the address of the fourth name list. Sarah Newgarden lived in a modern five story apartment building. Doc parked around the corner in a side street. Pulling out a spare mask he kept in his glove box he slipped it over his head. This face was of an average middle aged man; it was the kind of face you would forget a minute after you had seen it. Doc left the roadster and walked to the front of the apartment building. A quick look showed the lobby empty as well as the street nearby. The disguised Scar pulled out his set of master keys and tried the lobby door. He had it opened in less than a minute and slipped into the lobby. Striding to the wall of metal mailboxes he quickly found the name Newgarden. It was written on the box marked 4C. The Scar nodded and left quietly the way he had come.

He took a good look at the building from the street. There was a rear apartment with lights on that was probably 4C. He made his way around the corner to the fire escape that ran up the side of the building. A quick glance assured him that he was unseen. Jumping up he caught the underside of the ladder and beneath his weight it swung down quietly to the street. Thankfully the apartment building was fairly new and the fire escape well oiled. Climbing up the ladder the Scar let it swing up behind him. He then quickly climbed the metal stairs to the roof. It was cluttered with the usual maze of pipes, vents and the small structure that housed the stairs down into the building. That door was locked. Scar's master keys made quick work of it. He crept silently down the stairwell to the fourth floor.

Cracking the hall door showed a well-lit, but empty, hallway. The Scar made a quick tour of the floor and quickly established that apartment 4C faced out over the alley and the building behind it and was the apartment he had suspected. Back in the stairwell he swapped his forgettable faced mask for the fearsome features of the Purple Scar and quickly climbed back to the roof. Once there he took cover behind the stairwell structure. He checked his revolver and settled in to wait.

Time passed slowly. To keep alert and keep his limbs loose the Scar got up every few minutes and crept silently across the roof checking each side of the building and especially the fire escape. He was sure that an attempt would be made to acquire the final three swans. With Tommy covering the other address one of them would see action soon. Perhaps tonight, perhaps tomorrow but the Scar was sure the burglar would soon put in an appearance.

By four in the morning the Scar knew that it would not happen that night here at Miss Newgarden's apartment. He waited another hour until it was growing light. He climbed down the fire escape and crossed quickly to his car. Removing his mask he drove away. By the time he reached the final address to pick up Tommy the streets were beginning to fill with early morning traffic. Cruising down the street Doc looked for the address but was nonplussed to find that there was no such number. He circled the block to double check, but sure enough the address on the sales receipt did not exist. He checked the receipt again but there was no mistake. Thoughtfully he turned his car for home.

While headed back to Swank Street Doc changed his mind on an impulse and drove back to Simpson's apartment. He parked across the street from the building. Everything seemed peaceful. As he watched a man in a suit left the lobby, a briefcase in one hand. He walked casually to the corner. Doc was just about to start the car when his eye was attracted upward.

A curtain in the window of Simpson's apartment moved. He was disappointed that Simpson hadn't taken his advice when he realized that the curtain was still moving. Doc, looking closely, realized the window was slightly open. Doc's jaw tensed. So that was why it had been quiet at the Newgarden building the night before. The cat burglar had been here looking for Simpson's swan. He grimly hoped that Simpson had not been there. Doc wanted to go in and check the apartment but decided against it. Instead he would slip word to Dan Griffin to have one of his officers check the apartment. He drove away shaking his head; someday soon he would catch up with his elusive adversary.

Back at Swank Street he found Tommy waiting to report about the phony address. Doc brought him up to date. He then sent him to keep an eye on Newgarden's apartment. He did not think the burglar would strike during day time but wanted to be sure. After Tommy had left, Doc took a shower and changed clothes. He was ready to face a new day of patients when Dale entered his private quarters dressed in her crisp, white nurse's uniform, "How did things go last night, Miles?"

He shook his head as he adjusted his tie, "Good and bad. I acquired one more swan but also lost one." He told her about all that had happened the night before. When he had finished his tale Dale frowned, "So we have two swans and they have two for sure. But what about this false address?"

Doc replied, "I think whoever bought the last two swans is the person looking for the others. That's why he gave a phony address. If I'm right, he now has four swans. The only one we can't account for is the one bought by Sarah Newgarden. I have Tommy watching her place now." He shook his head, "The trouble is, with four swans it's very possible that our enemy has already found whatever he's looking for. There was nothing out of the ordinary about your swan. The odds are against us now."

Always optimistic, Dale asked, "Why don't we take a look at the one you got last night?"

Doc agreed and went to fetch it. A thorough examination showed nothing unusual about the statue. It was clearly designed by the same sculptor that had done Dale's swan. It was a slightly different pose but obviously part of the same set. Doc then X-rayed the swan. While the film developed Dale thought about the way Doc had bought the swan from Simpson, "You paid twenty dollars for it. I only paid twelve for mine." She laughed briefly, "I'll bet he would have paid the Purple Scar to take it just to get rid of him."

Doc looked hurt, "I went out of my way to not frighten him too much. He was startled when he recognized me but he was by no means terrified."

"Still, he will certainly have a story to tell, about the time the Purple Scar came calling." She laughed lightly as Doc went to the take the X-ray film from the developer. He held it to the light and stared at it. His stare went on long enough for Dale to ask, "Well, do you see anything unusual?" Doc did not answer immediately. Finally he asked in a quiet voice, "What do you think that is?"

Dale moved over to stand next to him and look up at the exposed film. The swan was perfectly outlined in light gray against the darker film. In the center of the light gray swan image was a white spot. It appeared vaguely triangular in shape with one sharp point and two more rounded corners. She cocked her head to one side and asked, "What is it?"

Doc didn't answer just mused to himself, "It's at least an inch and a half across...maybe more."

Impatiently Dale asked, "But what is it?"

Doc said thoughtfully, "I'd say it's a cut diamond seen from the side, cast in to the ceramic of the swan."

Dale was silent for a moment thinking she hadn't heard her fiancé correctly, "Did you say a diamond?"

"Well, it's the right shape and it's solid enough to show up brightly on the x-ray. Yes, I think it's a precious stone of some kind, and a big one at that."

"But, how can that be?"

Doc lowered the x-ray, "It was obviously cast inside the swan to smuggle it into the country. It makes perfect sense. A small but valuable item is easily hidden inside a cast ceramic. I'm sure it would breeze past customs inspection, especially if was part of a larger shipment." He picked up the swan and hefted it carefully, "This must be why our enemy is so desperate to get all the swans. He must be this mysterious Mr. Jones. Somehow he got there too late to buy all the swans. He later went back, murdered Hansen and stole the sales ledger."

Dale put in, "When I was there poor Mr. Hansen seemed surprised about the swans. He said he was expecting only a set of two swans, not seven."

Doc nodded, "Whoever shipped them got his wires crossed with this Mr. Jones. He must be pretty annoyed that all those swans got away before he got there."

"Well, the store was pretty busy that day. It's not a wonder that ceramics this nice wouldn't last long. So this Mr. Jones must be the cat burglar you've been tracking."

Doc shook his head, "Not necessarily. The burglar might be just a hired hand, kind of a mercenary working of Jones. But we won't know until I catch him tonight."

"Tonight? You seem pretty certain."

Doc smiled, "For the first time we have the advantage. We have the swan with the diamond. The enemy, whoever he is, has no doubt searched all his swans. The only ones he hasn't seen are yours, this one and Sarah Newgarden's. He'll come for that one tonight."

Dale raised an eyebrow and inquired, "And the Purple Scar will be waiting?"

Doc nodded, "He certainly will."

It was shortly after nine o'clock that night. Doc sat in his roadster parked a block down the side street next to the Newgarden apartment building. Tommy had watched the building most of the day. Dale had taken a turn as well. She had canceled his afternoon appointments so Doc could nap. She had also knocked on Sarah Newgarden's door on some pretext. While she had engaged the elderly widow in conversation she had managed to get a vague idea of the apartment layout.

Armed with this additional information Doc was ready for the night's work. He waited for a time when the street was deserted. He checked his pockets for the tools of his trade, double checked his revolver and quickly slipped the hideous mask over his head. With it settled on his face and his hat pulled down low, the Purple Scar slipped out of the roadster and walked casually up the dimly lit street. He reached the same fire escape that he had used the night before and in two minutes was on the roof looking down.

The routine was same as before. The Scar remained quietly in the shadows. Every few minutes or if he heard something suspicious he would patrol around the roof looking for an intruder. He was patient. He was certain the thief would come and stayed alert as the city settled down for the night.

Soon after midnight the Scar's sharp ears detected the quiet scrape of metal somewhere nearby. He stood up and made for the north wall above the fire escape. He took off his hat and craned his head over the edge of the wall just enough to see down. Sure enough a figure clad all in black was quietly climbing the fire escape. As he reached the fourth floor landing the figure stopped to listen and look around. Scar immediately pulled his head back. He counted five and hooked an eye back over the edge. The lithe cat burglar had climbed onto the fire escape railing and was pressing himself flat against the wall. The Scar watched in admiration as the burglar began edging sideways along a ledge a cat couldn't walk along.

His arms spread and his chest pressed against the wall the figure made good time. He reached the corner above the side street entrance to the alley behind the building and edged slowly around it. The Scar crept silently across the roof to where he could look down into the darkened alley. It took a moment for the Scar to make out the figure in the deep shadows but he finally made him out motionless against the building two floors below. As he watched the shadow clinging to the wall seemed to flow into the building below. Clapping his hat back on his head the Scar made for the fire escape. He clambered over the parapet and climbed down the steep escape stairs as quickly as he could while making little or no noise.

Reaching the second floor landing the Scar ignored the swing down final ladder. Instead he swung himself over the railing climbed down to cling to the lowest metal brace and dropped silently to the sidewalk below. He glided silently to the alley entrance and slipped inside. Pressed against the building just inside the alley the Scar looked upward. Silhouetted against the lighter, star filled sky above he could see the wall was empty. He moved further into the alley and across until he had his back against the six foot high brick wall that bordered the alley. On the other side of the wall was a narrow yard behind a three story building.

The Scar waited calmly. It was a gamble allowing the cat burglar into the widow Newgarden's apartment. Unfortunately there was no way of waiting for him there without breaking in and scaring the innocent woman himself. He felt the danger was minimal though. If he was surprised, the burglar would most likely flee as he had when Dale had confronted him.

The Scar had decided the burglar wasn't the man who had brutally killed Hansen. He had been chasing the burglar for only a few weeks. The smuggled stone and swans had been in the works for months. He was convinced the art dealer had been killed by whoever was attempting to smuggle the precious stone into the country. It was unclear if Hansen had

He...stayed alert as the city settled down...

been part of the smuggling or whether he had been killed to cover up the identity of the man who was desperately searching for his smuggled stone. The Scar suspected the latter.

Movement above caught the Scar's attention. Looking up he saw a dark form emerging from a fourth floor window. Drawing his revolver the masked avenger waited. Rather than work his way around the corner the black clad figure began to climb down the wall using the narrow cracks between the large stones to negotiate the wall. Again the Scar admired the skill and strength of the cat burglar.

The burglar quickly reached a point where his feet were no more than twelve or thirteen feet above the ground. The Scar could see that he was a wiry built man, no doubt very strong but trimly built. He could also see what appeared to be a small, black backpack across the thief's shoulders.

The figure stopped climbing and clung where he was to look down into the alley. Simultaneously the Scar raised his pistol; "All right freeze right . . ." The burglar caught sight of the movement below him and did not hesitate. He pushed himself strongly off the wall with hands and feet. In mid-air he pulled himself into a tight tuck, spun and landed briefly feet first on the top of brick wall behind the masked man. He was on the wall for a split second before he flipped backward off the wall into the dark yard on the other side.

The Scar spun around swearing, "Damn it!" He holstered his revolver and immediately threw himself at the brick wall. He scrambled up it and threw himself over the top. The dark clad burglar was just disappearing around the corner of the three story building to Scar's left. He was up and running immediately. As he reached the corner he heard what sounded like a gate slam. Ahead there was a six foot wooden gate. In the life of his alter ego the Scar had lettered in football while in college. His playing days came back to him as he lifted his shoulder and pulled his head down. His shoulder crashed into the wooden gate tearing the latch totally free. Boards also shattered crashing the Scar to the ground. He pushed himself up, shook his head and ran toward the street.

When he reached the street, he saw the figure he was pursuing duck around the corner of a building across the street. The Scar sprinted in pursuit. He reached the corner of the building. The burglar had jumped upward to grab the lowest part of a fire escape and was chinning himself up and onto the lowest level. As the Scar sprinted forward and made a jump for a piece of the escape, the burglar climbed higher. Grunting, the Scar pulled himself up in pursuit. He ducked under a railing and began climbing the steep stairs to the third floor landing. A floor above the burglar looked down. He stopped and changed direction. Climbing up on a railing he stepped off onto a six inch wide ledge that ran horizontally around the building and began edging along it, face against the wall.

The Scar reached that landing as the burglar was edging around the rear corner of the building. Swearing to himself, The Scar followed. He got his toes onto the ledge and spread his arms wide to grip the building and flatten himself against it. He too began edging sideways along the ledge, muttering to himself, "This is not a good idea." He edged toward the corner moving slower than the burglar but making progress nonetheless. He reached the corner and edged around it. He couldn't see the burglar but he couldn't move his head around easily either. Finally he chanced a looked to his left and saw the burglar transferring himself to a standing iron drain pipe that ran down the wall attached periodically to the wall by heavy, metal, wrap around straps.

Scar kept edging forward gritting his teeth as he did. The burglar was working his way down the drain pipe hand over hand. Reaching a point some eight feet away and with the burglar ten feet below him the Scar stopped. The burglar was in his element. On the wall he was faster than his pursuer. He was getting away. Realizing this, the Scar took a deep breath and threw himself sideways. He arced downward. As he brushed past the figure clinging to the drain pipe his gloved fingers scrabbled at the man's back. Finally he got one hand hooked in the burglar's belt.

With the sudden addition of 180 pounds to his back the burglar could not maintain his grip on the pipe. The two figures slid down the pipe six feet before they pulled away from it all together and fell away down the wall. Both men crashed into a pile of trash and overflowing garbage cans. They hit with a crash. The Scar landed feet first on top of a garbage can. The lid flew off, clanging into a wall. The masked avenger's momentum was mostly absorbed by the contents but his momentum knocked the can over and it rolled sideways the Scar half in and half out of it. The burglar crashed through a crate piled with carpet remnants. The crate splintered and collapsed, dumping him unceremoniously on his behind in the alley. He got to his feet but was immediately hit in the back of his legs by the rolling garbage can containing the Purple Scar. He went backwards over the barrel and landed hard on his back.

Squirming out of the barrel the Scar scrambled to his feet just in time to catch a wildly thrown punch from the burglar. He staggered slightly and the burglar turned to run. The Scar dove at him and brought him down in the trash his arms around the burglar's waist. They wrestled there in the filthy alley. The Scar caught an elbow on the jaw just as his fist connected with the burglar's head. He rolled to his feet the burglar did likewise but more slowly. As he reached his feet the Scar caught him with a left-right combination to the jaw and the burglar dropped unconscious to the alley floor.

The masked avenger rubbed his jaw through his mask and let out a long breath. From somewhere above him he heard a voice yell, "Hey! Who's down there?" Spurred by the thought of unseen hands dialing for the police he bent over the motionless burglar. He hefted the unconscious man up, bent forward and threw him across his shoulders. He then turned and scurried for the alley entrance. Out on the sidewalk it took him a moment to get his bearings. Finally he set off in the direction he thought his car was.

He reached it minutes later. He plopped the unconscious burglar in the passenger seat and jumped behind the wheel. He wheeled the car around and drove away with his lights out. Two miles away he pulled over on a quiet street when he sensed the burglar stirring. The Scar dragged the semi-conscious burglar into the shadow of a large building. He let him drop, then bent over and slapped his face to bring him around. The burglar moaned and his eyes fluttered open. The Scar reached to his hip and drew his revolver. The burglar raised his head, one hand held to his jaw and groaned loudly, "Ohhhh, what hit me?"

Brushing aside the man's hand the Scar pushed his gun into the man's face and hissed, "Wake up!"

The burglar's eyes grew wide as he focused on the gun barrel. From what the Scar could see of the man's face in the dim light he was not unattractive. He had dark hair slicked back from a widows peak. His face was thin and he had a fairly strong chin. Together with his lean stature Scar decided he was probably a lady killer…when he was not lying on a sidewalk with blood running down his chin and strongly smelling of rotting garbage. Or was that himself the masked avenger smelled?

The burglar's attention fixed on him; the Scar leaned in and grated out, "Do you know who I am?"

Lips pressed together the burglar nodded.

"Good, let's start with your name."

The burglar just stared stonily back. The Scar said nothing but thumbed back the hammer of his gun to full cock. The burglar flinched away and gasped out, "Flynn. My name is Flynn."

"All right Flynn, you're new in town but you've heard of me. What have you heard?"

Flynn swallowed and whispered, "They say the streets are yours after dark."

"What else do they say?" hissed the man behind the hideous mask.

Flynn paused a moment, "They say that most of the people you go after don't come back."

"That's right. You're good at what you do but now you're mine. So, if you don't want to disappear into the river you'll tell me who hired you to steal these swans." The Scar saw surprise flit across Flynn's face but he remained silent. A quick jab of the Scar's gun barrel into Flynn's soft throat changed that. He gasped out, "Frank. He calls himself Frank."

"Frank, who?"

Flynn shook his head, "I didn't get a last name. He heard about me and tracked me down a few days ago. He gave me a list of names and said I'd get five hundred for each swan I brought him."

The Scar gave this some thought then asked, "How did you make the exchange?"

"Uh, I had a phone number. I'd make a call and we'd meet somewhere at night. I'd give him a swan and he'd give me the money."

"Okay, what's this Frank look like?"

"He's big with brown hair. Looks like hired muscle but he's not dumb. He's smart and dresses too good for a hood."

After another thoughtful moment the Scar shifted topics, "You've been operating in town a few weeks. I've been looking for you and couldn't find you. How did Frank do it? You haven't been using the usual fences or hangouts."

Flynn honestly seemed at a loss as he shrugged, "I don't know. He didn't seem to have any trouble. You're right, I been holding on to my loot. It's just extra anyway."

Interested, the Scar whispered harshly, "What do mean, extra?"

Flynn thought for a moment. Then he reluctantly spoke, "I was working up north; Chicago, Milwaukee, Detroit. Things were getting a little hot and I was gonna move on but I meet this guy in a bar where I hung out. He seemed to know who I was. He says that Akelton is the place to go. Lots of sweet jobs and nobody like me working the town."

Now the masked avenger was really interested, "Who was this 'guy'?"

A shrug, "Never saw him before. He was well dressed and educated, I'd say. He just gave me an Akelton telephone number and told me if I ever showed up there to give it a call."

"So?"

"So I decided to give Akelton a try. I got into town and cased things. Sure enough it looked like pickings were good. I heard about you but I don't carry a gun and I figured if I pulled just a few big scores and didn't hurt anybody I could probably stay outta your way."

"What about the phone number?"

"Yeah, well I pull a couple of jobs and decide to give it a call. A voice told me that some people were looking for a high class second story man to pull some special jobs. When I asked what kind of jobs, the guy just said it was private stuff, papers mostly. I get what they want and I could keep anything else I found. They then buy what I stole for them and I could make out twice for every score."

Inside, the Scar was quite surprised to hear all this. It put a whole different light on Flynn's burglaries. He grated out, "How did you make these exchanges with Frank."

Flynn seemed surprised, "Naw, I never met Frank until a few days ago. Most of what I stole was papers, files, notebooks, that sort of thing. I was given an address and mailed them off. Money then came in the mail."

The Scar thought for a moment, "So you've held onto most of your loot?"

Reluctantly, "Yeah, it's back in my room."

Standing up straight the masked man gestured with his gun and growled, "Sit up and take off that backpack. Don't even think about trying anything. I haven't shot anybody this week and I'm getting kind of itchy."

Flynn sat up and did as he was told. When the pack was lying on the sidewalk, the Scar told him to rollover, face down. Flynn held up a hand and looked scared, "Hey, I told you everything I know. You don't have to plug me!"

"I'm not gonna shoot you…yet."

Keeping the gun on the thief Scar opened the back pack with his free hand. Sure enough a ceramic swan much like the others came out, minus its head. A little rummaging brought that to light as well. The Swan must have been broken when the two fighters had fallen off the building.

"Okay, Flynn. Now we're going to make a phone call and go meet your buddy Frank. But first I have one last question." The masked avenger stepped up to Flynn and straddled him. Bending forward at the waist, he ground his revolver into the back of the thief's neck, and whispered, "Tell me you didn't hurt that woman you just stole this swan from."

The answer came quickly, "No. I swear it! She was sleeping like a baby when I hit the joint. I was in and out without a sound. She's fine, yah gotta believe me!"

Now, while he was scared the Scar rapped out his last question, "If you don't hurt anybody then why did you kill Hansen?"

"Huh? I didn't kill anybody!"

The barrel of Scar's gun ground in a little harder, "No? Then where did you get the list of swan owners?"

"From Frank! Frank gave it to me!!"

This was the answer he had expected but the Scar had wanted to be certain. He was sure the thief was too frightened to lie at this point. Deciding his next move, Scar holstered his weapon. He then reached down, pulled Flynn's belt from his pants and used it to tightly tie his hands behind him. Next he grabbed him by the neck of his sweater and dragged him to the roadster. Opening the door he lifted him into the passenger seat. Grabbing the backpack the Scar got in and had the car moving in seconds.

Flynn squirmed around until he was face up in the seat and gazed fearfully up at his hideous captor, "You gonna shoot me now? I told you everything I know."

His eyes on the road the Scar replied, "Not yet. First we're going back to your place where you're going to call Frank and set up a little exchange. If you play things straight I might consider not shooting you and dumping your body in the river."

Flynn mumbled something unintelligible.

"What was that you said?"

The thief swore bitterly, "I'm sorry I ever left Chicago."

The Scar barked out a harsh laugh, "Not as sorry as you're gonna be."

A half hour later the two adversaries stood in the living area of a small non-descript apartment a mile or so away from the Down Street clinic, not far from *City Hospital.* Here the Scar found most of the stolen cash and jewelry taken during Flynn's burglaries just as Flynn had said. When they had arrived the Scar had Flynn write down as many names of the theft assignments and what he had taken as he could remember. The list was now in his pocket, and interesting reading it made. All the names had been of wealthy and influential men and women.

Now Flynn was dialing Frank's number. The Scar stood next to him so he could hear the conversation, his revolver barrel jabbing into the thief's side. The phone rang three times before a man's voice answered, "Yes."

Flynn spoke, "It's me. I got the next bird."

"What about the missing girls' bird?"

"Hey, you're the guy with all the connections. I went back there but the skirt's gone; her bird too. You find her and I'll get it, if I can."

There was the slightest of hesitations, "People are looking but we think she may have left town." The Scar was chilled at this reference to Dale. It was a good thing she was laying low.

"Okay. So where do we meet this time?"

The answer came quickly. Frank was prepared; "Yardley Park in a half hour; at the gazebo." There was a click as Frank disconnected. Flynn set the candlestick phone back on the table and glared at his captor, "Okay, you got what you want. You gonna let me go now?"

The Scar growled back, "I haven't decided yet when you're gonna be shot. Shut up and let me think." He was familiar with Yardley Park. He knew that the gazebo was in a large clearing surrounded by grass. It was dark and there only a quarter moon but the gazebo was still out in the open with little cover around. He stepped back and gestured to the empty back pack lying on the floor, "Put that on. We're going for a ride." Looking less than happy Flynn complied.

A half hour later the Purple Scar crouched behind a huge rhododendron bordering the clearing in Yardley Park. Flynn, wearing the back pack stood next to him, the thief's right arm held in his iron grip. This was as close as they could get without stepping out into the open. Visibility was good in the dim light and even now the Scar could make out a tall figure standing in the shadowy interior of the open sided structure. He was well placed. The nearest cover where the Scar and his captive stood was thirty yards away.

The Scar whispered in Flynn's ear, "All right, you march out there as if everything is great. I'll be right behind you. If there's any shooting, you hit the ground and stay there, understand?"

Flynn nodded.

"Good." Flynn took a deep breath and stepped out from behind the bush. He looked carefully left and right and then walked slowly toward the gazebo. He had taken only two steps when the figure in the gazebo stirred. It stepped to the edge facing Flynn. The open sided gazebo was built off the ground. Three wooden steps led up to the platform on all sides. The figure was wearing a long, trench coat and had his hands in his pockets. A hat cast his face in shadow. The Scar, his revolver held down at his side watched and waited.

When Flynn was half way to the gazebo he half raised a hand in greeting. The Scar tensed, thinking this might be some kind of signal but Trench coat stood unmoving as Flynn approached. The Scar ducked out from behind the concealing bush and ran forward with his gun up yelling out, "Don't move!" He swerved to his left to clear the burglar from the line of fire. Trench coat moved fast. His right hand came out of his pocket with a gun and fired. Scar felt the bullet's flight just past his head. He deliberately fired low in return, hoping to take the man alive.

Flynn had dropped to the ground as soon as he heard the yell. Back pedaling into the gazebo, Trench coat continued firing; a .45 from the sound of the weapon. Scar fired twice more. Trench coat had taken cover on the opposite steps of the gazebo. Firing low through the structure he let fly a flurry of shots. As the Scar returned fire Flynn the burglar cried out and sprawled forward. Scar ducked to one knee and fired twice more through the gazebo at the now fleeing gunman. He glanced to his side. Flynn was rolling around on ground groaning as he held his leg.

The Scar jumped to his feet and ran in pursuit. As he sprinted past the gazebo he flipped out the cylinder of his gun and tried to thumb in more cartridges. He got two into the cylinder while nearly dropping another before he realized the man in trench coat was gaining distance on him. The Scar stopped trying to reload and concentrated on running.

The gunman swerved round a hedge and onto a sidewalk at the other side of the park. Scar increased his pace. He dodged rounded the hedge in time to see the gunman throw himself into a dark colored coupe. He fired up the engine as the Scar took aim with both hands. He fired twice and his gun clicked on an empty chamber. He was sure he had hit the car, but seemingly unharmed the coupe tore away down the street driving without lights.

Scar walked back into the park thumbing fresh cartridges into his revolver. He holstered it as he reached the wounded Flynn. The burglar had taken a slug though his thigh and was bleeding badly. Whipping a handkerchief from his pants pocket the Scar pushed Flynn's hands aside

The Scar .....concentrated on running.

and pressed it hard against the wound. Flynn howled in pain. Scar grabbed his hand and pushed it onto the handkerchief, "Press hard, here!" As Flynn pressed the make shift bandage, the Scar whipped off his belt and wrapped it around the wounded leg. He tightened it across the handkerchief and told Flynn to keep the belt tight. He pulled the groaning man to his feet, bent forward and got him across one shoulder. He then ran as fast as he could back toward his car.

Less than ten minutes later the Scar pulled to a stop around the corner from the emergency entrance to City Hospital. Gathering up the unconscious Flynn he carried him around the corner to the night entrance. He placed Flynn down in front of the door. He pulled out his revolver and banged the butt loudly on the glass. Inside a nurse was talking to a doctor. They both looked up in surprise. Their expressions immediately turned to shock. The Scar turned and ran back around the corner. Jumping behind the wheel he accelerated away, smiling to himself that the appearance of the notorious Purple Scar with a gunshot man would quickly bring the police to the hospital.

+++

The next morning Doc was in his office catching up on paperwork when Dale knocked and stuck her head in, "Captain Dan is here, Miles."

Doc leaned back in his chair, "Fine. Send him in."

He had briefed both Tommy and Dale this morning on the night's activity. He had also called the hospital. Flynn was going to make it. He was recovering in a secure ward of the hospital under police guard.

The door opened and Captain of Detectives Dan Griffin entered. The two men shook hands. They were old friends. Griffin looked every inch a police detective. He was a big, square shouldered man. His black eyes looked out from his square face under a graying hairline. He had been best friends with Doc's older brother until he was tragically killed while investigating a murder. This terrible crime had sent Doc down the path to become the Purple Scar.

Settled into a guest chair Dan looked curiously at Doc, "Well, you've been busy it seems."

Doc nodded, "I understand you have Flynn in custody. He's responsible for the recent spate of burglaries and theft of these missing swans."

"But he didn't murder Hansen, you claim."

Doc shook his head, "No. He's pulled more than a few of these unsolved, high profile burglaries lately and he was hired to steal the swan statues but he did not murder Hansen."

Griffin looked confused, "Who killed Hansen then?"

Before Doc could answer there was knock at the door and Dale entered. She carried an x-ray. Doc motioned her to give it to Griffin. As he held it up to the light, Doc spoke, "That is an x-ray of one of the swan statues. As you can see there is something molded into it. I think it's a precious stone of some kind, possibly a diamond."

Griffin whistled softly, "Look at the size of that thing!"

"Yes, it's no doubt quite valuable. Someone went to a great deal of trouble to smuggle it into the country. Unfortunately when whoever it was went to Hansen's to purchase the bird, he found that there had been a mistake and a whole shipment of swans had been sent. And worse, some of them had already been sold."

"He killed Hansen to get the list of names of the other buyers. He then hired Flynn to steal the missing swans. I caught up with Flynn last night and forced him to lead me to his contact. Unfortunately he got away, but not before shooting Flynn and nearly getting me."

Griffin smiled at Doc. "This phone number you had me run down, it doesn't have anything to do with all this does it?"

Doc nodded, "It belongs to the gunman last night. Do you have an address?"

Griffin nodded and handed a slip of paper across the desk, "That phone number is assigned to a 'Sam Smith' at that address, probably a false name. The number has been in service for only a few months."

Doc nodded, "Good, the Purple Scar will be visiting Mr. Smith, alias Frank, alias whoever he really is tonight."

"Miles, why don't you let me arrest this Smith? I can have him under the bright lights in an hour. We can sweat him until he gives up everything he knows."

"No, Dan. He's a killer and good with a gun. There's too much of a chance that some of your boys could get hurt. Besides I don't want him arrested. It's better if I watch and follow him to whoever is behind all this. Did you check out Simpson's apartment?"

"Yes, it looked like it had been broken in to, just as you thought. Simpson wasn't there. He must have taken your advice and left town. We're trying to locate him now. Do you think Hansen was involved with the smuggling or was he just an innocent?"

"Hard to say, Dan. It'll probably come out in your investigation. Did you check on Mrs. Newgarden?"

"I sent two detectives around this morning. She's fine. Upset about her swan but fine."

Doc waved his hand to where the broken swan lay on a shelf, "You can take that back to her. I think it will be fine with a little glue. You won't need it for evidence. There's plenty at Flynn's apartment."

Griffin stood up, "I've already had all that hauled in. A lot of people will be very happy to get their goods back." He turned to go but looked back, "Anything else I can do?"

Doc stood up was well, "Keep some boys ready. I'll brace Smith tonight. Maybe I'll have some more arrests for you later."

Griffin nodded and took his leave. Dale looked at Miles and asked, "Are you sure about this Miles?"

Doc smiled and said, "As much as I am about any of this madness. I'll be all right. But we have to get back to work. I'd liked to take a nap before I go out tonight."

It was after ten that night. Doc was in his roadster parked on the street where Smith, or Frank, as Flynn called him lived. He was parked where he could see the lights in Frank's apartment. He had been there since before dark. He had seen the lights go on in the apartment and even caught a glimpse of the man himself once at the window. He was prepared to wait until the man either went to bed or left the apartment. He sipped coffee from a thermos and waited.

A half hour later the lights in the apartment went out. Doc sat up. Had Frank gone to bed? Perhaps, and perhaps not. He waited. Soon the ground floor door opened. Frank left and walked in Doc's direction. Doc was parked on the opposite side of the street but he slouched down in the seat until his eyes were barely able to see the big man walk past and down the street. Doc sat up and started his car. He drove to the corner turned around. Two blocks past Frank's apartment a dark coupe driven by a big man pulled out and drove away. Doc followed at a discreet distance without lights.

Frank was in no hurry nor was he worried about being followed. He drove casually across town. Doc, his lights now on, had no trouble following him through the late night traffic. Finally Frank pulled over in front of an older, three story office building. He got out and was opening a door in the building with a key as Doc drove past without slowing. He parked a block ahead and walked back carrying a cloth sack in his left hand. Outside the building he looked up. The only lights on in the building were two windows on the third floor.

The block long building seemed to be businesses on the ground floor; a butcher shop, a shoe store, a dry cleaner. The upper floors appeared to be offices. The glass door Frank had entered contained a dimly lit stairway climbing to the second floor. It was locked. Doc pulled his master keys out and opened it with the third key he tried.

Inside he climbed to the second floor. Everything seemed quiet here but he still walked by every closed office door listening and looking for signs of occupancy. Finding nothing he climbed the stairs to the third floor. He paced quietly along the front hall until he came to a door with dim light showing through the frosted upper half. The name painted in black letters on the glass read *Akelton Imports*. Doc listened. He could hear the low buzz of conversation but it was certainly not on the other side of this door. He set down the bag and went to work on the lock with his master keys. Moments later the lock clicked and the door pushed open to his touch.

Looking both ways in the hallway and seeing nothing Doc pulled out his mask and tugged it over his head. Settling it firmly over his face the Purple Scar replaced his hat and picked up the sack. He pulled his revolver and pushed the door open. Inside was a bare waiting room. A standing lamp gave dim illumination. The only other piece of furniture was a worn sofa on his left. *Akelton Imports* was a certainly a bare bones operation the Scar decided. He pushed the hall door closed silently behind him. The buzz of conversation was louder now. It came from a door to his right. Light showed under the door as well. He crept to the door and listened.

A voice was speaking, "So Flynn is dead?"

Another voice answered, "I hit him, but don't know if he's dead. I called every hospital in town today. No one answering his description was admitted last night. The morgue wouldn't tell me anything. He might be dead; if he is the Purple Scar got rid of the body. Or maybe he's got Flynn somewhere beating the truth out of him."

The first voice spoke up, "The Purple Scar! How did he get onto the swans so quickly? The police haven't even connected the swans to Hansen yet. He wasn't supposed to get involved in this at all!"

"Yeah, well he seems to know a lot about what goes on this town."

"Are you sure he can't track you down?"

"I doubt it. Flynn was our only contact and he can't tell the Scar anything."

"But how did he find you last night?"

"Must have followed Flynn."

There was a pause, followed by the first voice saying, "I still need to find the rest of the swans. Where are we on finding Simpson?"

"I've got people looking. He left town suddenly. He could be hard to track."

"I need that swan! I went to a lot of trouble to smuggle that gem into the country. I need the money and the credibility it will buy me. What about the girl's swan?"

At that moment the Scar decided it was time to put in an appearance. He set down his bag near the doorway but out of the way. He then grasped the door knob with his left hand. He took a breath and turning the knob shoved it open. The door swung wide. A big man wearing a trench coat over a dark suit stood to one side. He had brown hair and a hard but intelligent face. Directly ahead a well-dressed man of perhaps thirty five years sat behind a cheap desk. The rest of this office was as cheaply furnished as the outer office. The Scar barked out, "Freeze!" His pistol steadied on the big man's chest. The two men did not move. Both were shocked. At least the man behind the desk was. The big man was surprised but the Scar somehow knew he wouldn't shock easily. The Scar grated out harshly, "You must be Frank. Your aim was only so-so. You got Flynn but missed me." He swung his gaze slightly to the man behind the desk, "And you must be the man behind the smuggled gem. A good plan casting it into the swan; too bad it went . . ."

Frank was fast. He snaked a hand inside his open trench coat and came up with a gun. The Scar pivoted and fired just as Frank's gun came up. The slug drilled Frank in the chest. He staggered back and fired. His bullet burned across the Scar's side just above his belt. He put a second slug into the big man's chest next to the first. Frank's gun fired reflexively into the desk as he hit the wall and slid down it to the floor.

The Scar pivoted back expecting the second man to have gone for a gun but he was frozen into immobility. He stared at his dead associate for a moment and then swung his gaze back to the Purple Scar. He flinched away from the fearsome countenance, his face pale. He raised shaking hands in the air and begged, "Don't shoot!"

The Scar stepped forward his gun pointed between the quavering man's eyes, "Talk. What's your name?"

He opened his mouth but nothing came out. He swallowed and tried again, "My…my name is Pennington."

"Who are you?"

Pennington swallowed again. He was sweating hard, "I'm a lawyer." Looking over his expensive suit the Scar believed him. He laughed roughly, "So shystering isn't paying enough for you? Why did you set up this smuggling racket?"

The lawyer licked his lips and answered in a whisper, "I need more money…and I needed to show someone that…." He stopped and bit his lip.

The Scar digested that for a moment before continuing, "So you did this to prove something?"

Pennington shook his head, "Uh, I'm not saying anything else." He took a breath and seemed to get himself under control, "You can shoot me if you want. I'm not saying anything more. I…I can't." He licked his lips and then closed his mouth trying to look calm. The Scar decided that he didn't need to know anything more. He had reached the man behind Hansen's death and he knew why it had happened. Griffin could mop up the details. He pointed at the phone sitting on the desk and spoke harshly, "Take that phone." As Pennington pulled the phone toward him the Scar continued, "You're going to call the police and tell them your name. Then you're going to tell them there has been a shooting at this address."

Pennington lifted the earpiece with a shaking hand. He was reaching his other hand toward the dial on the candlestick phone's base when the Scar barked, "No numbers. Just dial 0 and have the operator connect you with the police." Pennington did as he was told. As he was being connected the Scar continued, "And tell them you're responsible for Hansen's murder while you're at it." Pennington did as he was told. When he was finished he hung up the receiver and looked at his captor. Keeping a close watch on the crooked lawyer the Scar reached back into the outer office and lifted up the cloth bag. He set it on the desk in front of Pennington who looked curiously at it. The Scar pointed his gun at the sack and laughed in his harsh grating voice, "That's the closest you're going to get to your loot." His eyes fixed on the bag, Pennington reached out for it with slightly shaking hands. He pulled the bag open and slid out Simpson's swan. He touched it reverently and then looked up at the Scar with sad eyes, "It was supposed to be so easy."

The Scar stepped over to the window. Keeping one eye on Pennington he peered out and hissed in his harsh voice, "Every crook thinks that.

You're no better than the worst thief. You just wear a better suit." His shoe crunched on something hard. Lifting his foot the Scar could see what appeared to be shattered plaster on the floor. He looked around and walked over to a large metal waste basket in the corner. Inside it was filled with broken pieces of ceramic swans. The Scar smiled harshly. He turned to Pennington. The lawyer was holding the swan and rubbing it gently with a strange smile on his face. The Scar asked harshly, "What's so funny?"

Pennington smiled absently not looking at his captor, "I was so close." Scar shook his head. Was the lawyer going into shock? A noise came to him. Stepping back to the window, the Scar could hear sirens. As he watched a police cruiser lights and siren going turned into the street. It was quickly followed by another. He watched as they pulled up just below him. As he walked past the lawyer he hissed, "The police are here. You can tell them everything." Pennington said nothing.

As he reached the door the Scar turned back, "How did you know Flynn was in Chicago?"

The lawyer looked up with a confused looked on his face, "Flynn, I didn't know Flynn."

The Scar grated harshly, "You brought Flynn here to pull burglaries for you."

Pennington shook his head, "I didn't know him. I just got his name from…" he trailed off and bit his lip again. He shook his head again. The Scar suddenly wanted to shake some more truth out of the lawyer. He knew that this point was important; but there was no time. Instead he turned and ran through the outer office. In the hall he could hear feet pounding up the stairs. The Scar turned and ran the other way. He ducked around a corner and headed toward the back of the building. A minute later he found what he was looking for at end of a hallway; a window that led out onto a fire escape. Lifting the window he climbed out onto the metal framework. As he swung his leg out over the sill he felt a twinge of pain. He knew his wound wasn't bad but it would need attention.

Moments later he had climbed down the ladder and was creeping down the alley behind the office building. He came out on a side street. Removing his mask he stuffed it in a pocket and walked away. It took some time but he eventually worked his way around to his parked car. Looking down the street he could see multiple police cars and an ambulance outside Pennington's office. He smiled as he climbed into his car. He started it up and drove sedately away.

+++

Two days later Dale and he were sitting in his office. Dale shook her head as Doc read over a patient's chart, "I don't understand it. Neil Pennington was a successful lawyer. He had a successful practice and a nice office downtown. Why would he want to smuggle in a huge gem in like that?"

Doc looked at her thoughtfully, "He said he needed money. It seems odd though. Everything Dan's checked out shows that he had no debts, no vices like gambling, or women. In fact he had plenty of money in the bank. And all the people that knew him claim he had no hobbies and was so absorbed with his practice that he worked seven days a week."

Doc thought a moment before adding, "What I want to know is who brought Flynn to town and who had Flynn burglarizing important people. And more importantly, how did Pennington learn about Flynn."

Dale answered, "Maybe the police can get him to talk."

"I doubt it. Dan says Pennington refuses to say a word and if they haven't broken him in two days of questioning him they probably won't. It's too bad that Flynn doesn't know more." He was interrupted by the telephone ringing. Doc answered it, "Dr. Murdock…Oh, hello Dan, what can I do for you…What? When? How?" There was a long pause as Doc listened intently. Dale leaned in, sensing something was wrong. Finally Doc spoke, "It's not your fault Dan. You couldn't have seen this coming. Yes, thanks for calling." Doc hung up with a dark look on his face. Dale asked anxiously, "What's happened?"

Doc looked solemn, "Pennington's dead. He was found in his cell an hour ago."

Dale looked shocked, "How could that happen?"

"Unknown. There was no sign of obvious injury. Dan will know more after the autopsy. Right now, he suspects poison."

"A suicide?"

"Maybe." Doc was silent a moment before adding, "There is another possibility. I think Pennington was working alone on the smuggling but he knew a lot more that he wouldn't say. There must be a way he managed to get in contact with both Flynn and his gunman, who still hasn't been identified. Maybe somebody didn't want him talking. There's more here that we don't understand."

Dale stood up to leave, "There is one thing I regret."

Doc looked up curiously, "What's that?"

"My swan. I only have one. That lawyer smashed the other one looking for his crummy stone."

Doc smiled, "The one you have is beautiful and maybe you'll find something nice to go with it."

Dale sighed as she opened the door, "Maybe."

Dale walked back to the front of the clinic. She was checking the schedule for the next patient when a uniformed delivery man entered the clinic carrying a large cloth covered box of some sort. He walked to the counter and set it down with a slightly metallic rattle. Dale looked curiously at it as he announced, "Delivery for Dale Jordan."

Surprised, Dale exclaimed, "Me?"

He handed her his pad, "Sign here, please."

Dale scribbled her signature on the pad and then turned to the receptionist who had just returned, "Do you have any change?"

The girl obligingly reached for her purse. Dale tipped the delivery man who thanked her and left. The receptionist asked, "What's that?"

Dale untied the cord replying, "I'm not sure." When she pulled the cloth covering off, a large bird cage was revealed. Inside were two beautiful brown and grey birds perched close together. Surprised Dale exclaimed, "Oh my!"

The receptionist looked up from the papers she was reading, "Oh, what lovely turtledoves!"

Dale did a double take from the receptionist to the birds and back, "Wait...What did you say they were?"

The girl replied, "Turtledoves. My aunt kept some of them when I was a girl."

Dale stared speechless at the two birds for a moment then raised her voice, "Miles!"

THE END

THE PURPLE SCAR RETURNS

It's been a long time since I've written a Purple Scar story...far too long. I've been trying to get back to the Purple Scar for quite a while but it just hasn't been in the cards. It's too bad because I've missed the fearsome featured avenger a lot.

When I came on board the Airship 27, Ron suggested I try writing a Purple Scar story. I knew nothing about the character but was willing to give it a try. Ron thought he had lots of possibilities and gave me some thoughts as to updating him. I started in and immediately realized that Ron was right about the Purple Scar. So I took his advice and wrote the Purple Scar as a masked avenger who terrorized the underworld with his fearsome appearance.

And I had a great time writing about him. I enjoyed writing that first story so much that six months later I wrote a second unsolicited Purple Scar story to be published in volume two. It seemed I had found a character that I was really at home with and one I had lots of ideas for. Despite working on other projects I continued working on Purple Scar ideas. I even worked up a detailed outline for a Purple Scar novel. I talked to Ron about this and he said it was not unusual for a writer to become especially attached to a specific character and encouraged me to write what I liked.

Unfortunately other projects soon intervened. Ron put out a call for Domino Lady stories as well as for The Phantom Detective stories. I certainly couldn't miss out on those. Then there were air adventures to be written. And then other editors came up with proposals. I also had ideas for original characters and stories that often demanded to be put on paper immediately.

Finally, just when I thought I could get back to some Purple Scar work along came the computer crash. That cost me my Purple Scar novel outline and nearly 14k words of writing in addition to a lot of other work. That hurt.

So despite my best intentions I haven't written a Purple Scar story for nearly three years. I can't believe it's been that long. Anyway, I recently found myself with a break in my writing schedule. No deadlines to meet, no desperate editors needing just one more story to fill a book. Instead I actually had time to finally revisit the Purple Scar. I was pleased, but what story would I write?

I looked through my files and found a story outline I had written a while back. It was a good little mystery that could easily be adapted to different characters; I decided it was perfect for the Purple Scar. In fact the story that I wrote for Phantom Detective volume one came about in similar fashion. I had had a generic mystery outline lying around looking for a home. I considered several characters before settling on the Phantom Detective. I used him and the story turned out pretty well.

So with a solid idea I set about writing my third Purple Scar story. The outline went well. In fact I had thought this one out so well and for so long that my outline was much longer and detailed than I usually write. The more detailed the outline the faster the writing usually goes. And this proved true. The story you hold in your hand was written in record time. Once I started I couldn't put it down. I set new personal bests in writing and finished the whole thing in three days.

I surprised myself by this blistering pace but it reminded me how important preparation and discipline is to writing. I write much better if I have given the story a lot of thought and have a really good outline. I'm not the only one; Robert Heinlein's biographer quotes the author as saying he did not sit down to write a story until he could actually hear the characters speaking their conversations in his head. Now that's thorough preparation.

I wish I could say that my story was brilliant and ready to go after those three intense days. Unfortunately I am not so good a writer that my work doesn't need proofreading and editing (Sigh!). So while three days sounds impressive it took a bit more than that to get *Seven Swans a' Swimming* ready for submission. But after some tightening and careful rewriting, it was ready to go.

So that's how *Seven Swans a' Swimming* came about. Purple Scar fans may have noticed it is slightly different than my other PS stories. Instead of the Scar fighting off a gang of criminals I wanted a different opponent; in this case a master cat burglar working for a mysterious criminal. I also decided to change up the pace of the story as well. Ron had felt the original Purple Scar stories were slow and his abilities wasted as a simple masked detective. I agreed and wrote my first two stories more as action pieces. For this one I changed the pace somewhat. So, the first half of *Seven Swans* is a little more like the original stories, with Doc Miles/ PS acting as a more of a masked detective. Think of this as my homage to the original writers of the Purple Scar stories. But rest assured there is plenty of action and striking fear into the Scar's adversaries in the second half.

I am actually quite pleased with *Seven Swans a' Swimming*. I think it stands up quite well alongside my first two PS stories. I hope you like it as well. With a little luck we won't have to wait three years for my next Purple Scar adventure. I've got some neat ideas for the Scar and hope they see publication soon. Thanks for reading and see you next time.

GENE MOYERS - studied European and Medieval history at the University of Oregon. He is also a U.S. Army veteran. He worked in the high tech industry for some time and ran a store front and internet hobby shop for several years. An avid military gamer and role player, his favorite game was *Daredevils* a pulp based roleplaying game set in the 1930s. His love affair with the 1930s and pulps in particular stem from his first time reading a *Shadow* novel as a boy. Although interested in writing since a teen he did not turn to serious writing until 2000.

He is the co-author of *GURPS Crusades* published by Steve Jackson Games. He has now written several stories for Airship 27 including stories published in *Ravenwood vol. 2*, *The Purple Scar vol. 1*, *The Domino Lady vol. 1*, *Black Bat vol. 3*, *The Phantom Detective vol. 1* and *The Legends of New Pulp Fiction*. He has also written a story for *Alternative Air Adventures* for Pro Se Publications and is soon to be published in two Moonstone Books anthologies.

When not working on various new pulp projects he is busy writing horror adventures for his colonial swashbuckler or his occult investigator, the *Dream Master*. Gene currently lives in Beaverton Oregon with his wife and two lazy dogs.

THE SCAR'S CLOSE SHAVE

FELIX CRUZ

Tommy Pedlar held the pistol pressed against Miles Murdock's temple. Miles was on his knees now, his eyes to the floor, looking away from his close friend and valet. He couldn't remember the last time he was uncertain on how to work his way out of a jam. But here he was. The famous plastic surgeon could only wonder now if Tommy would actually pull the trigger and send a bullet barreling through his skull.

"I'm sorry, Doc," Tommy said.

Miles gazed at the hardwood flooring that rested under his legs. The planks creaked every time Miles exhaled. The room was dark, and Miles wondered if eternal darkness would surround him in just a short moment.

Ten Days Earlier…

Dr. Miles Murdock was having breakfast with his nurse and good friend, Dale Jordan, at a diner just a mile or so down the road from his clinic.

"Something wrong, Miles?" Dale said, as she slipped a forkful of sunny-side up eggs into her mouth.

Miles hadn't touched his food in the five minutes since the waitress brought it to the table. His eyes held firm on a newspaper clutched in his hands.

"Eat your flapjacks. They're gonna get cold." No answer from Miles. "Miles, what's so important in that paper?"

"Sorry, Dale," Miles said, placing the newspaper flat on the table. "Just reading about this gang. Call themselves the Third Street Stompers."

"The Stompers?" Dale said. "Probably just a bunch of kids trying to get attention."

"Have you read the paper?"

Dale shook her head, making her reddish brown hair sway, then she sipped her coffee.

"Well, you should. These so-called 'kids' are turning this city upside down. In just a week they've robbed a bank, a pharmacy, and stole a police car." Miles sighed, running his hands over his face. "The Purple Scar needs to move on these guys. Fast."

"You need your rest," Dale said, lowering her voice a bit. She didn't want the handful of other patrons seated just feet away from them to overhear them discussing Miles' alter ego, the Purple Scar. "Dan can take care of things. That's his job. You've had a rough week with the patients."

"How can you say that, Dale?" Miles said, interrupting his nurse.

"I know, and I'm sorry. I don't mean to sound uncaring. It's just that I worry about you, and I see how tired you've been these past few weeks."

Miles stared at Dale. He knew she was right. He was exhausted. Besides being a plastic surgeon, he donated several hours each week working for free to care for sick people in the slums of his hometown, Akelton City.

"Don't apologize, darling," Miles said with a slight grin. "I love that you care so much. Tell you what; I'll play it by ear. I'll just stop by the precinct and see if Dan is all right dealing with the situation. If he seems to have things under control, then I'll leave the Purple Scar out of it."

"Now that sounds like a plan," Dale said with enthusiasm.

Not more than two hours later, Miles was walking along the avenue, heading for the 6th precinct, where his old friend, Detective-Captain Dan Griffin of the Akelton Police Department, was stationed. As he walked down the cracked and beaten cement sidewalk, Miles greeted the shop owners that he knew. One of them, Vincent Scagnetti, a barber in his mid-50s, was outside his shop, using a pair of eight inch shears to trim a tomato plant resting inside a small garden just below the window pane of his barbershop.

"Miles, my boy," the aged but tough barber said, "how are you?"

"Good, good," Miles said, stopping for a moment to greet the barber. "How about your girlfriend?"

Miles chuckled. "Dale? She's just a friend, but she's great. What about you, Vincent? Life treating you all right?"

"Just beautiful, Miles," Vincent said. "The sun beating on my face woke me up this morning. It's always a beautiful day when that happens."

Miles chuckled. "You're right about that."

"Ya know," Vincent said, "when I was in France during the war, I rarely ever saw the sun. Always rain and clouds, rain and clouds." He chuckled. "I guess that's why I love the sun so much."

Noticing the shears, Miles said, "Shouldn't those be used for cutting hair?"

Vincent laughed, sliding the shears into his back pocket. "I always carry a pair of scissors with me. You never know when someone needs a haircut. Speaking of, you coming inside for a trim?" Vincent said as he began polishing the spinning red, white, and blue striped-barber pole that stood beside the shop's window.

"Oh, no, not today. I have an important meeting this morning. Probably later this week or early next week."

"Sounds good, Miles."

"See you later, Mr. Scagnetti."

Miles continued toward the police station.

"Things are bad, Miles," Captain Griffin said.

"I was afraid you'd say that," Miles said, standing beside the captain's desk. "Do you know anything about this gang?"

"Nothing really. They're treacherous, I can say that much. They popped up out of nowhere a few weeks ago. I setup several operations in the slums with some of my best officers, but nothing doing. We haven't even been able to arrest one of them." The captain scratched the top of his head, confused.

"The map behind you," Miles said, motioning to the city map pinned to the board behind Captain Griffin, "is that related to the Stompers?"

The captain looked over his shoulder at the map, which had six pins pressed into certain parts of the city, most of them in the slums. "Yeah. Each pin represents a crime those punks committed." He paused as Miles studied the map. "I'm just concerned that it won't be long before they kill someone."

"No worries, Dan," Miles said. "The Purple Scar will see to it that they will never have that opportunity."

The rain was coming down hard on Miles as he slipped the rubber mask—resembling the death face of his murdered brother—over his head, becoming the masked avenger known as the Purple Scar. He was in a dingy alley as the full moon struggled to break through the heavy, dark clouds but continued to fail. He stood, hands to his side, pistols in shoulder holsters, and ready to do battle with any members of the 3rd Street Stompers that he had hoped to cross tonight.

After studying Captain Griffin's map of the crimes, he believed that the next crime the gang would commit may be in this section of the city. He patrolled here last night, and the night before that, but nothing happened. The streets were dead, just like tonight. Midnight had arrived, and all of the shops on the avenue were closed. Most of the citizens were home sleeping. So far, the only noise the Purple Scar could hear was the sound of raindrops crashing on the cracked asphalt just below his feet.

Then.

The sound of a window being busted filled the air.

The Purple Scar unfastened the belt of his trench coat, giving him easy access to the holstered pistols, as he marched toward the end of the alley. Peeking around the corner, he saw two men stepping into a dark jewelry store through a shattered window.

He waited until they were inside the store before he headed in their direction.

Moving closer to the store now he began to hear voices. One voice said, "Would'cha take a look at these rings? They're pretty swell looking."

"Nice. Bag'em," the other voice said. "Bag'em all."

The Purple Scar was at the busted window. He stepped into the jewelry store as the two thieves began shattering glass cases and bagging the goods.

The Purple Scar approached from behind, pistols drawn, as the first thief tried on a diamond ring. "Looks good on you," the Purple Scar said.

The two thieves were startled as their eyes locked on the Purple Scar.

The first thief tried to speak. He opened his mouth, but he couldn't utter a word. The Scar knew the grotesque appearance of the mask terrified the young hood.

The second thief said, "Whoa, mister. Li..li..listen, we don't want any trouble." He paused, watching the Purple Scar pointing the two pistols at him and his pal. "What are you?"

"A ghost," the first thief said, managing to squeeze out a short sentence.

"Put the merchandise back in the cases, or this face is the last thing you see," the Purple Scar said.

The two thieves nodded.

At that moment, the Purple Scar was tackled from behind and sent crashing into a display case as his pistols were jolted from his hands.

"Who is this punk?" a third voice said.

Disoriented, the Purple Scar tried to stand, but a large foot rammed into his stomach, dropping him back to the floor. He rolled onto his back, trying to catch his breath. His eyes widened as he gazed up at a massive four hundred pound man, who stood close to seven feet tall.

"This ain't no ghost," the giant said.

"How do you know?" First Thief said.

"Ya can't break a ghost," the giant said. "And I'm gonna break this rascal." The giant cracked his knuckles, moving toward the Purple Scar as he searched for his pistols.

"He's looking for his guns," Second Thief said, nudging the first thief.

First Thief rushed toward the smashed display cases, trying to reach the pistols before the Purple Scar. He was too late. The Purple Scar grabbed one of the pistols and fired a shot into First Thief's chest. He dropped dead to the floor.

Trying to flee, the giant and the second thief rushed toward the exit.

The Purple Scar took aim and fired another shot that dropped the second thief. Still disoriented, the Purple Scar tried to focus, but it was too late. The giant was gone.

If any other place in the city was seeing action right about now, it was the local dance hall several miles away. The Moonlight Ballroom saw its popularity explode since introducing the swing style of jazz music to Akelton City. Over a thousand people, most of them in their late teens and early twenties, came out to see Artie Shaw and his band, the Gramercy

Five, fill up the eight thousand square foot, two-story building with their most popular hits. As Artie brought life to the clarinet, energetic partiers stomped the dance floor with dances such as the Lindy Hop, the Charleston, and the Big Apple.

Two of the people on the dance floor, doing their best Jitterbug, were Tommy Pedlar and his date, Erma Schofield. Their smiles glistening through the sweat running down their faces showed that they were having a swell time.

To the right of the dance floor was a bar that stretched out, running the length of the wall. Smoke filled this part of the club, as tired dancers, wanting to catch a breath, and people who preferred to bend the elbow, sat and drank, or smoked, or both, whatever pleased them the most. It was a carefree time.

At the center of the bar, a man in his mid-twenties sat on a stool. He was dressed in a worn tan suit, glass of beer in hand, cigarette dangling out the corner of his mouth, as his eyes traveled the dance floor, studying the movers and shakers. His name was Jack. On Jack's lap sat his girlfriend, Trixie, lighting a smoke. She was wearing a white blouse, with a black, knee-high skirt, and her hair was blonde and short, made her look like Jean Harlow. To the right of Jack stood his old pal "Three-Fingered" Callahan, who got that nickname because he lost two fingers in a poker game. To the left of Jack were Ronnie "Ol' Man" Rivers, "Twisted" Dickie Sawyer, and "Boobie" Thompson. Ronnie, in his late thirties, graying at the temples, hence the moniker, sat with his back to the dance floor, tossing pretzels in his mouth and swigging ale. Twisted Dickie—the less said about his nickname the better—stood, a beer in hand, watching the young ladies with a smile on his face; he had a brown flat cap pulled tight over his forehead, trying to hide the unibrow that created a border between his forehead and eyes. Boobie Thompson sat with his face hovering above a large bowl of clam chowder, as he shoveled spoonfuls of the soup in his wide mouth—the guy was a slob and he didn't care.

No one in the Moonlight Ballroom knew Jack. No one knew that Jack was the leader of the notorious 3rd Street Stompers gang. No one knew that the five people surrounding Jack were members of his gang, but they were familiar with the chaos that the crew brought into town.

"Sweet Mary," Twisted Dickie said, "would'cha look at these dames." Paused. "Gorgeous."

"You fixin' on takin' one of these broads back to the pier?" Callahan said.

"One? I'm thinking it's too hard to choose just one. I may take two or three," Twisted Dickie said. "Whaddaya think, Jack?" He looked over his shoulder and saw Jack staring at someone in the crowd of dancers. "Uh-oh," chuckled, "the boy spotted a new dame. Time to hit the road, Trix."

Callahan laughed.

Trixie said, "Who you fooling? My baby's got all he needs right here with me." She pulled the cigarette from her mouth, stuck it beside the other cigarette between Jack's lips, and kissed his cheek. Pulling away, her mouth formed a sly smile after seeing that she left a red imprint of her lips on Jack's cheek.

"What's the problem?" Twisted Dickie said to Jack, who could not unlock his eyes off of his target.

Jack stood, forcing Trixie off his lap. "Everything's just peachy," Jack said. He handed Trixie her cigarette, "Wait here, fellas," and marched toward the dance floor. Twisted Dickie looked at Callahan and Callahan shrugged, confused.

As Artie's tune came to an end, the dancers began clapping. Tommy and Erma laughed and hugged each other. As Tommy embraced Erma, he saw the scrawny man, with a cigarette in his mouth and lipstick on his cheek, moving toward him. The man saw Tommy gazing at him, and he smiled. All of the energy drained from Tommy's face as he pulled away from Erma.

Erma noticed the change in his demeanor. "What's wrong, Tommy?" She noticed Tommy was staring at someone behind her. She turned and saw the man standing just a couple of feet from her, smiling at Tommy. Turning back to Tommy now, she said, "Do you know him?"

"Yeah," Tommy said, solemn.

Jack drew on his cigarette and said, "Hey, Tommy, whaddaya hear, whaddaya say? Long time no see, pal."

Three police officers stood outside the jewelry store as a couple of homicide detectives studied the bodies of the two dead thieves.

Captain Griffin stood at the corner of the street, discussing the crime with Miles.

"Did they look familiar?" Miles said.

The captain shook his head, "Nah, but they are definitely Third Street

Stompers." Miles squinted as if to ask, *How do you know?* The captain understood his expression and said, "They each have the number three tattooed on the palm of their right hand."

Miles nodded and said, "I see. Well, on the bright side, the gang's two members lighter."

"Sure, but how many are there? A hundred? Two hundred?"

"I doubt they're a very large crew. A gang that big in this city, they would easily be spotted. And these guys are doing a good job of staying hidden. No, my guess is they are a pretty small group. Less than twenty members, I would imagine."

"I sure hope you're right." Captain Griffin lowered his head, tired. He turned to see the morgue wagon pull to a stop in front of the jewelry store. "In the meantime, we'll see if we can get IDs on these bums. Maybe give us a lead, something that can point us in the right direction."

"Well, I'm going to take off," Miles said. "I'll see if I can track down the big fella. Hopefully he hasn't gotten too far. Just keep me posted if you find out anything."

Captain Griffin nodded and Miles walked off, vanishing in the shadows.

Tommy and Erma were at the bar now, surrounded by Jack and the rest of the 3rd Street Stompers. Jack offered to buy the couple drinks, but they declined. Jack ordered them drinks anyway.

Tommy could see Erma staring at him out the corner of his eye, so he was trying not to show her that he was nervous, because he knew that would only make her nervous.

Jack smiled, sipping his drink, as he stood in front of Tommy and Erma, his eyes holding on Tommy.

Finishing up the last of his pretzels now, Ronnie, sitting beside Tommy, looked at him, then turned to Jack and said, "You say you know this kid?"

"Yeah, you kidding me?" Jack said. "This here is Tommy Pedlar. We was in a gang about eight years ago. Ain't that right, Tommy?"

Tommy saw the surprised expression on Erma's face. He said, "Yeah," and paused. "That was a long time ago, Jack."

"Yeah, sure was," Jack said, as the bartender placed Tommy's and Erma's drinks on the counter behind them. "Fellas, let me tell ya, Tommy was the best pickpocket in the entire city. We called him the Sticky-Fingered Kid.

You could be staring right at him, and he'd somehow find a way to pick your pockets."

Some of the Stompers smiled, impressed. Ronnie said, "That's some skill, kid."

"Uh, thanks," Tommy said in a reluctant tone.

"So whaddaya say, Tommy, feel like shaking off the rust?" Jack said.

"What do you mean?" Tommy asked.

"He means joining up with us, ya screw," Twisted Dickie added.

Tommy let out a nervous chuckle. "Sorry, Jack, I've moved on."

"You don't like my boy, Jack?" Trixie said. "You think you're better than him?"

"Ain't nobody better than us," Three-Fingered Callahan claimed.

"It ain't that, is it, Tommy?" Jack pressed. "You don't think you're better than me, do you?"

Tommy wanted out of this place and fast. His nerves were making him antsy. He turned, grabbed the beer from the counter, and swallowed a huge gulp. His eyes went up to Jack, and he saw his former associate glaring at him, waiting for an answer. "I'm just not that guy anymore." He paused. "By the way, you have lipstick on your cheek."

A couple of the guys laughed. Boobie chuckled, saying, "Jack's getting all dolled up for us."

Trixie tried to wrap her arms around Jack, but he shoved her away, annoyed as he wiped his cheek. "Dumb broad." Back to Tommy now, Jack said, "So what've you been doing these days, Tommy?"

"I work," Tommy answered. "I'm a handyman."

"You don't say?"

"Yep."

"Guess you gotta pay the bills somehow, right?"

Tommy nodded as his eyes went to the large man approaching Jack from behind.

"Hey, Jack," the large man said.

Jack turned to see the massive Curley Jolson just a foot from his face. "Curley," Jack said and squinted. He saw the distressed look on the giant's face, then noticed that he was alone. "What happened? Where's Gus and Mel?"

"We got a problem."

+++

Still a bit tired from the late night at the Moonlight Ballroom, Tommy exited his bedroom in the mansion on Swank Street. He rubbed his face, trying to wake up, as he walked downstairs and searched around for Miles. No one was in sight, and the place was quiet. Then he heard grunting coming from the back.

He walked down the hall, pushed the door open to the gym, and saw Miles lifting free weights.

"Doc," Tommy greeted.

Miles was wearing shorts and a white shirt that was drenched in sweat. He placed the dumbbells on the floor and nodded. "Hey, Tommy. Good morning. How did your date go last night?"

"Well, Erma was the best. Um, Artie Shaw was the bee's knees. Best music I've ever heard." Tommy paused.

"Something wrong?" Miles sensed.

"Uh, I ran into someone last night."

"Who?"

"A guy I used to run with back when I was pickpocketing. I hadn't seen him in years."

"That's interesting," Miles wiped the sweat from his face with a small towel.

"I'll say." Tommy paused. "But it probably ain't as interesting as your scuffle in the jewelry store last night."

Miles' eyes widened. "How did you hear about that? It's not in the paper yet."

"That big guy that got away, he works for my old friend."

"Your friend told you this?"

"No," Tommy said as he sat on the bench in the corner. "The big guy—his name is Curley, by the way—well, he popped up at the ballroom last night. I overheard him telling everything that happened. Them busting in the store, you killing the two hoods, everything."

"Wait, wait, wait," Miles was confused. "You're telling me this guy from your past is associated with the Third Street Stompers?"

Tommy nodded. "He's the leader, Doc."

Miles was stunned. He stepped back and ran his hands through his hair. "Talk about being at the right place at the right time. So what's his name?"

"Jack Scagnetti. He's a year older than me."

"Jack Scagnetti." Paused. "Besides this Curley character, do you know of any other members?"

"Well, there were five others there with Jack," Tommy said. "Other than that, I have no idea."

Miles was quiet for a moment, staring at the floor and pacing the gym. "Doc, you okay?"

"Jack Scagnetti," Miles repeated. "I wonder if he's related to Vincent Scagnetti."

"Who?"

"Vincent Scagnetti. He runs that barbershop on Leonard Avenue."

"Oh, yeah, that's his pop."

"Really," Miles smiled knowingly.

That night, Vincent Scagnetti was sitting in the living room of his dimly lit apartment, eating his supper, creamed chipped beef with peas and some Italian bread. He laughed and chuckled, between bites, as he listened to *The Kate Smith Hour* on the radio. Abbott and Costello were guesting on the show tonight.

The old barber thought he was alone until he heard a deep voice say, "Good evening, Mister Scagnetti."

Startled, Vincent dropped his fork and grabbed the shears from the table beside him. He looked to the window at the side and saw a dark figure moving toward him.

"Listen, buster," Vincent said, defiant, "I may be a little old, but I'm thick as a brick, and I'll wipe the floor with you. I fought in France back in eighteen. I've seen it all, so I don't scare so easy."

"Relax," the voice said. "I'm not here to harm you."

"What do you want, then?"

The figure stepped out of the shadows, revealing his grotesque purple face to the old barber, who grew disgusted from the sight and had to fight for a moment to stop him from throwing up his dinner.

"I've heard of you," Vincent gasped. "They call you the Purple Scar, don't they?"

The Purple Scar ignored the question. "You have a son, Jack Scagnetti."

"How did you know that?"

"He's the leader of the Third Street Stompers."

Vincent shook his head. "I don't know. I haven't spoken to Jack in weeks, not since he came home."

"Where is he staying?"

The old man was growing agitated as he threw up his hands and said, "I haven't a clue. You're asking me questions that I don't have answers to."

The Purple Scar approached Vincent and stood just inches from him as he sat in his cozy chair. The vigilante placed his hand on the barber's shoulder. "Your son is responsible for multiple crimes throughout the city, and he must face justice."

Vincent just stared, growing a bit frightened, at the Scar.

"Find him. Tell him to turn himself in to the police. If he doesn't," he gripped the barber's shirt, "I'll find him. And I won't be as gentle as the police. You understand?"

The shears slipped out of Vincent's hand as he nodded, slack-jawed and stunned.

"Enjoy the rest of your night." The Purple Scar turned and walked toward the window. Vincent, tensed, watched as he climbed out and fled down the fire escape. Wanting to assure that the Scar was gone Vincent rushed to the rear window, stuck his head outside, looked down, and saw only the darkness of the narrow, filthy alleyway. He sighed and sat on the window sill for a moment, wondering about his troubled son.

When Tommy had spoken with Miles that morning, he'd given Miles the location of the old hideout that Jack and he used to lay low in when they would hide from coppers. That's where the Purple Scar was at now, an old warehouse in the industrial district of the city. He kept in the shadows as he moved toward the rear of the three story building, hoping to catch a glimpse of Jack Scagnetti and his crew.

After reaching the back of the warehouse, the Scar spotted three dock doors. The first dock door was empty and closed. The second and third dock doors were not empty. A Westinghouse box truck was backed up against the second door, which was opened. In the third dock door, beside a streetlight, was parked an unmarked box truck. The trucks were so close to the docks that he couldn't see through to the inside of the warehouse, but he heard several voices and the sound of containers being moved and dragged. The Purple Scar wasn't sure who was in the warehouse, but he was certain that they weren't supposed to be in there. It was time to get some answers.

"I haven't spoken to Jack in weeks…"

"Careful with that crate, Stumps," Callahan said.

"I'm sorry."

"Don't be sorry, ya dope, just be careful." Callahan was chewing on a huge wad of gum as he watched his workers, Stumps and Grady, carry wooden crates from out of the Westinghouse box truck and into the truck that they borrowed from Grady's uncle. "You bang that crate again, and I'm gonna crack that thick skull of yours."

"I can't help it," Stumps argued. "These things is heavy."

"I don't give a damn," Callahan retorted. "These ice boxes are worth a hundred bills apiece."

"Closer to two hundred," another guy named Terry corrected.

"A hundred, two hundred, just don't bust it up," Callahan said. "Jack sees any damage to the goods, and he's gonna blow his cork. I don't need him givin' me the business for your screw ups so be careful."

Stumps bit his lip as he glared at the weaker Grady. "Lift with ya legs, Grady. Geesh, I feel like I'm doing all the work here."

"Hey, shut up," Grady barked. "Youse just said you needed a truck. No one never told me I was gonna be busting my hump over some ice boxes."

"They're refrigerators, not ice boxes," Terry said as he stood nearby with Callahan, watching the two saps move the merchandise. Terry didn't look like he was part of the gang.

Callahan rolled a cigarette with his three-fingered hand, tucked it in the corner of his mouth, and lit it. "Who cares, Terry? Just let them move the crates so we can get the heck outta here."

Terry threw up his arms. "Listen, I'm just telling you, so you guys know what you're selling. These things aren't ice boxes, they're electrical. They're more valuable than some rinky-dink ice box."

Callahan shrugged and continued to enjoy his cigarette as Stumps and Grady struggled with the crates. He walked toward the second dock and peeked inside the Westinghouse truck. When he turned he saw Terry staring at him. "Just a couple more."

Terry nodded.

"What time you gotta have this truck back to your job?" Callahan inquired.

Terry shrugged as he removed his work cap and ran his hand through his hair. He was still sporting his brown Westinghouse uniform that all the warehouse employees had to wear. "I wanted to be back by midnight. Night security doesn't patrol that section until one o'clock or so."

"Yeah, you should be fine."

A loud thud was heard from inside the unmarked box truck, and then Stumps yelled, "Grady, you numbskull, you dropped it on my foot!"

Callahan sighed and shook his head. "Idiots."

"How long do you think it'll be before I get my share?" Terry asked. He was wearing a nervous expression. Callahan figured he probably had been trying to muster up the courage to ask that question for a few hours now.

"Maybe a few weeks," Callahan explained. "We're gonna work on movin' these throughout the city and see what we can make. Jack will cut you off your piece in time. Just be patient."

Terry nodded, "I will. I just really need this money."

Callahan smiled as he flicked the butt of his cigarette. "Don't we all?"

Terry was outside now, walking to the driver door of his company truck. As he opened the door and climbed in, he pulled out a matchbook and cigarettes and said under his breath, "What am I doing? Stupid. You screwed up big this time, Terry."

"You got that right, pal," an unknown voice said.

Startled, Terry's eyes darted to his side where a dark figure with a deformed face was sitting in the passenger seat. Before he could open his mouth, he saw a fist sail toward his face, then a flash of white, and then he was out cold.

Three-Fingered Callahan was following behind Stumps as he headed toward the unmarked truck. Grady walked in front of the truck, and passed the streetlight, as he made his way to the driver side. The three gang members entered the unmarked truck as the engine to the Westinghouse truck began to rumble.

Before Grady could start the engine, the Westinghouse truck darted out of the dock, traveled a couple of hundred feet, made a sharp U turn, and pulled nose to nose with the unmarked truck, blocking its path. The hoods were dumbfounded as the headlights from the Westinghouse truck blinded them.

"The hell is he doing?" Grady queried.

Stumps was sitting in the middle, cursing and covering his eyes.

Callahan was squinting and shading his eyes from the light. He managed to catch a slight glimpse of the driver's face. He declared, in an agitated tone, "That ain't Terry."

"What?" Stumps said.

"Just shut up and shoot," Callahan shouted as he pulled out a revolver and began firing through their windshield at the Westinghouse truck.

The Purple Scar was quick to drop under the dashboard as bullets began shattering the windshield and landing in the seat cushion behind him. He heard coughing and gazed at Terry, sitting unconscious in the passenger seat, as bullets slammed into his chest, causing his body to jerk with each thudding bullet, which triggered his work cap to slide off his head and land on the Purple Scar's leg. The crooked Westinghouse worker was choking on his own blood as the bullets ended his life.

For the moment, the Scar was trapped. The bullets were steady whizzing past just above his body. Every time one of the thugs stopped to reload, another was beginning to fire again. What's worse, he heard the creaking of the truck doors opening, so he knew they would be reaching him any second now.

As he scrambled for a solution, the Scar noticed the streetlight through the bullet-riddled windshield. He reached for the matchbook still clutched in Terry's hand, then grabbed Terry's work cap, and then he pulled out one of his pistols from the shoulder holster and fired a shot at the streetlight.

The bullet shattered the streetlight, drowning the scene in total darkness.

Callahan stopped moving. He was scared, but he didn't want to show it. He fired a couple of more shots as he slowly backed away from the Westinghouse truck.

Stumps and Grady stopped firing. "Callahan, whaddaya wanna do?" Stumps yelled.

Callahan didn't answer.

The Purple Scar knew this was his chance. He kicked open the passenger door, and dove out of the truck, using Terry's corpse to shield him from any incoming bullets. He rolled on the ground, away from the truck, then used the matchbook to torch the work cap.

As the flames grew, the Scar tossed the fiery work cap in the direction of the voices. As it landed, it gave off enough light to reveal two thugs, appearing frightened and confused, as they began to turn and run away.

The Purple Scar raised his pistol, fired two shots, and the thugs dropped dead. He heard scrambling footsteps and gave chase.

Callahan was terrified. He knew Grady and Stumps were down and probably dead, and he didn't want to join them. Breathing heavily as he hustled around the corner, Callahan bumped into a dumpster. He stopped, looked back, couldn't see anything, then he jumped into the empty dumpster and waited.

As the minutes passed, Callahan began to relax. He didn't hear any sounds. Whoever was chasing him was gone. But he wasn't taking any chances. He was going to sit in this dumpster, relax, and wait some more.

After what he figured was close to twenty minutes or so, Callahan climbed out of the dumpster. As he tried to shake off the cramp in his leg, he rolled another cigarette and stuck it between his lips. He reached in his pocket for a match, struck it against the dumpster, and brought the lit match to his face. That's when the mysterious figure behind him said, "Gotcha," and slammed Callahan's head against the metal dumpster.

+++

Jack waited and waited for Callahan to get back with the goods. Hours passed and he was tired of waiting. He had Ronnie drive him— with Twisted Dickie and Curley tagging along—to the old warehouse in Ronnie's beat-up 1929 black Adler.

Through the entire ride Jack didn't say much. Ronnie asked him a few questions, but Jack just grumbled. He was concerned that he may have lost an opportunity to make a few thousand bucks.

As the Adler reached the industrial district, Jack's eyes widened after spotting three police cars parked at the warehouse. He gritted his teeth, saying, "Stop the car."

"Why?" Ronnie wanted to know.

"Just stop the car, screw," Jack raised his voice.

Ronnie pulled the car to the side of the road and stopped.

"What's wrong?" Ronnie was confused.

"Oh, I see," Twisted Dickie said as he spotted the police activity.

"Coppers," Jack pointed. "But how? How would they know? Terry wouldn't say nothing."

Jack shook his head as a grim smirk crossed his face. "Tommy."

"What's that now?" Ronnie asked. "Who's Tommy?"

"You mean that fella from the dance hall?" Curley remembered.

"That dirty rat," Jack cursed. "He's the only one besides us who knew about this place." He motioned with his hand to drive on. "Let's scram. It's time to catch up on ol' times with my pal Tommy."

The Adler made a U turn and drove in the opposite direction.

An hour later, Callahan was sitting at a table in the dingy, dark interrogation room of the police station with Captain Griffin and Lieutenant Rick Riordan, dressed in a sharp gray suit with a fedora clutched in his hands, standing on the opposite side of the table, staring down at him.

"Youse guys gonna stand there all night gawkin' at me?" Callahan snarled.

"Yep, until you give us some answers," Lt. Riordan grinned, adjusting the shape of his fedora's brim.

"Three guys are dead," Captain Griffin said, "and you're the only one who can tell us what you were doing there. I know you're with the Third Street Stompers. I know Jack Scagnetti runs the gang. Now I want to know what happened, and, furthermore, I want to know where to find the rest of your crew."

"I already told you," Callahan repeated, "I was moving some ice boxes for my pal's company. That's it. Ain't no crime in moving ice boxes."

"They were refrigerators," Lt. Riordan said.

Callahan scoffed and dropped his head on the table.

The next morning, Tommy was at Audrey's Place, a diner several miles from the Swank Street mansion and his favorite place to grab breakfast. He ordered a couple of coffees and some codfish cakes and bacon for Miles and himself, and now he was reading the newspaper while he waited for his order.

After the waitress brought Tommy his food in a brown paper bag, Tommy tipped her and exited the diner to see Jack Scagnetti leaning against a black Adler that was parked across from the diner's entrance.

Tommy stopped and stared at Jack. Jack, tightening the belt on his trench coat, was wearing a deadpan expression as he said, "We've been looking for you all night, Tommy."

"We?" Tommy said, confused.

Jack motioned with his head, and Tommy looked over both shoulders to see two of the hoods from the ballroom the other night. He remembered their names as Twisted Dickie and Curley. They were standing behind Tommy, on either side of him, and the other guy, Ol' Man Rivers, was behind the wheel of the Adler. All four men were glaring at him, and none of them were smiling. Tommy was beginning to worry as the heat from the breakfast warmed his hand through the paper bag. Even though he was watching these thugs around him, he couldn't stop thinking of how the coffee and food would be cold by the time he got back to the mansion.

"I was about to give up," Jack continued. "The fellas here was tired. Ain't that right, boys?"

"Exhausted," Curley, the large one confirmed. Twisted Dickie responded with only a grunt.

"Yeah, then I got lucky. I figured we try this joint. I remember how much you used to love grabbing breakfast here. I just can't believe you still eat here after all these years. Let me guess, codfish cakes and bacon?"

Tommy nodded.

"Good," Jack smiled. "Me and the boys is starving. Ain't that right, boys?"

"Like a son of a gun," Ronnie agreed.

"Yeah, I could go for some bacon," Twisted Dickie added.

"Let's go, Tommy," Jack ordered, motioning to the Adler.

"I got my own car," Tommy didn't move.

"That's sweet. Now get in our car before the boys here break your legs in front of this fine establishment."

Tommy looked over both of his shoulders to see the two thugs standing just inches from him.

"C'mon, Tommy," Jack urged. "You really want us to do this in front of those customers in there? They're gonna see some bones getting broken, hear you scream, see some blood, then they're gonna lose their breakfast. Let's not do that. Think of them, Tommy. Don't be selfish, pal."

Tommy tightened his lips and began moving toward the Adler. He stopped in front of Jack and stared at him.

"Tommy, I've known you a long time. I know that look you're giving me. Don't do it. Don't even try to fight us. 'Cause as much as I know you, you know me. And you know that I won't hesitate to bump you off in front of those people in the diner. Then I'll bump them off for having the misfortune to witness a rat like you get plugged." He paused. "Now get in the car."

Tommy lowered his head and got in the backseat of the Adler. Jack got in the passenger seat, and Curley and Twisted Dickie followed in the backseat, sitting on either side of Tommy, while Ronnie began driving away.

"Where are we going?" Tommy questioned.

"Somewhere quiet where we can talk," Jack replied.

"Talk about what?"

"Well, I'm curious how the cops knew about the warehouse. You remember the warehouse, don't you?"

Tommy had to get out of here. He knew things were only going to get worse. He raised his left arm and elbowed Curley's chin. Curley wasn't fazed. He snorted, and Twisted Dickie was quick to stick a blade in Tommy's stomach.

A burst of pain erupted in Tommy's belly and his eyes widened.

"Dirty little punk," Jack said. "Now you messed up. Step on it, Ronnie. To the pier."

Tommy began to lose consciousness. Before he passed out, he turned to his side to see Twisted Dickie grabbing the paper bag with the breakfast.

"Looks like you ain't gonna be needing this no more," Twisted Dickie opened the bag and pulled out a codfish cake.

Tommy closed his eyes.

A little more than an hour later, Vincent was in his shop, with shears in hand, applying the finishing touches to the head of his first customer of the early day. They were the only ones in the barbershop as Duke Ellington's "In a Sentimental Mood" flowed out of the radio's speaker from the shelf behind Vincent. "I'm telling ya, Vinny. That Ross fight was the most exciting thing I've seen in years," the customer said.

"Yeah, I heard it on the radio. Barney's a heck of a fighter," Vincent admitted.

"Radio ain't nothing like seeing him in person, let me tell ya," the customer went on. "Next time there's a fight in town, you gotta come with me and the fellas. Deal?"

"Absolutely."

As Vincent applied talcum powder to the back of the customer's neck, the glass door of the shop swung open and in walked Jack, Trixie, Twisted Dickie, and Curley. Vincent's eyes were drawn to them for a moment, but he quickly went back to taking care of the customer.

"Hey, Pop," Jack greeted, "whaddaya hear, whaddaya say?"

Vincent looked at his son for a moment and stayed quiet as he removed the cutting cape from over the customer. Jack and his friends sat in the empty chairs across from Vincent. Jack was waiting for a response from his father.

Vincent finally said, "I hear plenty, but I say nothing."

"What the heck does that mean?"

The customer paid the twenty-five cents for his haircut, said his goodbyes, and left. Now Vincent was alone with Jack and the three hoods.

Jack approached his father as the old barber began sweeping the floor. "How about a haircut on the house?"

Vincent stopped sweeping and gazed at his boy. He noticed splatters of blood on his shirt. His eyes widened. "Is that blood?"

Jack tightened his lips and looked away from Vincent.

"Dear God," Vincent said. "What are you up to?"

Jack turned to his crew. "Let's skedaddle, fellas. Pop, I'll come back another day for that trim." The three stood and moved toward Jack.

"You're not gonna answer me?" Vincent said. "Jack, there was somebody looking for you?"

The group stopped in their tracks, and Jack looked at his father. "Who?"

"The Purple Scar. He wants you to turn yourself in to the police."

Jack squinted. "Who the heck is the Purple Scar?"

"He's a mystery," Twisted Dickie said. "Some people think he works for the police, others say he's a demon sent from hell."

"What?" Jack said. "You're kidding me?"

"This must be who attacked us at the jewelry store," Curley guessed.

Jack's eyes went to Curley, and he stared at him for a moment.

"You haven't been around for years, son," Vincent cautioned. "You don't know this fella. He means business."

"Boys. Go wait for me outside."

"Right, boss," Curley followed Twisted Dickie outside.

Trixie looked at him, holding his hand. "You too, Trixie. Scram," Jack snapped.

She smiled at Jack and his father, then left.

Alone now, Jack turned to his father. "Pop, I know what I'm doing. Ain't nothing gonna happen to me." His father stared, misty-eyed, at him. Jack nudged his chin with his fist in a playful manner. "I love you, Pop."

"I love you too, son."

Jack exited the barbershop. Vincent followed behind him and stood outside as he watched the group walk toward a black Adler that had its engine running.

"We going back to the pier?" Twisted Dickie asked.

"Is that blood?"

"Yeah," Jack replied.

They got in the Adler and drove away.

It was several minutes past one in the early afternoon at the Clinic on Down Street. Miles and a nurse were tending to a homeless man, who was suffering from a gash on his leg after tripping and falling down a small flight of stairs.

"You should be fine, Mister Howe," Miles told his patient. "The nurse here will patch you up. You can relax here for the day until you feel well enough to be on your way."

"Thank you, Doc," the man shook Miles' hand.

Miles smiled, gave brief instructions to the nurse, and exited the room. He walked down the hallway, toward his office, where he saw Captain Griffin waiting for him. The captain was wearing a grim expression.

"What's wrong, Dan?"

"When was the last time you saw Tommy Pedlar?"

"Yesterday. We were supposed to meet up for breakfast, but he never showed. I assumed he was with his girlfriend. Why?" Miles tightened his brow, concerned. "What's wrong?"

"Just come with me."

They were at Akelton City Hospital now, looking over Tommy as he lay unconscious in bed. Miles was fighting back tears as he listened to a doctor read him the list of injuries that Tommy was suffering from: a one-inch knife wound to his abdomen, three broken ribs, a broken nose, and a gash under his eye that required five stitches. "With that said, this man is a fighter. He will need plenty of rest, but I believe he will be fine," the doctor said.

"Thanks," Captain Griffin said softly.

The doctor nodded and left.

Miles, his arms crossed, tried to fight the rage growing inside of him. "Where was he found?"

"The station. He was dumped outside. Had a dead rat stuffed in his shirt."

"I think it's obvious who's responsible for this."

"Riordan is questioning Callahan again," Captain Griffin reported, "trying to see if he can break him—"

Miles screamed, kicked the door open, and left the room.

Captain Griffin was stunned. He had never seen Miles Murdock act this way. He left the room and saw Miles rushing down the hallway. "Miles! Come back!"

"Who's next?" Vincent, shears in hand, looked at the three customers sitting in the row of chairs lined against the wall of his barbershop.

An older gentleman stood and removed his jacket when the glass door burst open. Everyone's attention turned to see the Purple Scar marching toward Vincent. The customers panicked, one of them screamed, but Vincent was frozen in terror as the Purple Scar gripped his shirt and lifted him off the floor.

"Where is he?" the Purple Scar shouted.

"I..I..."

"Don't play games with me, Scagnetti! I want an answer now! That pathetic scum is going to pay for what he did."

"Don't hurt him," Vincent began to weep. "Please. He's a good boy. He just needs help."

"WHERE?!!!"

"He was here earlier. I thought I overheard one of his friends say something about a pier, but I—"

The Purple Scar didn't let him finish. He dropped him to the floor and stormed out of the barbershop. Vincent dropped his head into his hands and cried.

In the early 1900s, on the outskirts of Akelton City, the city's beach was a bustling place to spend the day with friends and family. The main reason for this was Marty's Pier, located near the end of the five-mile boardwalk. Marty's Pier had plenty of rides and games: a hundred foot tall rollercoaster called the Cyclone, Henrietta's Haunted House, the Village of Mirrors, and the Fun Time Ferris Wheel. All that changed in

1922 when a category four hurricane tore through the city and destroyed Marty's Pier, leaving only remnants of what was once a wonderful place. In the years since, the boardwalk and pier remained abandoned, with the city government rebuilding a new pier and boardwalk thirty miles away. Not a soul toured this section of the city, until the 3rd Street Stompers made it their new home.

The sun was setting in the horizon, and the sky was growing darker by the second as a storm was headed this way. The waves crashed against the abandoned pier, where two men, Boobie Thompson and his brother Franklin, stood outside the Village of Mirrors. The structure was partially collapsed, but it was suitable enough for the gang to use as a hideaway. Parked just off the pier, on the boardwalk, was Ronnie's Adler.

Inside, the walls were covered with mirrors, some of which were lined with cracks or completely shattered from the storm so many years ago. There was a section toward the back of the building that the Stompers cleared out to use as their meeting room. Past this room, against the back wall, were four doors leading to old storage rooms. These rooms were used as sleeping quarters for the members of the 3rd Street Stompers. Some of the members would sleep on the wooden floors, and others would sleep on old cots that they brought here from somewhere else.

In the meeting room, a metal table rested in the center. There were five large candles burning on the table, illuminating the center of the large room. The outer portion of the room was trapped in the shadows.

Jack stood on one side of the table, looking down at a map of the city. He was brainstorming, trying to come up with a plan to rob a second bank downtown. Trixie stood behind Jack, holding his lit cigarette for him. She was all smiles.

Curley was sleeping in one of the back rooms, while Twisted Dickie and Ronnie were sitting at a smaller table playing poker and drinking beers.

"I saw you slip the card outta your sleeve, wise guy," Ronnie said.

"What?" Twisted Dickie gave him a sly grin. "I ain't do nothing. You're seeing things, old man."

Ronnie pulled a knife from his jacket and pointed it toward Twisted Dickie, who continued smiling. "I catch you cheating again, and I'm gonna cut your hands off. Got it?"

"Would you two simmer down over there?" Jack shouted from across the room. "I can't hear myself think."

Outside, Boobie and Franklin were now pitching pennies against the wall, trying to past the time away. There was a small jackpot that totaled almost three bucks that they had piled up on the ground near their feet. They were bored and getting cold.

"Aw shucks, you win again," Franklin said.

Boobie laughed and crouched to collect his winnings from the ground.

Franklin tucked a cigarette in the corner of his mouth, and, as he lit a match, he noticed a figure walking out of the shadows and toward them. "Who the heck is that?" he said to his brother.

Boobie stood and squinted, and that's when a bullet hit him between the eyes. He dropped dead.

Franklin screamed, swallowing his cigarette, and scrambled for his revolver. He was nervous, aiming at the dark figure in the trench coat and fedora. Two additional gunshots erupted that hit the panicked young thug in his neck and shoulder.

Inside the house of mirrors, everyone was on their feet. "What was that?" Trixie gasped shaken.

Jack shook his head, alarmed. His eyes went to Ronnie and Twisted Dickie in the back of the room. "Find out what's going on out there."

As the two Stompers stood, the entrance door burst open and Franklin stumbled inside. Everyone was startled as their wide eyes darted to him.

"What happened?" Jack inquired, concerned. He could see blood running from Franklin's mouth and down his neck onto the front of his white shirt.

Fear and terror were in Franklin's eyes as he rushed toward the group and crashed onto the metal table, sending the candles to the floor, causing the wooden planks to catch fire.

Twisted Dickie screamed, "We gotta go! It's the cops!"

"No," Jack shook his head. "Cops didn't do this." He turned to Trixie. "Get the guns."

Trixie rushed to the corner, where a wooden crate of weapons rested. She grabbed a couple of pistols as Jack waited nearby.

The fire was spreading as the gang members were beginning to panic.

"Dickie's right, Jack," Ronnie said. "We need to take off. This place is gonna burn to the ground."

"Shut up, ya big baby," Jack took a pistol from Trixie. "If you wanna go, then go. But if you leave, you ain't a Stomper no more. Consider yourself dead to me."

Flames continued to grow, wiping the darkness from the main room. Smoke began to cloud around the gang members as they waited for the mystery figure to join the party.

"Come on out," Jack shouted, firing shots at the entrance. "I know it's you, Purple Scar."

As Jack stopped to reload, gunshots rang out, and a shot slammed into Jack's left side, dropping him to his knees. Trixie screamed and ran toward Ronnie and Twisted Dickie.

The Purple Scar entered the burning house of mirrors, and the 3rd Street Stompers all caught a glance of his mutilated face that shone in the light of the rising flames.

With no gun in hand, Ronnie screamed and ran toward the Scar, raising his fists to duke it out with the masked vigilante.

As Ronnie jumped at the Purple Scar, Twisted Dickie grabbed Trixie's hand. "We gotta go, Trix," he told her. "These guys ain't got a chance."

Trixie nodded and she and Twisted Dickie slipped out the side door as Ronnie occupied the Purple Scar.

Ronnie was swinging wide right and left hooks, but the Scar dodged everyone. He countered with a roundhouse kick that sent Ronnie flying back several feet. That's when Curley rammed his foot into the Scar's back, and he dropped to the floor.

The fire was surrounding the men as they had a difficult time seeing who was where. Jack was struggling to get to his feet as he readied his gun for action.

Curley grabbed the Purple Scar by his feet, spun him around several times, and tossed him against the wall, where he slammed and dropped to the floor.

Ronnie was back on his feet now. He rushed to Jack and helped him stand. "Let's go, Jack. If we don't go now, we die."

Jack nodded. Ronnie stood behind him, his hands on Jack's shoulders, steering him toward their escape.

The Purple Scar was dazed, but he saw Jack and Ronnie near the door leading to freedom. He fired a shot from the floor that hit Ronnie in the side of his head. He dropped like a stone on Jack, sending him back to the burning floor.

Jack was trapped under Ronnie's corpse. He screamed as flames began eating at his face and hands.

As the Scar shook off his dazed feeling and climbed to his feet, Curley slammed his open hand against his neck, lifting the hero from the floor, and clamping the grip on his throat.

"You ain't no demon," Curley declared. "Just some copper with an ugly face."

The giant had the Purple Scar pinned against the wall and over a foot off the floor. His eyes were becoming heavy. He knew he was losing consciousness. He needed to do something that would turn the tide of this fight. Using his jiu-jitsu skills, the Scar wrapped his left hand around Curley's wrist and pulled the giant's clamped hand an inch from his neck, allowing him to breathe again. With his right hand, the Scar slammed his palm into Curley's nose. The first strike only startled Curley. The second strike stunned him. The third strike caused his nose to explode in an eruption of blood.

Curley released the Purple Scar and stumbled back.

The Purple Scar was leaning over, coughing, trying to catch his breath as smoke filled the room. His eyes went to the crazed giant, who was now rushing toward the hero with a large fist leading the way.

Thinking fast, the Purple Scar ducked to his right, grabbed Curley's wrist, and bashed his forearm against Curley's elbow, breaking the giant's arm. Curley screamed.

"I'm done with you," the Purple Scar raised his pistol and fired two shots into Curley's chest. He collapsed.

The Purple Scar looked over his shoulder and saw that Jack was missing. He rushed out of the flaming house of mirrors to see Jack stumbling away, toward the boardwalk, smoke escaping from his burnt body.

"Jack Scagnetti," the Purple Scar called out.

Jack turned and raised a gun at the Scar, but the hero was quicker on the draw, whipping his pistol up and firing three shots into Jack's torso.

Jack stood for a moment as the Purple Scar approached. The vigilante saw his eyes roll up and then the leader of the 3rd Street Stompers crumpled.

As the waves crashed against the pier, the Purple Scar scanned the area and noticed the Adler was gone. The others had escaped.

He began moving toward Jack Scagnetti. As he walked, the black sky opened and a hard rain began falling, the large drops were beating against the Purple Scar. He welcomed this; it was cooling him off after the devastating battle in the blaze.

After reaching the gang leader, he watched the dead man's scorched face and wondered how the man's future would've turned out had he made better choices in life.

The Purple Scar removed his mask, and Miles tilted his head toward the dark sky to allow the raindrops to splash against his hot, sweaty face. The reign of the 3rd Street Stompers was coming to an end. He just had to gather up the remaining members. He was hopeful that they would turn themselves in to the authorities without their leader to guide them.

Miles was beaten and exhausted. He needed to rest, but his mission was not over.

+++

The next morning, Miles was in the kitchen, drinking a cup of coffee. He heard a knock at the door, then he stood and walked to the entrance.

He opened the door to see Vincent Scagnetti. The old barber was pale and drained of energy. His eyes were sunken, like he hadn't slept in years, and his hair was disheveled.

"Mister Scagnetti, what are you doing here?"

"Can I speak with you for a moment?"

"Absolutely, come in." Miles moved out of Vincent's path, and he entered the office.

"I know you're a plastic surgeon. That is correct, no?"

"Yes, it is."

"May I ask of you a favor?"

"Of course," Miles could tell that Vincent was reluctant, like he was afraid to ask Miles.

"My boy," Vincent began slowly. "My baby boy was brutally murdered last night." He paused, fighting back tears. "I want to give him a proper burial, but his face was destroyed in a fire." Paused again. "I was hoping…I was hoping you could fix it. Fix his face, you see? So that I can see him one last time."

Miles clenched his jaw and dropped his head. He wanted to help Vincent, but he couldn't forget what Jack did to Tommy. "I'm sorry, Mister Scagnetti. I truly am, but I can't help you."

Vincent's eyes widened. "Please, sir. I beg of you." He wrapped his hands around Miles' hands.

His eyes went to the barber. He saw a tear creep out the corner of his eye, then he pulled his hands away from the war veteran's grip. His tone was sterner now as he said, "I can't. I understand he was your son and you love him. However, your boy nearly killed someone that I care for very much. He beat this man. He stabbed this man. And he dumped him in the street like garbage. That attack is something I will never forget. If I were to do this for you, I would feel as if I had forgiven your son, and I can't forgive. Not for that. So, my apologies, sir, but I cannot perform this service for you." He waited for a response, but Vincent only stared at him. "Please, if there is anything else I can do or help you with, just ask, and I will be happy to—"

"No," Vincent said, interrupting. "I understand. I understand." The barber turned and walked toward the exit. Miles watched as he left. He noticed the shears tucked in the waistband of Vincent's pants, and it almost made him chuckle, even in this unhappy moment. He thought about Vincent's comment to him, several days ago, when he said that he always carried a pair of scissors just in case he ran into someone who needed a haircut.

As the barber walked down the path, leading away from the mansion, Miles watched him, wondering if he was being selfish in his decision not to help Vincent. For the first time in years, he doubted a choice that he had made.

The next day, Miles slept until the late afternoon. He was surprised. He couldn't remember the last time he stayed in bed for that many hours, but he felt refreshed and recharged to continue his mission to free the city from the dangerous 3rd Street Stompers.

After showering, Dale called him and they met at the hospital to visit Tommy. He was awake, but he was in excruciating pain. Erma also arrived with flowers for her boyfriend. Miles and Dale stayed with the young couple for several hours, then they left, so Tommy and Erma could have some privacy. They stopped at a food stand and grabbed a couple of burgers as a quick bite.

Miles and Dale chatted as they sat at a table near the square-shaped food stand, eating their burgers. Miles was regretful that he hadn't spent more time with Dale as of late, and he promised her that he'd take her to her favorite Italian restaurant for dinner later in the week.

Several miles away at a tenement in the slums of the city, Lieutenant Riordan was at a murder scene in one of the apartments on the fourth floor.

When he first arrived, he followed the police officer into the apartment and asked where the crime occurred. If he had just waited another three seconds, he would've never had to ask the question, because the splatters of blood covering the kitchen walls gave it away.

Inching closer to the kitchen, he spotted the body behind the table and near the sink. There was a pool of blood under the body. The body was that of a man, dressed in dingy brown pants and a white T-shirt that was covered now in his own blood. The man's face was riddled with deep gashes, and it looked like he suffered stab wounds in his torso area. Whoever did this was a very disturbed individual, Riordan thought.

After surveying the crime scene, and discussing the details with the two homicide detectives, the lieutenant and the detectives determined that the victim was twenty-three year old Dickie Sawyer, known to his friends as "Twisted" Dickie.

"Did you guys get a hold of Captain Griffin yet?" Riordan asked a couple of the police officers who were standing by the entrance to the apartment.

"We're trying, Lieutenant," an officer replied. "So far, nothing."

"Try the Old Madrid," Riordan suggested. "He may be there."

After Miles and Dale went their separate ways, Miles stopped at Old Madrid, a bar down the street from the police station where some of the officers would stop at after their shifts ended. That's where Captain Dan Griffin was at now, sitting at the bar, eating peanuts and talking to the bartender.

"Hey, Dan," Miles took a seat beside the captain.

Dan turned to see Miles and nodded. "How's the boy?"

"He's in pain, but it was good to see him awake. Any other news?"

"This Callahan fella isn't speaking at all. He showed no remorse over Scagnetti's death, and he wouldn't give us the names of the others who got away, so he's going to go down for the theft of the refrigerators."

Miles nodded. "I see." He paused. "I'll keep my eyes peeled for any kind of suspicious activity."

"Sounds good. I appreciate the help. We all do." He handed Miles a glass of beer. "For now, have a beer with me."

"Cap'n," the bartender shouted from the other end of the bar. "Phone call."

Miles sipped his beer as he watched Dan walk over to the phone and talk to whomever was calling for him. He noticed Dan was a bit annoyed at whatever was being said. After he hung up the phone, he walked back to Miles.

"Everything okay?" Miles asked.

Dan swallowed the last of his beer in one large gulp and shook his head. "Twisted Dickie Sawyer is dead. That name sound familiar to you?"

"No. Should it?"

"You tell me. The guy's got a number three tattooed on the palm of his right hand."

Miles' eyes went wide. "Third Street Stompers."

"Bingo. Why don't you come with me to the crime scene?"

Miles slid his full glass of beer away and stood.

At the apartment of Twisted Dickie, Captain Griffin and Doctor Miles Murdock were led to the mutilated body. They were stunned by what they saw.

"Who could've done something like this, Captain?" a police officer wondered aloud.

The Captain shook his head, unable to take his eyes off Twisted Dickie's face that was frozen in fear underneath all of his own blood. "Don't know. But we'll find out. We'll find out, and this maniac will face justice."

Miles watched Captain Griffin discussing the details of the crime with the two homicide detectives. Being that Griffin was the only one on the force who knew of his secret identity, Miles didn't feel it was his place to get involved in the conversation. To them he was just a doctor and Griffin's friend, nothing more. He leaned against the wall, his eyes wandering the room, trying to find clues. He noticed the front door didn't have any damage, so the killer didn't force their way in. If that was the case, Twisted Dickie may have known his killer.

After leaving the tenement, Miles was driving home. He realized how close he was to Vincent's barbershop and decided to drive past. He wasn't

"Bingo."

sure why, but he just couldn't stop thinking of the old barber and how he disappointed him.

The street was deserted. Miles was the only soul in sight as his car drove, passing storefront after storefront. As he approached the barbershop, his car came to a stop. He stared out toward the barbershop. The place was dark. The red, white, and blue striped-barber pole was still and lifeless.

Miles watched for a moment, looking closer he saw Vincent sitting in the barber chair with his shears beside him on the armrest. Miles watched him. The barber was wearing a solemn expression, gazing at himself in the mirror. "I'm sorry," Miles said under his breath. Then he drove away, trying to push the image of Vincent Scagnetti out of his head.

Two days passed since the murder of Twisted Dickie. After reading about it in the paper, Trixie cried for the rest of the day and into the night. Her friends were all gone, and she was alone. She was terrified since the night at Marty's Pier. Afraid of being caught by the police after they escaped the fiery house of mirrors, Trixie had Twisted Dickie drop her off at her Aunt Hattie's apartment in another tenement not too far from where he was living. She stayed hidden in her aunt's place ever since then. The small apartment made her feel a little safer and more comfortable, because she grew up here. Her aunt raised her after her parents were killed in an automobile accident when Trixie was still a toddler, so Trixie was familiar with the surroundings and the people in the neighborhood.

Her aunt left several hours ago to go on a date with a friend and wasn't expected back until after midnight. Before leaving, Aunt Hattie asked Trixie if she wanted to stay with the neighbor until she returned, but Trixie said she'd be fine alone until Hattie came back from her date.

Sometime after eleven, Trixie was awoken by a knock on the door. She had managed to fall asleep on the couch a couple of hours ago while listening to the radio. As the knocking continued, Trixie stood and drudged toward the door, wondering who it could be, because she knew Aunt Hattie took her key.

With the chain still in the latch, Trixie cracked open the door, recognized who it was, then removed the chain and opened the door.

Outside, just seconds later, the street was quiet, and most of the tenement was dark as the tenants slept. The quietness was interrupted when Trixie's body crashed through a fifth floor window and slammed to the street below, sending a loud splat echoing throughout the neighborhood.

A police officer, walking his beat, came running from around the corner and saw the mangled body of a young female lying on the sidewalk in front of the tenement. Shards of glass were sticking in her face, her arms, and her legs, and a pool of blood was collecting under her, swallowing up the other bits of broken glass that surrounded her body.

Long after midnight, Lieutenant Riordan and Captain Griffin had been interrogating Callahan for what seemed like hours, but it was probably closer to an hour and a half. Miles was sitting outside the room, nursing a cup of coffee, listening to the two high-ranking law enforcement officers shout threats and warnings at the jailed gang member in the hopes that he would help them with solving these murders, but he wouldn't budge. He gave up nothing.

Riordan stormed out of the room and down the hallway. Captain Griffin was slow to exit seconds later. He stopped and looked at Miles. "You want to take a crack?"

Miles nodded.

Captain Griffin motioned with his head. "Go on. No one else is around. I'll make sure you get a few minutes alone."

Miles stood and removed his mask from the pocket of his trench coat. The captain padded his shoulder and walked away.

Miles pulled the mask over his face and slipped into the dark room in one fluid move. After closing the door, he stood and glared at Three-Fingered Callahan, who was resting his head on the table. The room was dark except for a lamplight, just a couple of feet away from the table, shining bright on the criminal.

"Callahan," the Purple Scar said in a dark, disturbing tone.

The thug's attention was drawn to that haunting voice in the dark corner of the room. He could only see a shadowy figure and nothing more. "Who's that?" he said, frightened but trying to hide it.

The Purple Scar stepped out of the darkness and into the circle of light.

Callahan's eyes widened in terror. "Oh God, it's you." He paused, trying to fight his fear and put on a convincing tough-guy act. "Look, I ain't got nothin' to say, see? I'll tell you what I told them. Nothing." The mystery figure began taking slow footsteps toward Callahan. "Lo..lo..look..look, you can beat me all you want. I don't know any—"

The Purple Scar wrapped his hands around Callahan's shirt, lifted him off his chair, and slammed him against the wall. "I just may do that," his face just inches from Callahan's sweaty face. He pulled him away from the wall, then jolted him back against the wall. "Or maybe I'll just throw you out the window like they did with your pal Trixie?"

"I'm sorry," Callahan pleaded in a desperate tone. "But I swear I don't know who is doin' this."

"What about the rest of the Third Street Stompers?" the Purple Scar grippped Callahan's collar tight. "Where are they? We need to make sure they're safe and not next on this psycho's list."

"What are you talkin' about?" Callahan was confused.

"The Stompers. Tell me where they are before they wind up dead."

"The Stompers are done, see?" Callahan stated the obvious. "I'm the last one!" Callahan broke down in tears.

The Purple Scar watched him for a moment and knew that he was telling the truth. He released the defeated criminal and watched as he collapsed onto the chair, dropping his head into his hands.

"My friends," Callahan was crying. "They're all dead. I'm tellin' youse guys the truth. We didn't have no beef with any other gangs. I don't know who's doin' this. All's I know is I don't wanna die."

"You're not going to die," the Purple Scar said. "The police will protect you here. But you'll be paying for the crimes you committed."

Callahan nodded.

"Straighten out your life. It's never too late." He walked toward the door and stopped. "When you're finally released in several months, or a year, or however long you spend in here, stay on the straight and narrow. Because the moment you veer off and go crooked, I'll be there to meet you. We understand each other?"

Callahan nodded. "Yes, sir."

The Purple Scar exited the room and removed his mask as Captain Griffin approached from down the hallway.

"Anything?" Griffin asked.

"He doesn't know who committed the murders," Miles reported. The captain ran his hand through his hair, frustrated. "But he did confirm that he is the last of the Third Street Stompers."

"Well, that's a good thing. Hopefully that will put this murderer to rest. Now we just gotta track the lunatic down."

"Exactly."

"The detectives are interviewing neighbors to see if maybe one of them saw something unusual, or anyone who looked suspicious," Griffin added. "For now, we just have to stay on our toes."

Miles spent most of the following day caring for patients at the Clinic. Today was Dale's day off, so he was looking forward to their dinner later in the evening.

The Clinic had a couple of dozen people walk through its doors on what turned out to be a busy but satisfying day for Miles. He was always pleased to help the low-income citizens of Akelton City. As the day wound down, Dale called to make sure they were still on for dinner. He told her yes and that he'd pick her up at seven.

After closing the Clinic, Miles showered, got dressed, stepped into his sedan, and drove to Dale's apartment.

He was at her door now knocking, but she wasn't answering. He called out her name, but she didn't respond. He wondered if she may have stopped by the hospital to check on Tommy. He decided to go there, so he exited the apartment building and left, driving toward the hospital.

At the hospital now, Miles was walking down the hallway toward Tommy's room. He passed a doctor and several nurses whom he knew, so he greeted them and continued on his way.

Reaching Tommy's room, Miles opened the door and entered to find that the room was empty. Miles was worried. He searched the room and found no sign of them. He came out into the hallway and called for the nurse, who exited another room and approached Miles. She raised her eyebrows to Miles, giving him a look that said, *How can I help you?*

"What happened to the patient in this room, Tommy Pedlar?"

The nurse scrunched her brow and entered the room with Miles. "I don't know?"

"How long ago did you see him?"

"Only twenty maybe thirty minutes ago. A woman was here with him."

"A woman," Miles was becoming concerned. "With green eyes and long, kind of reddish, brown hair?"

"Yes, that's right."

"There was no one else with them? Are you sure?"

"Yes, I'm sure. Is something wrong, doctor?"

Miles ran down the hallway before the nurse could say another word. Seconds later, he was running out of the hospital and into the sedan.

He arrived at the Clinic. From outside he could see that the place was dark. The chances of Tommy and Dale being inside were slim, but he had to be sure.

As Miles approached the entrance to the facility, he heard a telephone ringing. Sounded like it was coming from inside the clinic, but it could've been coming from one of the apartments in the tenements that stood on either side of the clinic.

He rushed to unlock the door, the ringing sounding closer. As he entered, the ringing stopped. He was too late. He called out for Tommy and Dale. Nothing. He searched the facility. Nothing.

He stood by the front desk, contemplating his next move, wondering what could have happened to his friends. He decided to stop by the station to fill Captain Griffin in on what's going on. As he opened the front door to leave, the phone began ringing again.

Miles rushed to the telephone and grabbed it. "Hello?" he said in a vigilant tone.

"Miles."

"Tommy. Is Dale with you?"

"Yeah," Tommy sounded tired, "she's here."

"Are you safe? Where are you?"

"Come get us."

"Just tell me where, and I'll be there."

"One twelve bee, Leonard Avenue."

"I'm on my way," Miles dropped the phone, and ran out of the Clinic. As he jumped in his automobile and drove off, he kept thinking of his brief conversation with Tommy. Tommy called him *Miles*. Tommy never referred to him by his given name. He always called him *Doc*. The kid was smart and was trying to send him a subtle alert that he was in trouble. Miles would have his mask ready if needed.

The address was familiar to Miles, Leonard Avenue was a busy street. He traveled on it almost every day, but he wasn't sure what stood at 112B.

+++

As the sedan came to a stop, Miles looked across the street to see Vincent Scagnetti's barbershop. He knew the address was familiar; 112A was the barbershop, and 112B was Vincent's apartment on the second floor. What would they be doing in Vincent's apartment? Miles didn't have time to think it over. He was in too much of a rush to reach Dale and Tommy.

Reaching the door, beside the barbershop, which led upstairs to the apartment, Miles turned the knob. It was unlocked. He entered to see a flight of stairs leading up to the apartment door. A light at the top of the stairs was on, giving a bright glow to the entire hallway.

Miles walked upstairs and saw that the apartment door was cracked open. He nudged the door and it made a loud creaking noise as it opened to reveal a dark living room with Tommy, on the opposite side near the window, pointing a gun at Miles.

Miles was dumbfounded. "What are you doing, Tommy?"

"Step inside and close the door behind you, Miles," a voice said.

Inside the apartment now, after doing what he was told, Miles turned to his side and saw Vincent standing behind a petrified Dale, with his shears pressed against her throat.

"Vincent," Miles gasped. "What are you doing?"

"Just go over there with your friend," Vincent said in a low, depressed tone.

The entire apartment was dark except for moonlight beating through the front windows behind Tommy.

Miles walked over to his trusted valet and they stared at each other. Miles could see that Tommy had been crying. Tommy began to lower the gun.

"Keep that gun up and at Mister Murdock or I'll slit this darling's throat," Vincent threatened. Tommy raised the gun and pointed it at Miles. "Now, Miles, get on your knees and face me."

"Don't worry," Miles told Tommy in a low tone. "Everything will be fine."

"No, it won't," Vincent barked. "Don't lie to the boy."

"Mister Scagnetti," Miles replied, "whatever the issue is, I'm sure we can resolve it in a calmer fashion."

"On your knees and face me."

Miles followed Vincent's orders.

"Look at me." Miles directed his eyes to Vincent hiding in the shadows behind Dale, who was scared but tough. "You realize you're going to die tonight." Miles just watched Vincent. "Your pal here is going to kill you.

He's going to put a bullet in the back of your head."

"And what happens to them after I go?"

"I'm not sure, yet, but it'll be a fun surprise for all."

"It was you?"

"Me?"

"Did you kill Twisted Dickie and the girl, Trixie?"

Vincent was nodding. "Absolutely."

"Why? What did they ever do to you?"

"Nothing, and that's what will make their families' suffering all the more worse: to know that they died for nothing. But if my boy had to lose his life, I wasn't going to let them get away with enjoying the rest of theirs. And if that other fella wasn't locked up, I would've gotten to him too. I've lost enough in my life, brothers in the Great War, my loving wife, and now my son. That's too much for one man to endure."

"I can help you. It doesn't have to end this way tonight."

"End?" Vincent raised his voice. "It ends for you, not for me. Oh, no, I have plans. I may not have gotten that Callahan fella yet, but I'll get my chance. The other two were easy. You see, the night my son was murdered, I went to the pier to save him. I saw those two getting in the car and leaving the burning building. I thought my boy was with them, so I followed them. They led me right to their homes." He paused and glared at Miles. "You know this could've all been avoided. All you had to do was fix my boy's face," tightened his lips and squinted, "but your pride wouldn't let you do it, because of what you said my boy did to him," motioning to Tommy. "So you refused." He paused again and then screamed, "I begged!"

Miles lowered his head. He truly felt sorry for the barber, but he knew the man's suffering had driven him to insanity. He had to figure out a way to free Tommy and Dale, even if it meant sacrificing his own life.

Vincent's eyes looked like they were going to pop out of their sockets. He looked deranged now as he said, "Now it's time for you to beg me." He stood beside Dale, the shears still pressed to her throat. "Go ahead, kid. Shoot him."

Tommy had the gun pointing at the back of Miles. His hand was unsteady as he struggled to place his finger on the trigger. "I can't," Tommy sobbed.

"Do it," Vincent commanded, "or she gets it," pressing the pointed edge of the shears against Dale's throat, drawing blood.

Tommy stepped beside Miles and pressed the pistol against his temple. "I'm sorry, Doc."

Miles noticed that if he lowered his head a few inches, he would be out of the moonlight's path and in total darkness. This was his only opportunity. He had to give it a try. He leaned forward, lowering his head, as Tommy resisted pulling the trigger.

Out of the moonlight and in the darkness now, where Vincent didn't have a clear sight of what Miles was doing, Miles reached in the pocket of his trench coat and pulled out his mask. He pulled the mask over his face and raised his head out of the shadows. "Vincent Scagnetti," a frightening, dark voice shouted.

"I know that voice," Vincent stumbled back away from Dale. "Who is that?" As the mystery figure stood, the moonlight caught his face and revealed to the frightened barber that it was the Purple Scar. "No, no," he screamed, moving away.

"It's over, Scagnetti," the Purple Scar inched closer to Vincent.

"NOOOO!!!!!" Vincent raised the shears over his head and ran toward the Purple Scar. He brought the shears down, trying to stab the hero, but the Scar grabbed his arm, spun him around, and flung him toward the window.

The Purple Scar watched as Vincent Scagnetti crashed through the window, then he heard a loud thud echo from outside. He and Tommy rushed to the window and looked down to see Vincent Scagnetti, moaning in pain, with shards of glass stuck in his face, and his trusty shears lying close by.

The Purple Scar pulled his mask off and looked at Tommy.

"I'm sorry," Tommy said.

"You have nothing to be sorry for," Miles patted his shoulder. He turned to face Dale, who was standing right behind him. "You're late for dinner."

Dale smiled and wrapped her arms around Miles.

Several weeks later, Tommy was healing more each day and feeling better than he had since before the assault. He sat in the sedan, parked in front of the Swank Street mansion, reading the newspaper, with his feet resting on the dashboard, while the afternoon sun beat through the windshield, warming his face.

He heard a door open and looked over the newspaper to see Miles and Dale exiting the mansion. He dropped the newspaper on the passenger seat and stepped out of the sedan to greet the couple. As Miles and Dale approached, Tommy tipped his flat cap and said in a playful manner, "Good afternoon, beautiful couple. Welcome to my cab." He opened the back door and stepped to the side.

Miles flicked the tip of Tommy's cap. "Don't be silly, cabbie."

Dale laughed and Tommy's face turned red.

Dale stepped inside the sedan, followed by Miles, then Tommy shut the door, walked around, and got in the driver's seat.

Tommy looked over his shoulder, at the couple in the back. "Where to, kids?"

"How about dinner at that new restaurant downtown?" Miles asked Dale.

She shrugged. "Sure. Sounds good to me."

"Well, it's settled," Tommy turned back to face the road as he started the engine.

"Right, it's settled," Miles agreed. "We'll make it a table for four. How about we go pick up Erma?"

Tommy looked at Miles in the rearview mirror and smiled. "You got it, Doc."

That night, at the Akelton City Asylum, an armed guard was escorting a doctor to Cell Block E, which housed the criminally insane. As they reached the gate to the cell block, a second guard, stationed at the gate, pulled it open for the guard and doctor. The doctor thanked him and they entered the cell block.

As the second guard closed the gate behind them, he said to the first guard, "You take my scissors?"

"What?" the first guard shook his head negatively. "No. Geesh, that's the third time you asked me today. Did you ask Carl? Ask Carl. He's always stealing stuff from my desk."

"Yeah, right. I'll do that."

The first guard led the doctor toward the end of the cell block, passing room after room of screaming patients. They stopped at a locked door, and the guard opened the door. "I'll wait out here," he said.

The doctor nodded and entered the dimly lit, padded room. He stood by the door for a moment, staring at the patient on the other side of the room, then he approached the patient, whose face was pressed against the wall.

"Are you ready for your session?" the doctor inquired.

No answer.

"Mr. Scagnetti? It's time for your session. Are you ready?"

The man turned his head side to side.

"Vincent? It's 9:30. Remember? Don't you want to discuss what occurred? We can also review the incident involving your son."

"Vincent?" the man said in a low tone. "Vincent Scagnetti is gone."

The doctor stared at the patient, confused.

The patient turned to face the doctor. The doctor responded with a slight squint. He still hadn't gotten use to looking at the patient's face, which was covered in deep scars. Even his arms were covered in scars.

"You are Vincent Scagnetti."

"No," the patient chuckled. "You can call me the Barber," then he jabbed the doctor's throat with a pair of sharp, metal scissors. The doctor was mortified as a geyser of blood shot out of his neck and onto the padded, white wall behind the Barber. He collapsed to the floor, choking on his own blood.

The Barber pulled the scissors out of the doctor's neck and walked toward the door. He knocked on the door.

The guard opened and was stunned to see the patient, his hand covered in blood, holding scissors. Before he could reach for his weapon, the Barber slit his throat and stabbed him several times as he lay on the floor, dying.

The Barber leaned over, grabbed the guard's gun, and walked down Cell Block E, in a calm fashion, with the scissors and gun in either hand, as the insane patients cheered him on.

THE END

AN ARCH-VILLAIN FOR THE PURPLE SCAR

For every hero, there needs to be a villain. A villain is the yin to a hero's yang. The way darkness is to light, cold to heat, and death to life. In short, a hero may not want to accept it, but he needs a villain in his world in order for him to exist. The Purple Scar was no exception to this unwritten rule. With only four stories released between 1941 and 1943, there wasn't much time to introduce an arch-villain. But after 75 years, Airship 27 is rolling out that long-overdue introduction.

I had never heard of the Purple Scar until Ron Fortier sent me Airship 27's Heroes' Bible to choose a character to write a story about. I was beyond excited to tackle this assignment, and I was looking forward to delving into the world of one of the many fascinating characters that were available. After much digging and researching, I fell in love with Miles Murdock and his alter ego, the Purple Scar. The mysterious Purple Scar reminded me of a cross between the Shadow and Batman. He had that same mystique and passion to end crime that these other heroes had. I also believed that supporting characters like Dale Jordan, Tommy Pedlar, and Dan Griffin were interesting and further fleshed out Akelton City and the world of Miles Murdock.

While researching the characters, I discovered that there was something, or someone, missing. An arch-villain. For as badass as the Scar was, he needed someone like Shiwan Khan or the Joker. Someone that could stand toe to toe with him. That's when I realized that would be the story. Create an arch-villain for the Purple Scar, and this tale would serve as the origin story to this character. Lay the foundation for this arch-villain, so that he could be used in future Purple Scar stories.

When developing Vincent Scagnetti's character, I wanted someone who came face to face with death in his past, so that he wasn't easily intimidated by the Purple Scar. This was the reason for making the old barber a veteran of the First World War. Like Miles Murdock, the ol' timer had scars of his own. Scars that were hidden with the passage of time. Scagnetti fought in numerous battles, lost friends on the battlefield, and he took the lives of others during these skirmishes. Vincent Scagnetti was an unshakable and dedicated soldier of war during his time in France.

Life after the Great War was much kinder to Vincent Scagnetti, he married the love of his life, and they had a son. The years with his family softened the stern and rugged war veteran. He opened his barber shop and enjoyed what he had earned. Even after the passing of his lovely wife, Vincent continued appreciating each new morning. But that all changed once his traumatic experiences in *A Close Shave* transformed him into the Barber.

The Barber exists only to bring pain, suffering, and death to those he believes are responsible for the death of Jack Scagnetti. Unfortunately for Miles Murdock, the Barber includes Miles and his loved ones on that list. With his scarred face, deadly shears, and a thirst for chaos, the Barber will continue to bring terror to Akelton City until he gets his revenge, or the Purple Scar finally stops him.

I find it hard to believe that the Purple Scar had only a handful of stories released during the golden age of pulps. Having only four stories released in three years would be tough for any character to earn a solid audience. Having those same four stories released during World War II would arguably make it even more difficult for the creators of the Purple Scar. The vigilante never had a chance in the 1940s, and he deserved much more than what was given to him. However, with the popularity of pulp fiction increasing today with the help of companies such as Airship 27, the Purple Scar has a better chance than ever to gain fans. It is up to us, the writers to expand on his small universe, and create new characters that will bring new suspense, adventure, and thrills to Akelton City.

FELIX CRUZ - was born and raised in Philadelphia, PA. Besides his family, the two things he loves the most are writing and watching movies. He is a film junkie, watching all genres and everything from the classics to the cults. But get it straight; his favorite genre is the crime genre, with some of his favorite crime films being *The Public Enemy, Angels with Dirty Faces, Little Caesar, White Heat, The Asphalt Jungle, Le Cercle Rouge, The Taking of Pelham 123* (1974), *The Wild Bunch,* and *Lock, Stock, and Two Smoking Barrels.*

Felix credits his love of films with turning him on to writing, which he has been doing since he was a little tyke. He started out writing short stories, and then moved on to screenwriting. After discovering the books of Elmore Leonard and George V. Higgins, he shifted gears and began writing crime novels, beginning with *Rushing the Row* and moving on to *Daddy's Little Boys.*

He currently lives with his family in Philadelphia, where he is hard at work on his next novel. You can find him on Facebook, Twitter, Instagram, or on his website www.felixcruz.com.

GOLEM CLAY

MICHAEL F. HOUSEL

"**A**in't cha hot in that getup?" the high-heeled brunette in the red dress asked the figure in the gray-splotched coat, as they lingered at the alley's cusp. "It ain't winter, you know, but hey, whatever makes you comfortable. Anyhow, like I was saying, I charge more than the other dames round here."

It irked Paula Pasetti that his face was obscured by his wide-brimmed hat and if she was discerning correctly per the sporadic, neon splash, he sported some sort of facial sack. "All the same, this ain't the sort of thing I generally do. I prefer my appointments in advance with a set price. High-class all the way—that's how I operate."

The figure remained silent.

"In other words, I don't come cheap," she shrieked, catching herself a tad too late. She then lowered her voice and inquired, "You got the bread?"

The stranger nodded. From his coat pocket, he pulled what may have passed for a chalky wad of paper and with his pale, knobby hand, flapped it with a magician's finesse, forcing finer details to surface, in particular a green-fringed Ben Franklin.

Pasetti sighed. She had hoped he was broke.

"Great. We can get a room." She pointed back to the street. "The Boozer's Inn is a classier joint than most folks think. It's got clean sheets, a Bible in every room and a neon sign, for cryin' out loud. That oughta count for somethin.'"

The figure groaned.

"You don't like Boozer's? Okay, where you wanna go? We can hail a cab and—"

"I don't want to go anywhere," he seethed, his voice hoarser than when he had approached her from the surreptitious sidelines. He pointed behind her, at the queue of trash cans. "I want to settle this here."

Paula cringed. "In the trash? Say, what is this?"

He kept mum.

She looked him over and with a click of her fingers, deduced, "You don't wanna be seen. Sure, I get it." She eyed his "face". "You're deformed, aren't you?" She then whispered, "So, did it happen in the war, at work or were you just born this way? You can tell me."

With punctuating thrust, he rammed the spectral wad back into his pocket.

"Okay, all right, it doesn't matter. You got the funds. That's what matters." She forced another wink. "You're the customer. The customer's always right."

He pointed again at the alley.

"Sure, hon, sure, but I want half up front." She hoisted her pocketbook. "I'll stash it away, and when we're done, you shell out the rest." She glanced back. "For a special case like you, that's fifty up front and fifty when we're through. If you'd be so kind to tip, I wouldn't object."

She strutted toward the cans, the neon fading from her frame.

His breathing grew heavy, and he trembled in anticipation, sliding as he stepped.

"Watch it there, hon," she said, granting another glance. "Take your time." The aroma of the cans hit her and she whined, "Not for nothin', but I could make arrangements with Boozer's desk clerk and get you in the back way. Might cost you a few bucks extra, but for privacy's sake…"

He hobbled onward. "I told you—no." His voice had fluctuated from harsh to smooth. "A hundred upfront. A hundred when we're through."

She was stunned. "Really?"

"Yes…really."

In an instant, she quickened her gait, throwing some extra sway into it. "Like I said, you're the customer…"

She reached the cans and faced him, her smile clownishly wide.

"Don't know what you got in mind," she said. "There's not gonna be much room to get creative."

He dangled the hundred, but stopped a couple feet from her.

"Close your eyes," he insisted. "I'll take it from here."

"Fine…but don't forget the dough." She shook her pocketbook, as her eyelids dipped. "You fork it over, and we're as good as gold. Capeesh?"

He shuffled nearer, his hand aimed for the pocketbook.

She cracked a lid, saw him edging toward the unzipped flap. "That's right. Slip it in."

His leaned closer, but as he did so, he pretended to lose his footing and fell into her.

As she struggled with her balance, she noticed the deep, hateful red of his eyes and the gray seepage that curved beneath them.

"What...what in the world?" she stammered.

The hundred disappeared, as the gray gushed down the sack, onto her bosom, creating a thick, tightening web. She wanted to scream, but no sooner had her lips parted, the substance clogged her throat.

"I'm sorry," he said, his voice now as smooth as silk, his sack and coat slipping away, "but you've left me no choice."

Her curvaceous frame caved inward, her entrails greeting the forceful blast, showering her dropped pocketbook, its loose change and lipstick circling her feet. The trash cans popped and banged against the brick wall, until only a looming, amorphous mass stood before them, pumping like some great, gray heart.

The anomaly soon knocked loose the remnants of garbage and bone that it had absorbed, while its sloppy limbs reformed. With this, it pushed itself backward and with a buoyant thrust stood tall and clammy, the warm, night air drying it.

It waited a cautious spell before stumbling back to the alley's cusp and from an inconspicuous crevasse, yanked another coat, hat and sack. Between the neon flickers, it filled the attire like a liquid ghost and then slinked into the shadows...alas, still hungry.

Captain Dan Griffin, along with a handful of Akelton finest, inspected the scene.

"I don't get the hubbub," young Officer Bradford commented. "Looks like nice and dry, more an accident than a crime."

"Don't be hasty," the square-jawed Griffin informed the greenhorn. "There are signs of a struggle here, and this isn't the first to hit the area." He pointed to the quasi-melted, gray-globbed pocketbook. "This one might be the worst yet, though. Heck, even the bums were riled. This is their sleeping spot, you might know. They actually had the audacity to report the matter to the precinct—yeah, an official complaint, of all goddamn things." He clicked his tongue. "Guess we should've arrived sooner, but we assumed they were full of the sauce." He glanced up, the sun tickling his nose. "So, Bradford, any identification?"

"Yes," said the officer. "We extracted it from the pocketbook: Paula Pasetti. She's a known street walker. No great loss, if in fact, anything adverse has happened to her. We still don't have enough to label this an official homicide."

Griffin glowered and was about to give the young know-it-all a piece of his mind, when a garrulous spurt broke from behind.

Onlookers had gathered, a few daring to dash in, but the officers were quick to restrain them.

Griffin redirected his focus to the impetuous display: the same back-alley set-up, with only clay-splotched, personal remnants left to question. The previous, two females involved were still classified as "missing": a high-schooler and college sophomore, each with loose reputations.

As for the substance, testing had yet to confirm it as clay, at least in the traditional sense. He wondered what his friend, Doctor Miles Murdock, famed plastic surgeon and furtive crime-fighter, would say, since to date he had not offered an opinion on the matter.

"Third one this month," a familiar voice called from the crowd.

Griffin turned and caught the eye of Tommy Pedlar, formerly known about the seedy parts of town as the Sticky-Fingered Kid. In recent times, he performed as Murdock's faithful valet and jack of all trades. He was decked in jeans and a t-shirt, his typical gear in past years and now on his rare days off. "Pretty weird, don't you think, Captain Dan?" Pedlar tried to squeeze past a burly officer, but failed. "Gotta be a connection, I say."

"Whatever it is," Griffin hollered back, "we're on it. He wondered if Pedlar was present on Murdock's request or some snitch's scoop. "Now, please keep your distance—all of you." He looked to Bradford. "Don't just stand there like a wart on pickle. Keep those folks at bay. We don't want 'em trampling the scene."

With a snort, the young officer strutted away, granting Pedlar a clearer view.

He had not witnessed the prior scenes, but he knew their details from word on the street and even shared such with his boss. Maybe this latest strike would jar Doc into action. After all, this was more than an act of vandalism, and now with there being three in a row—three missing women, that is—how could his benefactor not take note?

Pedlar skipped away, deciding it best to comb the streets. Somewhere, someone had to know something about this strange chain of events. Even if it was only a measly tidbit he got, better that than nothing.

+++

Murdock finished his crackers and slid the *Akelton Daily Times* across the break-room table. Perhaps he should have placed more stock in what Pedlar had told him.

He was capping off a hard day's work at the Down Street Clinic, a humanitarian venture he had established for the impoverished and a counterpart to the less frequented Swank Street edition.

Folks visited the Down Street Clinic for various reasons, though Murdock's specialty was plastic surgery. He could mend any knife-slashed cheek, and in this austere realm, there were many to stitch. Often he wondered if folks didn't get themselves slashed just so he could make them look better than before their cuts and lacerations: a decent deal, considering that Down Street's services were pro bono.

He never complained, though. His gracious acts gave him substantial practice for the many anatomical sculptures and fabricated faces he created, the most noted being the Purple Scar: a rubber-mask reconstruction of his dear, dead brother's acid-torn face. The ripped-from-real-life design now served as a symbol to fear for Akelton's vile underbelly.

"Finished?" Dale Jordan, his chief nurse, operating assistant and longtime fiancé, asked.

Murdock stood and pretended to pat his lips. "All done, dear."

He would have liked to take her to dinner, if only there had been more time. Even more so, he wished he could take their relationship to the promised, next level, settle down and experience all those important things that defined the alleged good life. But that was impossible in Akelton, where danger lurked at every turn, far more than the police could ever handle.

"Crackers don't make a meal, Miles, but suit yourself. I could've grabbed you a sandwich from the deli."

"The crackers did the trick," Murdock assured her. "Besides, I was more interested in winding down with the evening paper. I like to keep abreast of current events."

"In other words, the city's crime rate." She removed her cap and stretched in an unintentionally provocative way, her bewitching, green eyes beaming. "Why upset yourself? You're doing all you can, whether playing respected surgeon, dashing humanitarian or dark avenger. Let Dan Griffin and the authorities handle the rest."

Easier said than done, thought Murdock. Things had gotten way too out of hand in Akelton for him not to intervene.

"I suppose you're right," he said. "How about we head out? I'll drive you home. The roadster's awaiting in the parking lot."

She consented, and they departed, granting the evening crew their gracious goodbyes, but no sooner had they exited into the stifling, August air, Murdock noticed his confidant, Tommy Pedlar pacing before the dilapidated buildings across the street, his thinning hair and t-shirt soaked with sweat.

"Looks like we've got company," Jordan acknowledged. "Looks urgent, too. Maybe he needs some advice on upholstering a chair…better yet, what to fix you for dinner."

"Be nice," Murdock replied, lamenting his employee's presence, but nonetheless waving him over. It was best to appear calm in the advent of bad news, and no doubt, that's what Pedlar would deliver.

"Hello, Tommy," said Murdock with a smile. "What brings you to this fine part of town?"

"Sorry to trouble you and Dale on your way out," Pedlar explained, giving Jordan a sheepish nod before pulling Murdock to the side. "I thought you might appreciate the scoop. I'm off tonight, as you know, and didn't want to wait until tomorrow to tell you."

"Sure, Tommy, sure…."

"It's about those missing women," Pedlar said, "the ones I told you about. There was another."

"Yes," said Murdock. "What gives?"

"That gray stuff—that clay, or whatever the heck it is—well, it's sure causin' lots of chatter. I talked to some folks, and they said they've seen traces of it near the old synagogue on Lanyon Avenue. They say there were footprints about the area—real strange and sloppy—but it seems they've since vanished due to the rain."

"If there's no evidence, Tommy…."

"But it's the locale, right? Lots of shady things happen there. Maybe it's worth a look. They say an old rabbi still occupies the joint. Maybe he knows somethin'."

Murdock considered the matter. "The Pasetti woman disappeared not far from Lanyon," he inferred, "and there must be a hub from where this strangeness stems. This could be a logical starting point. Maybe I'll pay this rabbi a visit." He patted Pedlar's back. "Good scoop, Tommy. Glad you came to me with it."

"Most obliged," said Pedlar. "By the way, the rabbi's name is Lieberman. They say he's long in the tooth, but who knows?" Pedlar then raised his voice, so Jordan could hear. "It's the least I can do, considering what you've done for me and my daughter, fixin' her up after the car wreck the way you did and payin' her tuition for boarding school. I'm forever grateful for that—willing to do anything you need, anytime you need it, Doc. Don't forget that—and I do mean anything." He bowed and backed away, bestowing Jordan a flap of his fingers. "Sorry again for the interruption. Hope the tidbit helps."

"Tidbit?" Jordan asked as Murdock returned. "Something juicy?"

"Maybe," said Murdock.

"Tommy seemed awfully nervous," she remarked. "He's not usually like that, and mentioning his daughter the way he did. Rather out of the blue, don't you think? With all due respects, it's old news. Wonder why."

"Who can say?" said Murdock. "Sure hope he's not hitting the hooch. Anyway, let me get you home."

Back in his Swank Street studio, Murdock prepared for that night's sojourn. He had donned his fedora, dark suit and accessories, but waited before applying the final piece. In so doing, he contemplated his mounted death masks, fabricated scowls and eclectic, hunting memorabilia. After all, a collection this vast was ideal for getting him into the vigilante mood.

Between a crossbow and rifle was his brother's framed photograph. In it, he wore his police uniform and smiled with unflagging confidence.

If only John had lived longer, there was no telling what great strides he and his old pal, Dan Griffin may have achieved on or off the beat.

Nevertheless, John had fallen victim to Akelton's heartless scourge, shot six times in the spine, stripped and erased of his distinguishing traits (hands, soles…face) by sulphuric acid, his body then deposited into the river, where it festered in the greasy grim for two days before the Harbor Police retrieved it. It was because of John's unjust fate that the Purple Scar was born, not only physically but mentally. Because of his brother's murder, the disgusting way his body had been defiled, a part of Murdock had become scarred, as well. And now John's disfigured persona acted as an eternal warning and symbol of comeuppance to the criminals who beheld it: the perfect form of twisted fate.

Murdock pulled the mask from his pocket and unfolded it. Each blister, bloody boil and stony tooth radiated with angst, intensifying Murdock's need to set things right…

Pedlar's concern was just one in a long series of those rights to be wronged, and the Scar should have moved on it sooner. Three women were now missing: no ransom notes, no indication that they were alive.

With this incentive, he slipped on his second skin, suckling its rubbery scent. He glanced across the room, into the long, wall mirror. The Scar glanced back, with "flesh" feverish and eyes undaunted for yet another night of parabolic revenge.

The Lanyon Avenue Synagogue looked like a war-torn tower under the muzzy moonlight.

The Scar wandered along its side, beaming his pencil flashlight upon the concrete stretch, detecting only meandering cracks. He needed to delve deeper. Too bad his skeleton keys had not worked on the entrance's mass of locks and chains, but a nearby window beckoned.

The glass behind its boards was shattered, but offered enough room for entrance. With athletic finesse, he shot past its marginal opening, landing inside on the balls of his feet, his trusty light aimed.

He fanned the light over a series of collapsed pews and onto a splintered bema, beyond which a subtle flickering caught his eye—candlelight streaming from the room behind.

He began to approach it, when something struck his ankles, making him tumble.

"What gives you the right?" a craggy voice bellowed. "Why you here?"

The Purple Scar shot the light upward, catching a glimpse of the cane set to strike. He dodged it by springing upward, his beam catching his attacker's face.

The gray-bearded man blinked behind his tiny spectacles, giving the Scar enough time to yank the cane from his hand.

"Damn you," the old man growled. "You can't let me be, can you? There's nothing here for you—nothing left to steal or destroy." He flailed his fists. "To hell with this rotten-to-the-core city. Is nothing sacred anymore? Go on, then. Do me in, if you want. Crack my head open for all I care."

"Settle yourself," the Scar croaked. "I'm not going to harm you." He held out the cane. "Go on—take it."

The old man did so and pressed it against his black-robed chest. "Who are you?" he asked. "My taxes are paid in full, straight from my lifelong savings. City Hall knows I'm here—permission granted."

"I'm not visiting to collect or inspect," said the Scar, keeping himself shadowed. "However, I do require some information."

"Information?" the old man bristled. "What information?"

"For one, your name?" the Scar said. "Might it be Lieberman?"

"Lieberman, yes," the old man confirmed, "Joseph Lieberman. I'm the rabbi—or rather was at one time—of this once eminent establishment. And you are?" The Scar hesitated, which prompted the rabbi to slam the cane into the floor, causing an eerie echo throughout the capacious chamber. "If I'm to share information, I demand that it must be tit for tat. Come now—tell me."

"A guardian angel," the Scar quipped, "curious about three women who've disappeared. A peculiar substance was found among their belongings…gray like clay. Some say that traces of it were spotted about the synagogue. Does this sound accurate, Rabbi Lieberman?"

The rabbi's face became drawn, his eyes watery.

The Scar's voice grew gruffer. "Do you know anything about this?"

The old man bowed his head. "Take that light off me. I can't concentrate with it in my face."

The Scar lowered the beam, though still kept the rabbi lit.

"I need to sit," the old man grumbled, "have a moment to catch my breath." He pointed toward the rear. "We'll go to my study…not that there's much left to study…the texts either trashed or donated to those who could care less. I was eating some bread when I heard you scuffing about outside…figured you'd make your way inside. Anyway, follow me. Maybe… maybe I can help."

The Purple Scar trailed him to a small set of creaky steps, which led into the chamber, where the Scar stationed himself away from a shelf of cupped candles, next to a near-bare bookshelf, opposite a table tiered with torn pieces of bread.

The rabbi propped his cane against the shelf and into a wooden chair flopped, gesturing his visitor to take the one opposite him.

"I prefer to stand," said the Scar.

"Whatever you fancy," the rabbi grumbled and flung a crumb into his mouth.

"So," said the Scar, "do you know what's become of these women…who may have taken them?"

"'Taken'?" the rabbi scoffed. "An odd choice of words, with all considering."

"Please, explain," said the Scar.

"This clay, as you call it," the rabbi went on, "has acute, absorbent properties. Even its residue can prove infectious during the short time it lasts. Yes, I know all about the substance: what it is and how it came to be. But believe me when I say, I've had no part in its murderous manifestation."

"Murderous? Then, you're saying these women were murdered."

The rabbi's eyes widened. "Absorbed—that's the better term."

"By the clay? Come now, how?"

"In the wrong hands, this substance can—and will—cause dire consequences. Personally, I'd prefer a carved agent for retribution, if I were ever to seek retribution, but this clay...this clay is tricky. Even one versed in Kabbalah technique can still miscalculate. When molded per a pompous novice—oh, my!—the worst of the worst will hit sky high. There's no telling what attributes the thing may possess, how it may perceive its purpose, not to mention its means to survive. Such are the ways of rogue golems."

The Scar was well aware of the Hebrew myth, but surely the rabbi was joking. "You're saying a golem is behind this?"

"A man is behind it," the rabbi corrected him. "The golem is only ever an instrument, but there are times when the lines blur. A man and his instrument can end up synonymous, their actions and desires one and the same."

"Do you know this man's name?"

The rabbi scratched his beard. "A name, you want?" He looked to the ceiling, rolled his eyes. "A name...a name. I don't think I have a name. I can't quite remember his face, either, but I do recall his manner of speech: educated and refined. I also recall what he asked me."

"And what's that?"

The rabbi grinned. "How and where he might procure the clay."

"And you told him?"

The rabbi glowered. "In no way did I." He tore a chunk of bread and twisted it. "By its very nature, the clay is wicked. I told you that—told him that. Oh, he tried to tempt me with his cash, but I didn't cave." The rabbi shrugged. "In any event, it matters little what I did or didn't do, or so I tell myself time and again. He got what he wanted, as the signs now show."

"Who supplied the clay?"

The rabbi crushed the bread with his thumb and regarded it with disdain. "It appears it was my nephew. He funnels all sorts of illicit goods through his godforsaken curiosity shop. The authorities should confiscate every last, unholy speck of it and yet the smug, little bastard gets away scot-free."

The Scar recalled such a shop. "Is it on the corner of Loew and Wegener, the one called Lenny's?"

The rabbi beamed with sardonic jollity. "Yes…yes it is. Have you been?"

"Not as of late," said the Scar, "but I know the layout: a novelty center for eccentrics and kids, no more or less. And yet…"

"And yet if you knew what to request…if you had the monetary means and the proprietor was low on morals… That's how these unsavory things happen." He shook his head. "And here, this money-flapping buffoon comes to me after the fact, asking if I can reverse the process that my nephew commenced. Yes, I know the basic doctrine, the basic dynamics to initiate the ritual, but that's the grand extent. Reverse the process—please!"

"How long ago did this man return?"

"Not very long…a week maybe," the rabbi conjectured, twisting more bread.

"Did your nephew ever converse with you on the matter?"

"My nephew could care less if I lived or died," the rabbi exclaimed. "When I knew he was the one who sold this character the clay, I told the damn fool to deal with Leonard exclusively. Demand a refund, I said." The rabbi smirked. "He didn't take too kindly to that."

"So this character let you be after that point?"

"Indeed," said the rabbi, "though his absence didn't make me feel one iota better. After the intrusion, I locked everything up—gave some neighborhood ruffians money to board the windows, shackle the front doors. I can unchain the back if I ever want to get out, but for now, I have enough supplies to succor me for several months. Should have locked myself away long ago. I don't like to be bothered, neither by those of flesh and blood nor fabrication." He placed the bread to his lips, took a nibble and frowned. "Even so, I'm confident he won't return."

"I do hope you're right," said the Scar.

"Oh, I am," said the rabbi with a confident grin. "An old geezer like me…I'm not his type. He prefers the young ladies. You understand, don't you…um, what was your name again?"

Long in the tooth, indeed, thought the Scar. "Angel," he improvised, "as in Guardian."

A calm overcame the rabbi. "Ah, yes, a guardian angel. We certainly need more of those in this decrepit zone."

"Tell me about it," said the Scar and stepped to the threshold.

"So this character let you be...."

"Wait—where are you going?" the rabbi asked, springing from his chair. "I know I said that I don't like to be bothered, but there are times when a man does need company. Please—don't go."

The Purple Scar cocked his masked face from view. "I've a friend," he said. "His name is Murdock...Doctor Murdock. I'll ask him to look in on you."

"But...but when?" the rabbi asked. "I don't like to be surprised."

"Soon," said the Scar.

The rabbi grabbed his cane and shook it, "I'll hold you to that, Mister Angel. You hear me? I'll hold you..."

The Scar darted through the window and granted the exterior a final scan before wandering on to the rear.

He studied a stretch of lumpy grass, a series of conspicuous ridges. It looked as if something had stomped or dragged itself across it...something malformed, perhaps heavy.

The Scar trailed every patch of roughened earth, dented fence and open gate along the way, until he came to Loew and Wegener.

LENNY'S CURIOS looked as dismal and desolate as the other battered shops on the strip. Such was Akelton's woeful lay of the land these days.

A cardboard sign in the window read CLOSING SHOP...EVERYTHING MUST GO. From the looks of things, everything had.

The front door was ajar, and so the Scar entered, his light catching a headless, ventriloquist dummy in the corner, a few whoopee cushions on a rack ...scuff marks along the floor.

The rear office and adjoining, living space were in even greater disarray: an overturned desk, couch and chairs, broken plates...a torn, tourist poster of Florida dangling from the wall. He spotted an empty box on the floor and illuminated its rubber-stamped insignia: EXOTIC WORLD MUDS, LAKE TECHIRGHIOL. ROMANIA.

He noticed a door on his left, opened it and gasped. A nauseating stench attacked him: decaying flesh, doused by some foreign seasoning, or so his expert sense of smell discerned.

"Great," the Scar moaned and descended, the light capturing each wobbly step until a leg appeared, its ankle twisted, its socked foot laced with blood. He then highlighted the bloated face and bludgeoned crown, a portion of milky brain exposed.

He then swung his light past the body and saw several wall mounts queued with small urns, bowls, spoons...stirring sticks. Not far from them were large canisters, lidless...ready to be filled. Boxes flanked them, more from Romania, others from Egypt, India...the Czech Republic.

He returned upstairs and poked about for a phone, yanking one from under the desk...

"Hello, Dan...It's Doc. I've a juicy tidbit for you..."

"You don't really think it's some living statue, do you?" Griffin asked, as he and the maskless Murdock stood near the front of the store. "It's got to be some crackpot, just playing the part."

"It's possible," said Miles, if only to appease. Griffin was still shaken by the odor, his eyes ruddy, his nose dripping.

Attendants ushered the stretcher past them, triple-sheeted, but that did little to mollify the stench. Meanwhile, the milling officers pinched their noses and cupped their mouths, except Bradford, who strut confidently about.

"It's a psychological contrivance," he formulated, "all smoke and mirrors to conceal a basic crime. The same goes for those splotches we've seen. I bet there's even a logical explanation for our missing women. It'll all come out in the wash, so obvious that if it were a snake, it would—"

"Clam it, Bradford," Griffin snapped. "I've had enough of your speculative bull for one night. Do something constructive. Help sort the evidence—anything but bend my ear."

The young officer gave Griffin a haughty onceover and drifted away.

"Kind of hard on him, don't you think?" Murdock asked.

"Easy for you to say," Griffin retorted. "You don't have to work with him. Everybody's so damn ambitious these days." He motioned Murdock to exit the shop. "It would be nice for once if folks just did what they're told."

It felt good to be in the warm, fresh air, even though the stench had followed them.

"Could go for a cigarette, if I only had the appetite," Griffin remarked, watching the body get hoisted into the coroner's car. "I still want to talk to that rabbi. Don't care how senile he is. He's this clown's only immediate family. He might spill the beans."

"I wouldn't count on it," said Murdock.

"Whatever. By the way, when the reporters arrive, I'll keep things short and sweet, try to sidestep how we came upon the body. We don't know how any of this connects, but there's no denying a connection exists. We just have to streamline it. Too bad there wasn't a receipt log. We could have used the names for questioning. No matter. I'm hoping our ol' friend, the Purple Scar will nab this fanatic and get those gals back home, assuming the creep's a kidnapper. Let's hope that's all he is. We'll see, in any event. Maybe the ol' Sticky-Fingered Kid can make the rounds. He's good at that sort of thing, and since he's been sticking his nose into the case…"

"I'm certain Tommy will oblige." Murdock glanced at his watch. "It'll be sunrise soon. I've got to change before heading to the Clinic."

"Yeah, sure," said Griffin. "Get your head nice and clear while you're at it. You've had a humdinger of a night. We all have." Griffin patted Murdock's back. The department's most appreciative, Doc. Hip, hip hooray, the Purple Scar comes through again."

Murdock crossed his fingers. "Now, let's just hope he can end this."

"Do what you always do, Tommy," Murdock said, as the two chatted in the doctor's studio. "Prick up your ears, ask around."

"Okay," Pedlar consented, trying to look assured in his oversized, tweed jacket, "but what if I come across somethin' that can't wait?"

"You tell me about it, no different than last night, or tell Dan Griffin." Murdock tightened his tie and then fastened his cufflinks. "Why are you making such a big deal out of this?"

"Sorry, Doc. Sometimes I think I'm goin' around in circles: some silly slob lookin' in from the outside, but never gettin' into the nitty-gritty."

"Leave the nitty-gritty to the professionals, Tommy."

"But I used to be in the thick of it, Doc. You treat me like some delicate flower now. I can make a difference beyond pickin' up tidbits. Really I can—and like I said, I owe you."

Murdock sensed the depth of his confidant's concern. Maybe it was time for him to gather more than just the facts.

"Dan will check the area," Murdock explained, rushing the words before he might change his mind. "That's always his first move when a criminal is on the loose. He's probably initiating the surveillance right now. He'll need plenty of eyes to make it click." Murdock walked over to his desk drawer, pulled out a long, wiry mustache. "It's a tad frayed, but let's see how it looks."

Pedlar held the moustache under his nose and unleashed a hardy sneeze.

Murdock shook his head. "Well, at any rate, we'll see what Dan thinks. Perhaps I can coax him into letting you participate. Sound good?"

"Gosh, Doc, I can't thank you enough," Pedlar beamed. "You won't regret it. I'll make you proud. I swear."

"Okay, then, we'll head to the station. I don't have much time, though. I promised Dale I'd give her a lift."

"Gotcha, Doc," Pedlar handed back the mustache.

"Keep it, Tommy. Consider it a souvenir to commemorate your prospective career."

"Career, eh? Well, what do ya know? Finally—the nitty-gritty!"

"He'll screw it up," Griffin yapped. Murdock and Pedlar occupied his office, along with a brunette in heavy makeup. "Turn around, dear," Griffin told her. "I want to see how convincing you are."

She obliged, her blue dress twinkling under the light. "So, am I convincing?"

Griffin shook his head and slipped her a stick of gum. "Here—try this."

She unwrapped it, slid it into her mouth and gnawed.

"Now, that's more like it…"

"Dan, please," said Murdock. "I'm not asking much. The more eyes you have out there, the better your chance for success."

"And I know this turf, Captain Dan," Pedlar pleaded. "You know that I know it. I've a keen eye for anything that looks fishy."

"You're the one who's fishy," Griffin snapped and then lowered his voice to a whisper. "Come on, Doc. Why put me on the spot? I could get canned for something like this."

"You'll make the allowance because you're my friend," said Murdock, "and my brother's best friend. That holds weight, thicker than blood one might say."

Murdock knew that mention of John would strike a chord. The sight of John's corpse at the harbor—the way his once handsome face looked, all mangled and dissolved—it was not something one could ever forget or dishonor.

Griffin sighed. "I don't know" he said, sizing Pedlar up. "Maybe we can find him a role. He'll have to adapt the required look, of course." He pointed to his gum-smacking subject. "Take Officer Harrington, for example. She's the bait—and meticulously rendered, at that. The missing ladies were brunettes, as well: our resident concubine, Paula Pasetti; the college gal, Freda Farrell; and the high-schooler, Betty Bannon. They were known for flaunting the flash. Their newspaper photos more than tell the tale, if you've seen them. Also, per reputation, they were known to be low on dough. In other words, they weren't adverse to a back-alley rendezvous. The culprit evidently likes that type, and so, there you have it." Again, he looked Pedlar over. "Now, I'm figuring you for a wino. We get you shabby clothes and a glued-on beard. You crunch down somewhere, between the garbage cans, nice and camouflaged-like. If by chance you're seen, it's of no big consequence. You're a mere fixture, a wino, no more or less, but in truth, an eagle-eyed sentinel, who can signal the others if and when trouble strikes."

Pedlar nodded. "It'll be a breeze, Captain. Trust me, I'll be the best, fake wino you've ever seen."

"Now, that's the spirit," said Harrington, still chewing.

"There you go," Griffin guffawed, giving Murdock a wink. "Encouragement straight from our pseudo lady of the night. Can't ask more than that."

"You'll take it from here, I trust," said Murdock. "Dale and I are due for the Clinic: not a place to be fashionably late."

"No problem," said Griffin. "And speaking of Dale, tell her to be careful. She may not be the flashy sort, and she's not a brunette, but at night, she sure might pass for one. She doesn't want to end up in the wrong place at the wrong time, not with this crackpot on the loose."

Murdock nodded and exited to find Jordan waiting outside, adjusting her nurse's cap.

"Hey, there, Dale," Murdock chirped. "Dan said—"

"I heard," she stated. "For a police station, you'd think the doors would be a tad more sound proof. Anyway, I appreciate the sentiment, but I'm more concerned about Tommy…"

Murdock took her arm and they headed down the hall.

"Tommy wants to get more involved. Can't say I blame him. There comes a time when a fellow has to take the initiative."

"That's all well and good, Miles, but Tommy is known out there. People know he's loose with the lips and shares with the police. It's bad enough he romps around Akelton without a care in the world. One of these days, I fear someone will do him in. He's come close already. You pay him well for rudimentary work. Why can't he be satisfied with that? Need I remind you that he has a daughter—one you've assisted more than once. You could be positioning both of them in harm's way. Is that what you want?"

Jordan was right. In much the same vein, he had often distanced her from his investigations. It was why, though she wore his ring, they had never tied the knot. To think of the danger he had subjected her to, whether directly or indirectly, made him cringe.

Now, here he was throwing caution to the wind with his trusted aide (a man who looked upon him, as he had looked upon John). He was using the poor fellow like some pawn in a chess game. It was bad enough Pedlar had sustained a bullet during that confounding, pharmaceutical caper: "the German Connection", as Murdock had come to call it. To boot, Pedlar had already put his life on the cliff-hanging line several times over. Sure, their bond was mutual (with one owing the other as much), but as with any taut relationship, its string could—and probably would—unspool.

"I see your point, Dale. Let's just let it ride for the moment, okay? Again, the Purple Scar is on the case. He'll keep a sharp eye on Tommy—on everyone involved."

"I'm sure you will," Jordan mumbled.

There was no point beating the bush. The minutes were ticking by, and he had to get to the Clinic to commence the daily routines. The sooner such was done, the sooner he could focus on the case.

Murdock dabbed the stitching above the bald bruiser's black eye, when someone knocked at the door.

"Yeah," Murdock called while pressing a bandage onto the stitches. "What is it?"

"Sorry to bother you, Doctor Murdock." The coroner attendant stuck his head inside. "We've got the body. I'm assuming you want it on ice."

"Pardon?" Murdock patted the bruiser's shoulder and motioned him toward the door.

"The cadaver," the attendant said, as the big guy squeezed past him. "The fellow donated his remains for study. You signed the paperwork, made the arrangements, remember?"

"Oh, sure," said Murdock, "but the body was to be delivered to Swank Street, so I could store it until display in my operating odeum. I believe I left instructions to that effect."

"We took it to Swank Street, knocked on the back door, just as you specified, but no answer. We figured that fellow, your assistant, would be there."

"Yes. Well, we can't store the specimen here." He pulled off his gloves and flung them into the receptacle. "Let me get out of these duds, and we'll head to the estate. Really, if it's not one thing…"

Within minutes, Murdock was traveling in his roadster, disgruntled and disappointed, not only in Pedlar but himself. By the time the coroner's car reached the rear, his agitation had peaked. He jumped from his vehicle and ushered the men and the body inside.

"Place it in the side room, in the wall compartment. You know the drill: no different than the city morgue." He then heard someone enter the hall and looked to find Pedlar making his way down it, his gait confident, smiling from ear to ear. .

"Glad to see you could make it," Murdock jeered.

Pedlar's smile faded, as his memory jarred. "Oh, gosh, I'm sorry, Doc— real sorry. Guess I lost track of the time. Captain Dan had me try on different disguises. It took longer than you'd think. We're stickin' to the wino routine for tonight. Stashed the goods near the front door, so I'll be all set when the time comes. Anyway, let me give you a hand…"

"Never mind, Tommy," Murdock grumbled and returned to the attendants.

Pedlar listened to them grunt, push and clang, then watched the men depart. When Murdock re-emerged, he appeared apologetic.

"Sorry I snapped at you, Tommy. It's not your fault. I forgot about the arrangements, as well. I'm just glad the attendants knew where to find me."

"I got the whole afternoon to make up for the mishap," Pedlar suggested. "I could head back to the street, maybe rub a few more elbows. I'm sure there's a ton of chatter since Leonard Lieberman's murder hit the mornin' paper."

Murdock shook his head. "Why don't you just tidy up around here and save your energy for tonight. I'm going back to work."

Pedlar frowned and let him depart without further word. He then sulked about the medical rooms and ultimately, the freezer chamber, where on a whim, he slid open the wall's metal slab, curious to see if the corpse was young or old, male or female.

He let the compartment's icy breeze engulf him, the result of the apparatus' coolant vents: a high-powered version of what Murdock had commissioned for his abode and its adjoining work stations, keeping all sections nice and fresh throughout the year.

Pedlar lifted the sheet. Male...middle aged. If standing, the cadaver would have been about Murdock's height. Probably a heart attack did the poor bugger in. Of course, it was his head that Doc would tinker with, in order to give his visiting students those essential pointers on facial reconstruction. Still, not a bad lookin' guy.

Damn shame to be struck down in one's prime, Pedlar mused. One had to make the most of life while it lasted. Even in his own right, he was no longer a spring chicken. That was why he wanted to latch onto this case, dig deeper into the investigative intricacies of it, do something more challenging for a change.

He moved on, checking the rest of the premises, finding nothing in need of immediate tending or mending. So be it.

He snatched an *Exciting Mechanisms* from the magazine rack and wiggled into one of Murdock's big, comfy chairs, next to a side table with a quaint, reading lamp and a bottle of dandelion wine.

He flipped to an article on radio-controlled robotics, "...their construction and related purposes in the future". He poured some wine into its accompanying glass, took a sip, absorbing the articles' details, finding the content fascinating and surprisingly practical. Doc had some spare steel stacked out back, he recalled, and replenished the glass and took another sip...then another. Maybe he could construct a mechanical butler to do the chores. Now, wouldn't that be a hoot, even if the damn thing did put him out of a job...

He felt a yawn come on and decided on some shuteye before the evening's venture.

His lids grew heavy, the magazine slipped from his hands, and into the warm, cushioned softness, he sank.

Rita Harrington considered how many nights she would have to play the decoy, how many wardrobe changes she would be allotted for her performances, how many matching pocketbooks…how many sticks of gum. She was adamant not to shell out for any of it. No ifs, ands or buts, she would stomp her stiletto at any such suggestion.

Earlier that evening, she had been propositioned by a couple old coots who she dissuaded with an extravagant price: a walloping, five bucks each to get a mere peck upon the smudgy brow. At least the coots didn't push the issue and left without incident. Still, if this was any indication of what was in store, the stretch would be a long one…

She eyed the officers stationed about the area, all within careful view: one in the window of Denton's Diner (the antithesis to Akelton's prestigious Blue Moon); one in the window lobby of the Haystack Hotel (Boozer's prime competitor among the seedy sect); one loitering near the Tick Tack Five & Dime…and where was that wino? Wasn't he supposed to be stationed at Laramie's Liquors? For the life of her, she could not pinpoint him. Perhaps for the sake of their clandestine dealings, it was just as well.

As the moon grew more prominent, more men came around. Some struck up conversations with her; others hinted at something more. Perhaps she looked too officious for any to dare seal the deal.

There came a point, however, when nothing but crickets and passing cars characterized the atmosphere. She considered signaling Griffin, if he was even about, to cut the shenanigans short and pick a livelier spot for the next night.

It was then that this weird guy in a floppy hat and coat crawled from out of the shadows. Griffin had said the suspect might be lugging some clay, buckets or canisters maybe, but if this was the guy, he must have hid them away.

"So, honey, how ya doin'? Looking for some fun, some action on this hot, steamy night?"

The man glanced about and lowered his head. If only she could make out his face.

"Cat caught your tongue?" She smacked her gum and clicked her way toward him, but not too close. "Now, don't be shy. My name's Rita. So, you lookin' for a good time or what?"

The figure nodded.

"Swell. What's your name?"

He hesitated and then whispered, "Mudd."

"Mudd, you say. If memory serves me, a fella named Mudd had somethin' to do with John Wilkes Booth and Honest Abe, but then I ain't no historian." She laughed. "It's a good name, though. Memorable…

Anyhow, whatcha have in mind, Mister Mudd?" She cocked her head and gave a couple suggestive chews. "It's anything goes for ol' Rita, as long as you got the money, and if you do, I guarantee you'll come away smilin'."

"I don't want to talk here," he answered, his voice now neither harsh nor smooth, maybe a little of both at different times and perhaps, if she was hearing right, tinged with a certain femininity. "We can go to the alley, out of the moonlight."

"I like the moonlight," she said, stalling. "Moonlight can be romantic."

"I don't like it," he grunted with a dismissive swat of his pasty hand.

"Sure, okay, have it your way." She fluttered her lashes. "Why don't you take the lead?"

"I insist you go first," he said.

Maintaining a smile, she turned, her eyes shifting toward the diner, the hotel...the five and dime. Come on, guys. You watching? You with me?

She clicked her way to the alley's cusp. "Okay, here we are."

"Farther," he said, "where it's dark."

Harrington's heart raced, but she clicked onward, into the garbage and the smell of piss, cheap whisky and wine.

She glanced back and then discerned the pillow-case sack on his head. His eyes glowed behind its crooked holes like ruby gems, hypnotic and commanding. She felt dizzy, but was it out of nervousness or something else? She felt magnetized, too, as though her bodily fluids were being scrutinized, juggled and prodded, but how? Why?

"Okay...all right, I'm reasonable with my...my services," she explained, looking past him, again for a sign of rescue. "If you tell me what you want—and please do take your time and be specific—I'm sure we can come to an agreement."

He tapped his pocket. "I've the cash...plenty of cash. I'll show you."

"I'm sure that you do, sweetie. I've no doubt of that, but it's the specifics that I need. I need you to tell me precisely what—"

She saw crescents of gray building under his eyes, dripping onto the sack, curling like tears.

"Oh, dear God," she gasped. "Oh, dear—".

Fast footsteps clacked across the rooftop, followed by a great swoosh. In an instant, a stealthy, dark figure had fallen upon her aggressor, knocking him to the ground.

Her rescuer raised his fedora, a spurt of invading moonlight revealing his face—purple and scarred. His intense gaze met Harrington's, as if to say all would be fine, except that her perpetrator had found the strength to rise, elevating the Scar, who then sprung off with fists poised.

"Hold your ground," the Scar snarled, noticing the fresh, gray splotches that began to form about his adversary's stony feet. "I mean it. It's over now, Mack!"

At this point, the undercover officers rushed in, Griffin in the forefront, his badge gleaming, pistol aimed.

The aggressor turned to face them, revealing the heeled indentations where the Scar had landed.

"You heard the man," Griffin shouted, shocked by the character's semblance. "Hands up. Don't make this difficult."

The fiend groaned, as he turned back to the Scar, the sack now one with the enveloping mush.

"What's wrong with him?" Harrington squealed. "His face—it's...it's melting."

The Scar scanned the entity's semblance, which looked like an amateur's take on a Classic Greek statue, neither male nor female.

With reciprocal awe, the entity regarded the Scar, eyes glistening in respectful kinship and cautious fear, its husk crimping and shifting.

"You're in pain," the Scar stated, hoping the empathetic gambit might coax it. "I can tell. It's all right. Turn yourself in. We can help—"

The thing answered with wailing and flailing, sliding toward the officers and even inspiring one to fire.

A slimy chunk blew from the thing's shoulder, but the spot appeared to reform no sooner than it had splashed, leaving the creature more outraged than hurt.

It charged, but the Scar interceded, landing at its feet, hoping to trip it, but instead it glided around him and then the officers.

"Stop," Griffin shouted, "Stop in the name of the law..."

This time he fired, though the thing averted his bullet, stretching like lightning along the sidewalk, merging with the brick walls, using both shadow and light to its insidious advantage to disappear.

"Where'd the bastard go?" Griffin cried, stomping about.

Frustrated, he marched back to his men, teeth bared, nostrils flaring. "Who asked you to fire, Bradford? Who? Not me—that's for damn sure."

Bradford, garbed in faded flannel and patched dungaree, returned his gun to his concealed holster. "Sorry, sir, but under the circumstances—"

Griffin landed a rock-hard right to the know-it-all's chin, knocking him flat on his ass.

The other officers pressed in, begging Griffin for restraint. Meanwhile,

Harrington stumbled out of the alley, her bosom heaving like a freight train.

She spit out her gum. "That wasn't real, was it? It...it couldn't have been." She turned to Griffin, but his attention remained on the young officer.

"You screwed up everything, Bradford," the captain growled. "You brassy, little bastard. The Scar had it under control. He could have subdued that...that lousy freak. He could have—" Griffin looked about, but the Scar had departed. "Goddamn it all to hell."

To add fuel to the fire, Pedlar then appeared behind them, sporting his glued-on beard and hoisting a bagged bottle of grape juice.

"Sorry I'm late," he said. "Did I, uh, miss anything?"

It was hard for the Purple Scar to track the entity. For something that may have been dissolving, in need of nourishment, it mustered astounding agility.

It traveled the sidelines, sliding low and close to the curbs, slipping in and out of alleys and open yards. However, when it skidded into a stretch of high grass, the Scar was able to catch up, thus throwing if off track, as it rubbed against a nearby wall.

Like a ball of blubber, it flexed outward upon its pursuer's approach, its small head tottering above its oversized torso, ready to bolt. But before it could, the Scar unleashed his toxic pen, squirting its "face" with a black splash, hoping this would prove more effective than a mere bullet.

The substance stained the thing's clammy exterior, and it twisted and shook.

"You're cornered," the Scar asserted. "Now play nice and come clean. Who's pulling your strings? Who set you in motion?"

Its head cocked to the side, revealing an uneven ridge about its brow, where a hat had once rested. The black fluid flowed like a Rorschach blotch down its left cheek and up again.

"Give me what I need," the Scar threatened, again poising his pen. "Who controls you? Who's your master?"

The thing steadied, seeming to contemplate its circumstance and then in a voice as meek as a child's, whispered, "No one."

The Scar leaned forward. "What did you say?"

Its throat constricted as it re-conjured the words. "No one." Once more, it gurgled. "I am my own master…my own device." A red eye slid forth, fixing on the Scar, absorbing the pursuer's mangled cavities. "And what may I ask, are you?"

The Purple Scar was struck by its odd articulation. "An angel," he replied in homage to the rabbi.

The thing looked at the pen, as the stain subsided. Another eye then emerged, pushing the first a few notches across, so that the two became aligned.

From its thin, crinkling mouth, the creature cackled in a way that was more fairy-like than monster, "I don't think so... I believe you're more mortal than angel."

"Perhaps," said the Scar, "but I'm not the one in question. Women have gone missing. Why?"

The misshapen form shrugged. "I must…stay alive."

The Scar cringed at the implication. "I know a doctor. His name's Murdock…Miles Murdock. He specializes in deformities…their remediation. He's the best in his field. If anyone can help, he's the one. I'll lead you to him…"

The creature hesitated, giving the Scar hope that he had reached it, but then it began to quake again. The Scar felt its vile vibrations pressing against his temple, as if his thoughts were being scanned, leaving the thing to purr in evident satisfaction.

"I said I'll take you to him," the Scar continued, shaking the strange sensation. "We can take a back route if you—"

Before the Scar could finish, the thing had jolted like a ball of jelly onto the asphalt and in a staggering swoop, accelerated onward.

The incensed Scar followed, hoping again to impede its path, but the thing had adapted an irregular, zigzagging pace, becoming harder to detect among the shadows and light. In little time, the Scar had lost sight of it and in shameful regret, abandoned the chase.

He contemplated the wracking situation. This golem (if that was the right classification for it) hungered like a germ, and no germ ever resigned its ravenous spread without an antidote. Even if he could capture it, how the hell could he—or anyone—cure it, let alone put it out of its monstrous misery?

+++

The creature hesitated...

"How's Doc?" Pedlar asked, creeping into the kitchen. He was still in his shabby costume, traces of spirit gum and fake fuzz globbed on his checks. "I'd rather not bother him, Dale, but the better part of wisdom tells me I should."

Jordan was still in her nurse attire, making sandwiches. Murdock had phoned her that there had been some strange altercation, but she knew he really only desired her presence.

"He's in his studio, Tommy." She didn't look up. "I was about to head there. I'd ask you to go along, but I don't think it's wise."

"Gotcha," Pedlar slouched. "I don't know what's wrong with me, Dale. I wanna do good, and I've been doing good, and yet somehow or other, I still mess things up. Boy, did the captain ever blow his stack when I showed up late. Wouldn't even tell me what had happened. Can't say I blame him. No doubt Doc will do the same."

"Sit down," she said, revealing her strained, emerald eyes. "Have a bite. I'm sure you're hungry."

As Pedlar sat, Jordan slipped him a napkin and plate and then took the chair opposite him.

"I know you want to do good, Tommy," she said with maternal grace. "However, there are certain things you should stray from. For one, you don't have the training that Miles and Dan do, not to mention the police. You're good at gathering information. That's great, but even that's risky, considering your sources. I mentioned all this to Miles, only out of concern for you. You're a father. You need to be more careful, and there's nothing wrong with taking some extra time off when you can."

"I hear you, Dale. It's just that…"

Jordan gave him a scornful stare. "You're well paid, Tommy. There's a lot to do around the place and within the reasonable hours that you're assigned. There's always something in need of repair. Deliveries get made. They need to be signed for…"

He looked down and sighed.

"Your basic services are important, essential even. I know you'd like to do more, achieve more, but you're not helping if you reach too high and let promises slip. I don't know exactly what happened tonight, but it seems you missed the mark. You should stick to what you do best and be content with that. That's all Miles has ever wanted of you. Understand?"

"Sure I understand," he conceded. "Believe me, I do, but I can still do more than just fixin', cleanin' and signin' for stuff. I was just lookin' through this magazine that Doc has, readin' this article on remote-control robotics: none of it's as tricky as you'd think. Doc has some scraps out back. I was figurin' he'd get a real boost if I…"

Her frown spoke volumes. Tommy swallowed hard, lifted his sandwich, but had lost his appetite.

"Know what, Dale? I appreciate the sandwich and all, but maybe I'll head home. Hope you don't mind."

"Not at all, Tommy." She patted his hand and smiled. "Just remember, no matter what you do, I'm proud of you."

He smiled back and stood. "Thanks. I appreciate that. See you later."

He exited the kitchen, touched by her kindness but feeling like a jerk even so. Maybe he should just cut everybody a break and quit.

With head hung low, he headed into the hall, when suddenly he heard a pounding at the door. He hesitated, listening as a prolonged squeaking ensued, as if the door was being unhinged, followed by a clamorous thud.

"Say, what's goin' on?" he asked. "Is that you, Doc?" No answer, only an unsettling silence. "I say, is that you?" He then heard an odd shuffling. "Come on—answer me."

He saw a shadow stretch into the hall: bulky in one way and yet at certain angles, slender. Could it be what he thought? Griffin and the officers had kept him in a lurch, but he still overheard them whispering about some strange person or thing that sprung out at them. But no—this had to be a trick of the light.

"Who's there? Come on. I mean it, I'm not playin'."

It dragged itself nearer, prompting Pedlar to take a few steps toward it, at which point its full, frightening form came into view.

With a slit of a mouth, it grinned, its crimson eyes bulging. Was it male…female? That was the scary part. It was impossible to tell.

"Tommy," Jordan hissed, scampering behind him. "Tommy, what's going on? Who are you talking to?"

"Get back, Dale," Pedlar warned. "Don't come any closer. Get Doc. Get him now."

Jordan was set to do so, but from behind the creature, the acrobatic master of the house had already made his entrance, having swung his way down from the studio, onto to the front porch.

"May I help you?" Murdock asked.

The thing stiffened and spun around.

"It is you." The creature gurgled. "Miles Murdock—the man behind the mask." It gurgled some more. "Your internal workings…I can sense them …just as I did on the street." It gave a sloppy bow. "I am honored, sir. Sorry for the delay, but I decided to take a private path to your home. I knew where to go. The Murdock estate is...renowned."

Murdock savored its presence, fishing for a means to trap it.

"I said I'd help," Murdock replied, "but with all due respects, a simple knock would have sufficed."

"Forgive my brashness. I've grown a tad anxious. I have no desire to be splashed again by your trusty ink pen." It croaked a coarse chuckle or was it more a giggle? "The fluid did rather sting."

Murdock glanced at the knuckle-smeared door: some splotches thick, others now fading. There were also subtle punctures along its top and bottom: marks that suggested an attempted seepage.

"I've no time for jest," Murdock resumed, his expression taunt, his voice borderline Scar. "Again, if you require my help, I'll grant it, or else…"

The thing slumped, throwing its hands down as if to shove them into its pockets, if it still had any.

"What will it be?" Murdock demanded.

Its eyes turned a woeful pink. "I'll accept your help, Doctor Murdock." It restrained a burgeoning laugh. "As you can see, I'm in no position to argue."

Murdock had directed his guest to a surgical bed, where it now lay sheeted (an awkward means for modesty, since the cloth had already gained splotching), its tendril-like arms and stubby feet hanging from the sides and ends.

Though Murdock had donned his gloves and medical apparel out of professional habit, he evaded his surgical mask. True, the entity might be infectious, and if so, the damage was done.

"You're alive," Murdock informed it, "breathing and such, but your physiology is beyond my range. An X-ray might reveal more, though I doubt it, not to mention an exploratory probe, but for the moment, we'll tend to what we're given. Your face is pliable, with the obvious inclination for both subtle and drastic change. There's still some bone structure stationed beneath. I can't categorize your gender, due to your apparent lack of genitalia. Whatever has altered your framework has also deleted the distinction."

The creature appeared transfixed by the globed, ceiling light under which it rested. For the interim, it had become inarticulate.

"I don't know how you came to be," Murdock continued, "but I presume you encountered a severe, chemical imbalance. It likely caused your mutation, along with your accelerating drive. A verbal account would be helpful. It appears you're more communicative at certain times than others. It's probably due to the fluctuation of your throat and tongue...an absence of teeth. You were emoting quite well a while ago. Might you give it another try?"

The golem opened its mouth, but only emitted a vague pant.

"I see... Might you participate in a hypnosis session, then? I could possibly cull some details that way. You'd be surprise what the power of suggestion can do." He moved to the side of the bed and waved his gloved hand before the creature's unblinking eyes. "I neglected to mention, in addition to being an ace plastic surgeon and nocturnal crusader, I'm a psychologist." He lowered his voice, turning his tone drawled and smooth. "So, are you game...ready to try?"

It mustered a halfhearted twitch.

"Good. Now, you appear to fancy the light. That's a start. I want you to continue gazing at it. As I count, you'll grow sleepy, and then when I ask, you'll answer my questions accordingly..."

Murdock's murmured instructions only reinforced the surreal state. It was as if he were speaking to a prop. If not for the thing's prior, calamitous behavior, he may have scoffed at the current scenario. Was he a doctor or Geppetto?

"Mudd—that's not your real name, is it?"

Its mouth moved, but nothing came.

Murdock tried again. "Tell me your name...your real name."

Again its mouth moved. "Brennan," it then said with crisp succinctness. "Brennan Millgate."

Murdock was impressed and wasted no time to seize the moment.

"How old are you Brennan Millgate?"

"Thirty-eight."

Murdock smiled. "Your occupation..."

"Professor."

Murdock raised an eyebrow. "Do tell. In what field?"

"Philosophy...archeology...art."

"Which do you prefer?"

"Art... I...I sculpt."

"I've been known to dabble myself," Murdock confessed. "Do you prefer a special type of clay?"

It nodded.

"What kind?"

It frowned, the sides of his mouth caving inward. Perhaps at this point, the topic was touchy. Murdock decided to backtrack.

"Are you married?"

It shook its head no.

"Have you ever been?"

It paused, then said, "Yes."

"Your wife's name..."

It gurgled, then cooed "Maria," as if it were the most beautiful utterance it could make.

"Maria Millgate," Murdock stated. "Lovely. Where might she be?"

"Dead."

"May I inquire how she died?"

"Cancer."

"My condolences... How long ago did she expire?"

It raised its hand, extending a long, clubby finger.

"I see, a year... You miss her, do you, Brennan?"

It seemed displeased, as evidenced by the putty-ish curls about its eyes.

"Sorry, I was merely hoping to get a better notion of—"

Before Murdock could finish, the golem had sprung up, its shell seeping of moisture. Murdock was baffled by the reaction and expected the worst, but the thing just sat there, looking straight ahead, immersed in its agitation.

Murdock decided it was too risky to continue. He would recommence later.

"I'm going to count backwards. When I do, you'll lie down...rest until I say otherwise. In the interim, you'll have no recollection of this sojourn..." Murdock watched the moisture recede. "Ten...nine...eight..."

It fell back and shut its eyes, its lids as smooth as polished steel. Perhaps it now looked more female than male. It also appeared tranquil, thank goodness. "You sleep that deep sleep," Murdock suggested, "dream only pleasant dreams."

He then exited the room, only to find Jordan and Pedlar standing close by, ears arched.

"Listening, eh?"

"Couldn't help it," said Jordan. "How horrible. It had a wife...a life... What suffering it must have endured."

"I'm sure you could say the same of the women it consumed," Murdock added, throwing his gloves into the contamination bin.

"I didn't mean to sound unsympathetic," she said, as Murdock moved toward the sink. "I saw what it did to the door. I can only imagine…"

"Can you?"Murdock began lathering up. "Its disease, if one can call it that, isn't even on the books. Somewhere along the line, it played with fire, and boy, did it ever get burned, not to mention those who've crossed its flame." He looked at Pedlar. "Tommy, I want you to chain the door. Can't say that'll be enough to keep it contained, but it's worth a shot. I'm only hoping my hypnotic inducement will last." He turned back to Jordan. "I want you to leave. You're too close to being dark-haired for comfort. Like Dan said, this character prefers that type. How much you want to bet Maria was a brunette?"

"Well, I've no desire to put myself in danger," Jordan assured him.

"Then you'll keep your distance until I give you the okay."

"Still, you need assistance around here," she argued. "Tommy can't help you with the medical end of it."

"What medical end of it? I'm playing a mere mesmerist until I figure out what else to do." He pointed to a nearby chair. "I'm planting myself by the door tonight. When I'm not here, Tommy will fill in."

"Why not ask Dan?"

"The time isn't right to pull Dan in. I need this thing quarantined, for select one-on-one analysis. Besides, in that unlikely chance it should awake...should attack, I've enough ammo to put the police to shame, though it appears guns won't do much except rile it. No matter the situation, I can rely on being nimble and quick to avoid its wrath. Remember, my dear, I am the Purple Scar." He tapped his temple and winked.

"Maria Millgate...yeah, I got the scoop," Griffin said, performing like his old, cocky self, but beneath the surface, Murdock knew last night's calamity still hounded him. "She's connected to the mud monster, obviously. That's why you dropped the name, as well as her husband's."

"The surname surfaced through basic inquiry," Murdock explained.

Griffin stepped from his desk. "You mean, the Sticky-Fingered one got the digs." He looked Murdock in the eye. "I probably shouldn't place much stock in it, then."

Murdock ignored the remark. "So what do you know about Millgate… either one?"

"For the wife's sake, she was an alleged looker in her time and yes, a brunette, but later down the line, a sickly sort. She got breast cancer…died."

"What else?"

"It may not have been the cancer that did her in. Somethin' may have beat it to the punch."

"Like what?"

"She fell down a flight of stairs, cracked her head. Anyhow, the coroner's report says it was an accident, but some suspect she was pushed. Neighbors said her husband was real temperamental. A professor, no less. No doubt still is—a temperamental professor, that is." He laughed at his cleverness. "Anyhow, I got the scoop straight from the captain in Pleasantville. He's a real good buddy of mine."

"What else did your good buddy say?"

"Oh, it gets juicier. It seems that her husband, Brennan Millgate, is this spongy, little guy—no Clark Gable, if you get my drift—but if some young thing wanted to secure a good grade, he wouldn't turn a blind eye to the prospect. He knew how to fling around the academia to impress, particularly weird folklore and sexual taboo. Hey, whatever works, right? It ended up where two universities, Radwell and Cyprus Hall, had to terminate him. Faculty talked. Students gossiped. Parents complained. Was the result so surprising? Before Mrs. Millgate met her demise, Doc Millgate claimed he was unable to make ends meet. Seems, though, he had a decent sum in the bank, and yet lingered at this fleabag apartment in the worst part of town. How's that for oddball behavior?"

"Delightful," said Murdock, meshing Griffin's description to the slumbering shape he had locked away. "What of the fleabag apartment?'

"Ah, it's been rented out several times since to fly-by-nighters. The landlady says she was going to toss Millgate out anyway. Too noisy, she said, but who knows? She even claims she heard Maria Millgate moaning up a storm, and this was after she died. Go figure. Anyway, she told my buddy that Millgate's junk—old clothes, books, parchments and such— were tossed into the trash once he flew the coop after some big, floor-stomping rant. She also claims he had these little, clay figures he was working on—all women, same design, sculpted from dime-store putty, or so one presumes. His wife's photos were clustered along with them, evidently. Weird and worthy of notation for this case. Anyhoo, no point in tracking the stuff down. It's no doubt buried deep in some landfill, left of Timbuktu."

"Has anyone seen Mister Millgate since?"

"No word on that," Griffin replied. "Considering his state of mind, he might be hitting the flop houses, sleeping in alleyways, maybe the sewer for all we know...rounding up dames for some whacky ritual. Your guess is as good as mine."

"I see."

"And so I ask you, my other good buddy, how's this connect? There's the clay angle, but still, is Mister Millgate our guy or just some sideline eccentric?"

"I'm not sure."

"I know you're fibbin'," Griffin smiled. "You want dig into this on your own, don't you?" He slapped Murdock's back and chuckled. "So, did Sticky get any more than the names? Best to come clean, chum."

"Tell you what, I'll toss you something when I have it. Really, Dan, I'll be in touch—promise."

"Sure thing, Doc," Griffin put out a vinegary pout. "Oh, and by the way, our lab boys still can't make heads or tails out of Lieberman's stash. The content's pretty esoteric, they say..."

Murdock nodded and dashed off, wracked by confusion and perhaps a decent heap of fear. If the golem was not an incidental victim of poisonous judgment, then what? Had Millgate played the poverty-row part only so he could someday pay for an exotic substance? Indeed, what were the motivational hows and whys? He had to know.

"I fixed the front door as well as I could," Pedlar reported, sitting at his post, holstered pistol on his hip and *Exciting Mechanisms* open on his lap. "It's creaky, though. We'll need a new one." He cocked his thumb at the lab. "That door's a lot sturdier. Lots of intertwining chains and girders to keep it in place. I reinforced it with some odds and ends I grabbed out back."

Murdock regarded the complex arrangement.

"Oh, you wanna get in, sure," said Pedlar. "Allow me..."

Pedlar leapt from his chair and popped loose the intricate bracing he had applied with several curt twists and snaps, allowing the frame to slip onto his chest.

Impressive, thought, Murdock, and he may have complimented Pedlar on his unorthodox ingenuity, if not for being impatient.

Pedlar set the contraption against the wall and gave it a proud rub.

"There you go, sir." He then turned the knob and with caution, cracked the door. "Haven't heard a peep. I assume we're okay." It was obvious he wished to regain Murdock's favor. "I'll head in with you, if you want."

"That won't be necessary, Tommy. I intend to pick up where I left off. If you sense anything amiss, re-latch the door. It doesn't matter if I'm inside. Do what's necessary."

Pedlar agreed, though he looked more uneasy than compliant.

Murdock walked in, clicking the door shut in such a way that it should have disturbed the mound. No question, hypnosis was a grand sedative, unless he was being conned.

He walked to the bed and eyed the creature's head.

Its features had smoothened: the cheekbones a trifle higher, the brow smaller. Indeed, all the more female than male. Maybe even closer to human than monster...

"Brennan...Brennan Millgate...do you hear me? Remain as you are, restful and relaxed. Do you understand? If so...nod."

It did so.

"Good. I have additional questions for you. Please do answer them." Murdock waited, if only to fortify the psychological ambiance and asked, "How did Maria die?"

It said nothing, its calm, cold countenance only adding insult to injury.

"Was it the cancer that did her in? A simple yes or no will suffice."

Again, nothing.

"How did you feel after she died? Were you lonely? Did you miss her?"

The thematic inquiry caused the golem's lids to shift, implying thought.

"Come now, how did you feel?"

The golem moaned its moisture remounting.

"Sit up if you'd like. It's fine by me. Whatever prompts a reply..."

The bed rumbled, and with this, the golem sprung up, though its trembling was subtle this time, while the moisture streamed more heavily. In fact, Murdock had to leap away from its uncanny spray, but that wasn't the only unnerving consequence. His heart began to beat in fervid skips.

Despite this, he kept a placid facade, while extending his deep, vocal command. "I asked...how did you feel?" but much to his dismay, his vision blurred. When he looked again, he was startled to find that the golem had changed form.

It was definitely a "he" now, but more precisely, a little man in a patched suit, squinting through a pair of oval-shaped lenses. His head was round, his skin pocked and to say the least, his physique spongy.

Reversed hypnosis, Murdock deduced. This was not good. He was supposed to be the one pulling the cerebral strings, not the creature. On the other hand, this might be a means for him to get the information he desired.

"Are you who I think you are?" he asked the little man with feigned innocence. "I presume you're Brennan Millgate...the true Brennan Millgate? Am I right?"

The little man offered a confirming smile.

"So, Brennan Millgate, would you be so kind to answer my questions? Would you tell me how you felt when your wife died?"

He rolled his eyes and in a sharp, squeaky voice replied, "Angry, terribly, unconditionally angry—that's how I felt."

Murdock appreciated the honesty, even felt the little man's contempt, absorbing it as if it were his own. "So, sadness held no part?"

"After a time," said Millgate with matter-of-fact panache, "sadness did come. I missed her to the point that it hurt. She was such a striking, caring lady, optimistic in spite of the penultimate cancer. Poor, sweet thing... never understood what she saw in me, but on occasion, she said it was my artistic ability, the way I forged beauty from clay that lured her. She also said that I was the kindest man she had ever known, the sort who wouldn't harm a fly, but it was all a lie—my lie. I harbored hatred the whole while. I couldn't contain it forever. Sooner or later, it had to manifest. When it did, it spread like wildfire, as did the lust, the greed, all those vile things that make any man bad."

"And Maria—she never saw that side of you?"

The apparition smirked in a way that was chilling. "Of course she did. I abused her, verbally mostly and endlessly so. I believed she hampered my ambitions. I took everything out on her, but through it all...ah, through it all, she remained at my side, seeing only what she wished to see: the man who wouldn't hurt a fly." He laughed and slapped his knee. "Meanwhile, I scrimped and saved, but never once let on that all was fine. Sooner or later, I would make my great escape, burrow my way into some exotic, foreign land and mingle with the fairest of the fair. Would she go with me? Maybe, but probably not."

Murdock's dislike for the man grew. He despised the hate Millgate shared. He hated the man's jubilant selfishness. He was an ugly, little specimen, on the inside and out—and far uglier than the androgynous monster he had become.

"Tell me, Millgate, what prompted you to push Maria down the stairs?"

The little man squirmed. "Pushed her, you say?"

"Yes, pushed her."

His face scrunched in disgust, his hatred doubling, tripling, pounding Murdock in a merciless wave.

"I explained all this to the police. I told them she was frail. They saw that she was frail. She lost her footing, hit her head. Accidents happen."

"You killed her. That's the gist of it, isn't it?"

Millgate folded his hands, dousing his petulance enough to say, "And what if I did? One does one's best, except that I struggled fiercely as the days crawled by in that doleful apartment. I did love her in my own particular way. It's just that when a man is tempted by young brunettes, he loses track of what's right before his eyes. Maria was once one of those beauties. Ironic that I should find in others what she once possessed and no doubt still possessed, if only I had taken the time to look for it. Without her, I realized how much I needed her, no matter the cost, but this time as spry and lovely as she'd once been...more or less."

"And how were you to achieve this lofty goal?"

The little man contemplated the matter. "I couldn't resurrect her. There was no hope of that, but perhaps I could refashion her semblance in some specialized form. I knew of the Hebrew legend, the one of conjuring life from inanimate properties." He held up his hands and wiggled his fingers. "I had a way with clay, but for a tip-top result, I needed a material unlike any I had used before. I needed that magical, archaic blend. The question was, where might I find it in this modern age?"

"And so you asked around," said Murdock, letting the little man's memory penetrate his thoughts. "You had connections throughout the academic world. One led to another. Joseph Lieberman was said to know. You took your cash, waved it at him, but he dismissed you. No matter. He was said to have a nephew, a skilled smuggler of sorts, who dealt in cryptic merchandise. Why not give him a try?"

"You've pegged me all too well, Murdoch. Leonard had learned much from his uncle, too much perhaps and yet not enough. He procured the scrolls for me and promised the rest thereafter. We fixed a price. It was high, mighty high, but I was eager to invest, especially after he shared all the details."

There came a moment drawn and stressed, wherein the two did little more than regard each other, their thoughts and emotions swamped and prickling.

"The canisters were heavy as hell," the clay man continued, "but I got each and every one to the apartment. I rolled up the rug, threw down a sheet and placed as many photos of Maria as I could around my work station, but it was the thrust of my memory, my passion that guided me. As I had done with many, smaller prototypes, I molded her in the nude, right down to the smallest detail, just as she looked in years gone by: subtle curves, right height, a wee goddess, even if a pale, solid gray." Millgate paused and then uttered in a breathy whispery, "I swear, I could hear her voice, only to realize it curdled through my own." He giggled. "Ah, the sweet allurement of anticipation..."

"And once the sculpture was done," Murdock surmised, "you recited the words from the scrolls."

"Oh, yes," Millgate concurred, "straight from them, all enunciated with my reasonable, broken Hebrew, not a note missed. Then, I waited...and waited. I prayed...and prayed. But no matter how hard I looked upon it, the statue didn't move. It only seemed to harden and cool. Damn it to hell, I thought. After all that effort and money, what was I to do?"

"You slept on the couch," Murdock extrapolated, envisioning the scenario with uncanny clarity. "The hours ticked by, and then—"

"I felt her." Millgate's eyes twinkled behind his lenses. "She was cold yet warm, the clay like skin. I looked straight into her pupiless eye, and I kid you not, she smiled. Alive—she was alive."

A sick churning filled Murdock's groin. "You kissed her, embraced her." He cringed. "You—oh, dear lord."

"It went on for several days, several nights," Millgate boasted, "over and over. That my flesh grew damp and raw was of no consequence. That there came an intense itching about my wrists and along my thighs—what did I care? I never once considered infection. It only mattered that she did what I asked, time and again, absorbing my lust, my hate, my very essence. In the process, I overlooked the fact that she was withering away, just as the original Maria had, and yet she wasn't so much fading as she was merging with me." He tapped his chest. "By mating with me, she was becoming me and in the reckless interim, I was becoming her...or that is, her reproduction. One morning, she was gone, if only in the visible sense, but when I looked in the mirror, at my hairless, pallid skin, the breadth of my bosom, I knew the truth, and it startled me to no end."

"Who could possibly help you at that point?" Murdock asked.

"Leonard Lieberman, perhaps. I approached him before he closed shop one night, revealed what I had become. He was frightened, denied he was to blame, asked me to leave, and so I did, despondent, afraid...then hateful

"By mating with me..."

again. I kept returning night after night, banging on his door, the spread of the clay defining me. He kept turning me away, said he was closing shop for good, moving to Miami or some such place. He told me to see a doctor, join a circus, perhaps do myself in. His condescending attitude only intensified my rage. When I could take it no more, I broke in, went after him. He headed for the cellar, probably thinking he could seal himself away." Millgate raised his fist. "I caught him, though—struck him." The little man hammered down and grinned, a touch of red enflaming his eyes. "I guess I didn't know my own strength. He was dead, and I was still the same. Then in desperation, I went to his uncle, but of course, the old cretin was of no more help than when I first approached him. And that's when those strange urges started: thoughts and feelings I couldn't comprehend. I yearned for Maria, and she yearned as much as I did... for precisely the same thing. Instinct dictated that we stay replenished, and what better way than to seek the young, dark-haired females we desired. We could live through the absorptions. The trick was to find the right candidates. They were the only ones that instinct...that passion...permitted us to devour. No others would do."

"Your selfish desires painted you into a corner," Murdock murmured, sickened by the scenario, "and now you're a freakish conglomerate with a hunger that worsens. But it's always been Brennan Millgate who's pulled the strings. You're your own sick puppeteer, cursed by your own, misguided cravings."

Millgate only emitted a conceited stare.

Murdock rubbed his eyes, desperate to shed all aspects of the nightmare. When he looked again, the little man was gone. The golem, moist and dripping, fell back upon the bed. Its eyes closed, wearied from its confession.

Murdock sprung from the room and found Pedlar waiting, his face ashen and drawn.

"I could hear, Doc. Can't believe it. A murderous male and female, trapped as one. How can it be, Doc? How can it?"

Murdock motioned Pedlar to re-shackle the door. "I don't know, Tommy. Where does one begin and end on something this strange?"

+++

There was much to consider as the hours passed, and because of it, no time to waste.

Murdock returned to the lab with some food (apples, oranges, a slice of beef). He asked the creature to awake and eat, but what Murdock offered was not what it needed or desired.

Would a lack of nourishment cause its dissipation? At this phase, it wasn't changing its basic formation, not shrinking or expanding. There was no sign of regurgitation or excrement. Beyond its ability for telepathic projection, would this be its permanent guise?

For hours, Murdock paced, the propped masks in his studio regarding him, mocking him, including that of the Purple Scar. He held it to the light, contemplating its etched ugliness. Thank God his brother did not sport the hideous face when alive. If he had, what would he have done? Hid away like the golem...committed suicide?

These ghastly considerations forced Murdock to plunge deeper into morbid thought. He felt the urge to scream, smash, do whatever indignant thing Millgate would do. There was no doubt that the spiteful, little man yet affected him, just as the clay had further propelled Millgate's resentful rage.

And then, as if the timing could not have been more imperfect, someone knocked on the door.

"Yeah, what is it?" Murdock snapped, assuming it was Pedlar. "You're supposed to be on watch."

A meek, nervous voice replied, "Miles, it's Dale. I know you said you didn't want me here, but I've been worried. I used the key to get in. Tommy doesn't even know I'm here. You weren't at the Clinic today or the hospital, and I know you're prone to go out at night. I didn't know if I'd catch you. Anyway, may I come in, please?"

Murdock flung the mask to the side, brushed back his hair and adapted a pretentious glow. In truth, he didn't want to see her, but to turn her away might only worsen the situation.

"Sure, Dale, come in."

She slipped past the cracked door, moving with a quiet pace. She wore a fashionable, green dress, which complemented her soulful eyes and lush, auburn hair. Was it auburn? In the dim light, it looked darker somehow. Even so, there she was, all dolled up with nowhere to go, except...

"I hope you're not angry with me, Miles. I know I'm going against your orders, but this situation is so surreal. I'm scared, as you can well tell, though not as much for me, but for you."

Murdock was taken aback, perhaps even insulted. "By now you should know, Dale, I can take care of myself."

"But that...that thing..."

"I thought you felt sorry for it," he chastised, but just as soon regretted his terseness. "It's confined, Dale. I don't think we'll have a problem."

"So, you don't think it'll change its mind...try to get loose?"

"I didn't say that." He was growing frustrated. "I mean, why take an unnecessary chance? I couldn't live with myself if...come on, you understand."

She stepped closer, her eyes lit with yearning. "I got dressed up for you. I wanted to look nice."

"You always look nice, but I don't think this is the right moment, Dale."

She moved close enough to place her cheek upon his shoulder. "Hold me, will you? I'm not asking much."

He resigned the fight. She was here. Why not make the most of it?

"Please, Miles, I need you..."

Her warmth consoled him. He wished to reciprocate, but there was something brewing beneath the surface, beyond what may have been love, lust or the insinuating scent of her favorite perfume.

He heard her heart thumping in unison with his own. How peculiar.

As the seconds ticked, the situation grew even stranger, for he then sensed the passionate rush of her blood. It was as if their souls, their very essence, were beginning to intertwine. Was he as weary as he claimed? Was he still under the influence of that jarring, golem exchange?

He pushed her away. Her expression was unreal...fabricated, leaving him to infer, "This is a ruse, a lousy trick." He jutted his fingers out to her, cutting through her gossamer neck, leaving her image to totter and crackle, and then like a puff of smoke, it was gone.

Murdock ruptured with rage—yes, that ol' familiar, Millgate rage—and recognizing its influence incensed him all the more.

Try as he may, he could not stand still. He had to get out of the house, get away from this intoxicating spell or else go insane, if he had not already.

In his ardent fervor, he grabbed his fedora, gloves, guns and coat and of course, the mask, and with an insatiable urge to purge, hastened into the moonlight.

+++

The air felt like pea soup, but compared to the fiery tension of Swank Street, it was a cool, crisp paradise, where he could run with unabashed gusto, evading the weird phenomenon he had experienced. Before long, he caught wind of a crime, and with a stamina culled from his old, football days, darted across the rooftops.

When the perpetrators' Ford Sedan cascaded in sight, he landed with precision upon their roof, startling its driver enough to hit a stop sign. Steam seeped from the car's hood. The driver and his confederates leapt out, looked up with guns cocked, as the Scar somersaulted over their heads, onto the street, as limber as a cat.

They fired upon him, too distraught to notice his demonic scowl, only the remarkable manner in which he dodged their bullets.

The Purple Scar may have just as well snatched his handy .38s, but it was evident these fools were hasty amateurs: faces exposed, gestures erratic... all wearing light-colored clothes. Why waste ammo on them, thought the Scar, when it was more fun to kick the driver in the chest and whack the others across their chins?

His rapid assault dazed the fools, but did not disable them, leaving them with enough mettle to fire some more. In a flash, the Scar disarmed them one by one, swatting each to the ground, positioning them on their backs.

He fed off his rage, his brother's memory hitting hard. The Purple Scar now made certain the culprits saw his brother's wounds, striking them over and over as he did so, energized by inexhaustible, emblematic revenge, and he may have battered them forever and a day, if not for the sirens' collective wail.

The squad cars screeched to a halt, prompting the Scar to sprint to the shadows. With bruised-jaw Benson leading the way, the officers pointed their guns at the ravaged crooks, ordering them not to budge, as if they could.

The Scar, meanwhile, reached into the vehicle and grabbed a strung sack of cash.

"Tough one, eh?" said Griffin, swaggering forth, cocking his thumb back at the brutalized men. "Maybe we should take them to City Hospital instead of the pen."

The Scar tossed the sack into Griffin's chest. The violent assault had rejuvenated him, and he was glad for having made the unrepressed jaunt.

"Thought it might be our clay creep," Griffin confessed, juggling the sack from hand to hand. "The report referenced a disturbance at Gary's

Groceries: broken glass, kicked-in door and such, but that was all. In any event, I had to see for myself."

As the officers led the cuffed crooks away, the Scar took a few steps back, hoping to truncate the exchange.

"I've done my part here," he said with gruff finality. "I'll be in touch."

"Hold on, will yah?" Griffin insisted. "Any new leads?"

"If I had any," snapped the Scar, "I'd have shared them."

"Well, I talked to that rabbi. Wasn't easy—pried my way past the synagogue entrance. A real pain in the ass and against procedure, mind you, but what's done is done. Anyway, the old fool was of no help—senile beyond repair. The name Millgate didn't ring a bell, either. All in all, a waste of time."

"Sorry to hear," said the Scar, backing farther into the shadows. "Something will surface. Give it time."

"I can't keep a lid on this forever," said Griffin. "The sooner we settle this, the better. Folks will start demanding answers, especially if more incidents occur. With what we've got, who'll believe?"

The Scar didn't reply, resuming his sojourn into the night. Indeed, he didn't believe any of it either, even though he engaged it firsthand.

He cut through the alleys and side streets, his mind buzzing and brewing, hoping for another chase or altercation. Either would be ideal for him. After all, fighting the good fight did ward off those infiltrating thoughts and visions—all in John's memory, of course.

Yes, it was all for John...well, perhaps the both of them...Dan Griffin, too. Anyone who had been scarred one way or the other by the city's sinister scum. How he wished to smash, pound and kill every last one, and if he played his crusading cards right, he might yet have the chance. And if not, what was the point?

While his thirst to vengeance prevailed, he also considered the rabbi. Such a poor, tormented soul. Why not pay him a visit? After all, the Purple Scar possessed superior, interrogative tact than Griffin, skilled though the detective was. If he could regain the rabbi's trust, perhaps he could also gain more insight.

Regrettably, when the Scar reached the synagogue, his intent sank. Not only were the entrance's boards and chains pendent (Griffin's doing, no doubt), the structure invoked a troubling emptiness.

He triggered his light and entered. "You there, Joseph Lieberman?" he asked, his voice fluctuating between Scar and Murdock. "I say, are you there?"

He swung the light throughout the decrepit decor, illuminating the woeful dust and rubble, but as he entered the room, he realized the truth.

The rabbi was seated with eyes and mouth open, head cocked back, a slash of browning blood across his neck. On the floor was a ruddy puddle, containing his cane and a carving knife.

Among the table's crusts of bread, next to a seeping fountain pen, the Scar spotted a note:

To Those Who Find My Carcass:

I am forcing enough clarity upon myself to leave this farewell message, in that I cannot halt the creature's heedless deeds. The haphazard thing my nephew helped create will continue to seek and absorb living matter without reprieve, all to sustain and increase its demented drive. I should have stopped this abomination—convinced the man who desired the formula to abandon his reckless pursuit— but due to my short-sightedness, the horror now spreads.

The monster will not die. Bullets or any related form of artillery will only cause it temporary pain. It knows instinctively what to avoid and what to consume—nothing much more than living flesh and some accompanying bone. An abundance of anything dead or inorganic could prove fatal, but it is too shrewd to be fooled. This is its impregnable, insatiable advantage, an innate means to thwart any hindering element. By now you know all this, for surely you have made your acquaintance with the demon.

I tried to push its existence from my mind, pretend it never came to be, but guilt has overwhelmed me. Because of it, I have decided to take the coward's path and end my wretched life. Forgive me for what I have done, or rather did not do.

Sincerely,
Joseph Lieberman

The Scar bowed his head in regretful respect. Was he not as bad (and as mad) as the rabbi, for having eschewed the situation's urgency?

He considered the scribbled commentary, despising yet relishing its content, in particular the phrase, "nothing much more than living flesh and some accompanying bone". Well, it certainly consumed clothing, but clothing was soft and porous, perhaps incidental to its overall composition and perhaps easy to regurgitate per a disgusting deposit.

It had reacted negatively to the ink, though the formula had only triggered a fleeting reaction. What if the thing were dipped into a vat of it? But what was the practicality of such a stunt? It would take too long to accomplish. And the longer the thing lingered, the craftier it could become.

On the other hand, if it was as evil the rabbi claimed, why would it request help, let alone find solace in incarceration? In less than a day it was prepared to absorb another female: a sign of enormous need. Why the change of impulse, the inexplicable restraint...the telepathic ploys? Indeed, what ulterior motive did it have up its clay-caked sleeve?

Perhaps it was hoping to find a host other than its raven-haired maidens, and what better way than by luring the Purple Scar. But was the Scar the right match...was Miles Murdock? Maybe it wished to weigh its options before deciding, ensuring that the one it absorbed would possess the right properties to grant it a lasting, physical constitution. Maybe, just maybe...

Somewhere within his pondering, Murdock then realized the utter folly of his crazed spree. It was fine to use anger to achieve a goal, but if his actions were unstable, that made him no better than the wrongdoers he tracked. For the Scar's crime-fighting crusade to succeed, coherence was paramount. Thank goodness he was far enough from the creature's influence now to realize it.

As such, he could not allow the ghastly thing to maintain the upper hand. Miles Murdock possessed the incomparable, mental prowess to hold his ground, to turn the tables on any opponent. It was only a matter of how and when.

His thoughts peaked and faltered, but by dawn's advent, he had a plan: by no means full-proof and without question, cursed by kinks, but a plan nonetheless.

Hours passed. Murdock had worked with fearless diligence, making certain everything went to plan.

As such, the lights flashed. Droning words were dealt. Red eyes opened, closed.

Murdock counted backwards...snapped his fingers.

The golem looked up in petulance.

"Why all this light?" it asked, its voice husky yet sweet and more so than before, tinged by Millgate. "I fail to see the point."

"I'm initiating the next phase," Murdock explained, adjusting one of several, surrounding hospital lamps he had commandeered from City Hospital. "I prefer to work in stages, or did you miss plucking that particular nugget from my head?"

"I'm no mind reader by habit," it said, "but I do seem to have a penchant for tossing about emotional baggage. I imagine it's part of my auxiliary physiology. Through my newfound nature, I absorb and if the variables are conducive, toss back. That's all."

"Toss as much as you wish," Murdock encouraged. "I've decided to record our sessions for scientific posterity." He edged away. "If you don't mind, I'll be back with the equipment."

The golem sprung up, swinging its lumpy legs off the edge, its hip protruding with pronounced femininity. "And if I refuse?"

"You're under my care and therefore, my command." Murdock smiled. "To use your words, you're in no position to argue."

"I'm cognitive," the thing countered with a slippery smirk, "fully autonomous. I evidently regained my senses when you snapped me in and out of that superfluous trance."

"I'll reinstate the process." Doc Murdock promised. "It shouldn't prove too difficult. Really, how hard is it to count backwards?"

With immense distaste, it said, "I would prefer that you not."

"As you wish. I'll still get what I desire, as will posterity."

The golem groaned and wheezed, slimy moisture spurting from its pores. The lamps shook as if from an earthquake, and then as if by an invisible hand, Murdock felt himself being dragged across the floor.

"What the—" he exclaimed, swiveling into the bed, catching his balance with a deft turn of his heels. "Ah, I see," he admonished, regarding the thing with enraged astonishment. "Your powers are, indeed, greater than you pretend, but it only goes to reason. You prompted that image of Dale last night and filled me with enough rage to make me leave the estate. You wanted to see how far your influence would extend, before taking it to the next level."

"You combed the city of your own accord," the golem negated. "As I said, sometimes I toss back, but in this case, the manifestations were of your own design: lustful, hateful spawns of your subconscious mind."

"Your acknowledgement of the details clinches my claim. You are, therefore, to blame."

The golem grimaced. "Inferring something and causing it are two separate things, Doctor Murdock. A man of your intellect should know that."

Murdock shrugged. "Why should I place stock in one who murdered his wife and then used her essence to murder others?"

"Rationalize all you want," the golem simmered, its eyes reaching a rich red, "but I won't comply. We're equals, you must realize. I may be the veritable monster, and you merely a man who masquerades as one, but our intentions connect. We both hold an insatiable urge for control. I can't master the need because of my physical impediment. You can't because, unlike your phantasmic facade, you're merely an anguished man. However, if we were to come to terms, we both might gain what we desire. Akelton could be our oyster, devoid of its present foibles and flaws: paradise made real, Doctor Murdock, and without any want for the Purple Scar. Think of the possibilities. Think of such for posterity's sake: a surgeon by day and a malleable crusader by night, with only one face in the forefront. However, for the process to work, for your intellect to mend unconditionally with mine, you must willingly share it, with every ounce of sharpness and insight it contains. I can't take it from you…force it from you, or else the merger will be as muddled and imperfect as those that have preceded it."

Murdock wavered and placed his hand to his brow, hinting that the creature's words…its thoughts…resonated.

With a slobbering flick of its wormish tongue, the golem slid off the bed, the crusty sheet falling to the floor, revealing the gamut of its globular form.

"You're skilled on many levels, Doctor Murdock, but sooner or later, you were bound to tumble. You can ensure that your crusade was not in vain. I could give you that much, if you'd only share with me." It presented its limp, mushy hand. "To the best of both worlds, Doctor Murdock. What do you say, my good man?"

At this point, Pedlar wandered in, looking stressed. "The equipment's all set." He kept a decent distance from the thing, avoiding its gaze and to Murdock whispered, "Don't listen to this devil, Doc. We've got a plan—document everything from this point on. No stone left unturned, remember?"

Murdock gave Pedlar an uncertain glance, but that was as far as their exchange went, for his assistant was then tossed from the room per the golem's telekinetic hurl.

The lights flickered fast, initiating a long, electrical buzz, before settling on a series of slow, methodical flashes.

Pedlar moaned. Murdock budged, but the golem's suctioning grip kept him stationed.

Into his ear, it whispered, "My way is better. Think of it. You even get to keep the girl. I know how much you desire Miss Jordan. Our merger would secure your time together, all without fear of consequence...a lifetime devoid of threat or danger. Isn't that what you want? Of course, I'd only ask for one compromise: that she dye her hair shiny black."

Murdock watched Pedlar rise from the floor, rub his rear...straighten his hostler. He glanced at his employer as if to say he was okay, but then ambled off.

"You talk a good talk," retorted Murdock, "but none of your absorptions have endured. Why would this be any different? There's little chance that my semblance would permeate, let alone my consciousness."

"You're wrong," the golem exhorted. "The answer came to me as I dreamt: sharp and clear. Only the ideal physiology can remedy my progression and grant us enough sustenance to rule as one. I know what strength and fortitude you hold. I've tasted it, want it as much as when I commenced Maria's simulation. It's not a coincidence that our paths have crossed. I'm certain it's destiny."

"I don't believe in destiny."

"But you do," the golem emended. "You sought it when you fled last night, running with your torment, pretending to enjoy it. You'll never be at peace, Miles Murdock, unless you take an alternate path." It pulled the surgeon close, its coldness penetrating his warmth. "A man who wears a mask to hide from his true self—a man who puts his life on the line night after night—possesses little more than a death wish. You now have the chance to embellish your life, with all the comforts you've garnered."

The lights continued to flicker, making the room bounce and bend.

"All the pain, all the guilt will fade," the golem promised, "as if none of it had ever existed, just like the clay, a means to an end."

Murdock hesitated, as if fighting the urge, but then slipped his hand into the golem's.

"Send the handyman home. Let my words settle in. When you're ready, you know where to find me."

In silence, Murdock departed, the lights perpetuating their solemn beat.

The golem grinned, its dripping husk tingling with anticipation.

"It will be mine," it trilled, "all mine."

+++

A short while passed before the shouting commenced.

"Good—fire me. I don't wanna work here anymore—not with that damn freak callin' the shots."

"It's your choice, Tommy, and good riddance. You're on your own."

Angry footsteps followed, the slamming of a door. The golem rubbed its hands, depositing gray flakes upon the floor.

Minutes ticked by...then hours. All the while, the golem transmitted its thoughts in tune with the flashing lights, believing such would fortify its subject's loyalty, but why was it taking so long?

Then just when it thought the endeavor might prove in vain, Murdock called from the adjacent room: "Millgate—I'm ready."

The golem grinned and followed the voice, cutting through the hall with a confident swing of its hips, toward the side door.

"Millgate—where are you?"

The golem turned the knob...lumbered in.

The chamber's opulence was inspiring, with surrounding seats of high, elegant tier, and in the bare, operating center stood Murdock, garbed as the Purple Scar. He hoisted his arm in acknowledgment, his trusty fedora shading his upper face, the bottom blurred in smeary violet.

The golem's face sagged, missing the point.

"I wished to put old habits to rest," Murdock announced, his voice lower (though devoid of the Scar's usual acridness), a trifle muffled perhaps and distanced, as would be the case under rubber. "Do you object?"

Millgate sniffed the air, drawing Murdock's omniscience, which encircled the prodigious chamber with voracious zeal. "Not at all," it conceded. "For the sake of embarking change, the symbolism fits."

With a gleeful, sloshing gait, it waddled nearer, admiring the man's sturdy frame. Too bad he hid his face behind a fright mask, but no matter. The right face—the perfect face—would soon become the one and only.

The golem sniffed the wafting sweat of Murdock's suit. "The threads will melt," it said and regarded the mask. "The same goes for the disguise. Neither substance is potent enough to impede the process, though their insertion may make us dizzy for a spell, but not to worry. We'll shed the excess easily enough."

Murdock raised his other arm, signaling his willingness to comply. "The sooner, the better, Millgate."

Murdock's essence spread, oscillating with a peculiar, close-yet-far dynamic. Tempting yet taunting—how charming, the golem mused and straightened its back to match its partner's height and stance.

The Scar's hands extended, landing upon the golem's slippery shoulders.

"That's the idea," it said, its voice in lilting juxtaposition. The theater's lush, circular scope furthered its hunger. Its stomach rumbled. "Mine...all mine."

A cloudy spray soaked Murdock's suit and in turn, bled through the cloth. The golem looked pleased, ramming its innards into the fabric at full steam, but in so doing, it then sensed a telling chill and took note of the corpse's cold, pinned eyes.

"No...no—noooo!" it yowled.

This was death, not life: a carcass in lieu of a living man. In exasperation, the golem shook from side to side, snapping the corpse's puppeteered braces.

"The inanimate made animate," Murdock proclaimed, stepping into the chamber in his smoking jacket and tie: so cool and at ease, the envy of any man or monster.

"No...no," the golem cried, its eyes phasing from bruised brown to panicked yellow. If only it could retract the flow. "You...you tricked me."

From the other end, Pedlar appeared, smiling as he held a small, levered device, looped with coiled wires.

"I apologize for the switcheroo," Murdock teased. "The poor gent donated his body to science in good faith. I do believe his wish has been fulfilled. There can be no cause greater than your demise."

Millgate sank farther into the flaccid cadaver.

"It was easier than I thought," Murdock bragged, "a clever combination of mental fortitude, hypnotic suggestion, ventriloquism and hours of triggered lights: the latter a reinforcing drill to make you believe you had found the solution to your predicament. Really, did you think I was so disgruntled to become your sacrificial lamb? And those see-through gloves sure came in handy—so much for any infectious stain." He rubbed his palm and sneered. "However, my favorite moment will always be how you took the bait. You may have consumed life in order to live, but now death defines you, Brennan Millgate."

The golem sprung up, its muddied shell severing the cadaver, while ascending the Scar mask high upon its bulbous tip like some devilish trophy.

"I presume this quells your absorption pangs." Murdock shook his head. "May you now starve for an eternity in the bowels of Hell. It couldn't happen to a nicer...thing."

In one, mighty swoosh, the mound struck the floor, its repugnant layers kicking and writhing, limb twisting over limb, until only a headless hill remained, like that which it consumed, dormant...dead.

The mask glided toward Murdock per a lonesome, gray trickle, inviting him to retrieve it, but he let it be. He had plenty stored away.

Pedlar switched off his device. "Well, I'm glad my control panel worked, Didn't know if it would over the long haul, having to lift the arms and all. It's not as if you gave me a whole lot of time to test the waters, Doc. Riggin' those lights was tricky enough."

Murdock patted Pedlar on the back. "You did good, Tommy...real good. I'm proud of you."

"Shucks, Doc, that's why I'm here. It's all part of the nitty-gritty and of course, my prospective career."

Some days later, in the precinct's back room, flanked by queues of filing cabinets and cartons, Griffin regarded the uncloaked heap of interlocking appendages.

"Looks like abstract art, but then those clay splotches did, too." He took a drag of his cigarette. "I've never been keen on modern art. It always gave me the willies."

"Well, this one should prove the ultimate case in point," said Murdock. "I'm surprised you'd insist on keeping it, but considering it's evidence, as you say. Where will you store it?"

"Right here. Probably in a nice, steel crate, where no one'll monkey with it." He blew smoke at the thing and chuckled. "Still can't fathom how you managed it, but I'm glad you did. Even so, I'm not keen that you were so hush-hush about harboring a monster, but as long as it was for the good of Akelton's citizenry, I won't complain."

Bradford entered the room, a stack of folders braced under his arm. "Oh, sorry, Captain. Didn't know you were here." He nodded at Murdock. "Wanted to do some filing." He looked at the repulsive sculpture. "Wow... weird. Would make a swell centerpiece for Halloween."

"You're telling me," said Griffin. He paused and sized up the young officer. "By the way, Bradford, I was informed you did an exemplary job exposing that real-estate scam. You prevented a lot of folks from getting swindled. Excellent work."

Bradford blushed. "Thank you, sir. Appreciate it. I'll come back later to finish up, and thanks for the compliment."

"Why, that was decent of you, Dan," Murdock remarked.

"Ah, why hold a grudge, especially considering your update on ol' Tommy-boy? Everybody deserves a second chance."

"Or a third or fourth," said Murdock.

"Don't push it, Doc," Griffin barked.

They then took a further moment to contemplate their hideous souvenir.

"It troubles me to keep those gals on the missing-persons list," Griffin complained. "Doesn't give much closure to the families, but I've come to realize, there's sometimes no practical way to unveil the truth. And as far as the rabbi goes, too bad we couldn't have intervened, but such is life... and I dare say, death."

"I know," Murdock agreed. "At least the golem is out of commission. We can savor that much."

"All the same," Griffin thumbed his chest, "I'm keeping a report on the ordeal for my personal archives, right along with all that other concealed-from-the-public stuff."

"You don't say?" said Murdock. "Many cases?"

"Many?" Griffin laughed. "You're darn tootin'. Got 'em stashed under the letter 'P'—you know, 'P', as in my good buddy, the Purple Scar."

THE END

A SCAR BY REQUEST

How could I say no to Ron Fortier when he asked me to contribute a story for a new, Purple Scar anthology? Fortier has done a lot for me. People read my stories because of him and of course, his trusty partner, Rob Davis. To fashion a tale was the least I could do and above all, a huge honor.

If the truth be known, I became fond of the Purple Scar when I read Fortier's novella, *Faces of Fear*: a Scar/Black Bat crossover. I am also drawn to dark avengers in general, as long as they don't fly too far off the righteous handle. As such, my writing a Scar story seemed a natural fit.

But I wondered, what type of Scar story should I tell? Should it be crime based or something give-or-take supernatural?

Decades ago, I had drafted a short story about a golem. I believed it was effective, but abandoned it when a pompous pundit proclaimed it substandard. Nevertheless, my unpolished yarn haunted me over the years, along with such beloved fables as the silent classic, *The Golem: How He Came Into the World, It!* (aka *Anger/Curse of the Golem*) and the coming-of-age *Snow in August*.

I thought it might be interesting if the Scar combatted a classic creature. Why not a golem? But not a standard golem. My old draft featured a golem that manifested per gross miscalculation. It was also female in form. (To be honest, I always fancied that scene from *The Mummy's Curse* where Virginia Christine's Princess Ananka rises from the mud. Indeed, she was not a golem, but for all intents and purposes...) Anyway, I believed the concept could present a chilling challenge for the daring Doc Murdock.

To rattle Murdock's nocturnal chains further, I decided to add homages to John Payne Brennan's "Slime" and its famous, Irvine H. Millgate knockoff, *The Blob* and brushed them with a generous coat of *Kolchak: the Night Stalker*.

Whether in its original design or as a New Pulp melodrama, "Golem Clay" emerges not only a man-vs-monster parable, but a tale of addiction, selfishness and greed: those unwholesome ingredients that have come to distinguish Scar lore.

I hope my contribution works its creepy charm: that you, the reader, have had as much fun absorbing it, as I have had writing it.

MICHAEL F. HOUSEL - is the author of the Airship 27 novels, *The Persona, Vol 1: Enter—the Persona*, its sequel, *The Persona, Vol 2: Green-Fleshed Fiends, Mark Justice's The Dead Sheriff, Vol 4: Purity* and the novella, *The Hyde Seed*. Housel is a faithful fan of offbeat fiction, movie monsters, and fantastic films. He resides in Trenton, NJ with his wife, Donna.

THE BLACKMAIL HEIST

FRED ADAMS, JR.

Sonny Marmont knelt beside the big steel vault in Bilvane Machine's payroll office. The little man took off his rimless spectacles and put his ear against the thick steel door.

"Hurry up," the big man behind him hissed. "That watchman could be back around any time."

Sonny crouched beside the safe and impatiently waved him away. "He's on a Detex. He has to make a full circuit to each key station before he gets back here again. It'll be forty minutes. Now shut up,, Buzz. I can't listen to you and the tumblers at the same time." He pressed his ear against the steel door as his spidery fingers delicately turned the dial.

The cracker was annoyed at working with Buzz Miller. He was used to working alone, but the boss insisted that Buzz tag along. The muscle head talked too much, he desperately needed a bath, and his white knuckled grip on his revolver told Sonny that Buzz was way too edgy for this kind of work. He'd have to ask the boss to send somebody else with him in the future.

The safe was a Kenzler, an old one but made with German pride in precision. The stair-step door was machined to fit so perfectly into the frame that only a hairline crack defined it; one inch locking bolts on three sides, external ball bearing hinges, and a big brass dial with tic marks from zero to a hundred etched on its face to work the safe's six tumblers. A work of mechanical art.

Sonny Marmont was probably the best safe cracker in the trade, and had somehow managed to evade the law for over ten years, largely because he chose the jobs he'd do and the ones he wouldn't and because Sonny wasn't greedy. He stole only enough to live in relative comfort and to care for his polio-stricken daughter Julia. This time was different. Mobster

Marty Holbein put a gun in his face and said, "Work for me, or I'll put a bullet through both your hands, and then I'll put one through your daughter."

Click. Sonny gently rolled the dial between his fingers. The tumblers fell into place. Click. Click. Click. He reached for the spoked handle and spun it counter-clockwise. He felt the rods slide back, and gave a tug with his finger. The door to the big Kenzler swung open. Perfectly balanced, the three-hundred-pound slab of iron swiveled away smoothly without a sound.

Buzz shined his pocket torch inside and whistled in spite of himself at the stacks of banded bills. Their info was right; the payroll cash was delivered two days early this week to fool would be robbers.

Sonny reached into the safe and methodically rifled all of its drawers and compartments. "They're not here. Time for the backup plan." Instead of grabbing all the money, he counted out a specific amount, and put it in his tool satchel. He started closing the safe and Buzz clamped his meaty hand on the edge of the door.

"What are you doing?"

"There's a lot of money in there, Sonny. What say we take a bundle for ourselves?"

"You know the deal," Sonny said. "The boss told us how much to take, no more, no less."

Buzz frowned and stuck out his chin. "So we take a little extra and split it fifty-fifty and don't tell? Look at all that green." He put his gun into his pocket and started reaching into the safe.

"No."

Buzz's eyes narrowed. "No? You don't want it, I'll keep all for myself."

Sonny reached into his tool bag and pulled a revolver of his own. He aimed it at Buzz's forehead and cocked the hammer. "Back away."

Buzz snarled, "Why, you little rat. What do you think you're doing?"

"Following orders, you moron. Back away. Now. Hand over your gun – butt first. Don't make me kill you."

"You couldn't kill anybody."

"Want to bet your life on that? Hand me your piece – between your fingers."

Buzz did as he was told. Sonny pocketed Buzz's pistol and switched hands with his own. He nudged the door shut with his shoulder, turned the toggle, then spun the dial, wiping his prints as he did. Keeping his eyes on the thug, he wiped Buzz's prints from the door of the safe. I ought to leave them there and let the cops have him, Sonny thought, but he'd give me up on his way to the station.

"Now let's get out of here before the watchman comes back. He sees us, we shoot him, it queers the whole deal and the Boss'll kill both of us" He gestured with the gun. "Now move."

Buzz backed out the door, hands still away from his pockets. Sonny realized that he would do what he was told for now, but the look on the thug's face told him that Buzz would deal out payback at his first opportunity. He was too used to his muscles calling the tune. The pair slipped out the way they came, made the street without incident, and two blocks away, climbed into the big maroon Buick sedan where Mike was waiting.

"You up front," Sonny said, gesturing with the pistol in his pocket. Buzz sat in the passenger seat and Sonny in the back. "Drive," Sonny told Mike.

"Everything okay?" Mike said, stepping on the starter.

"For the moment," Sonny replied. "Let's get out of here."

As the big car rolled away from the curb, Buzz felt the cold steel of Sonny's revolver under his ear. Mike's eyes twitched over and saw the gun. "What's going on?"

"Insurance. Just drive."

Across town, the Buick pulled up to a darkened warehouse. The weathered sign overhead, lit by three shaded lamps read, Central Shipping. Mike flashed his headlights, two short, one long and waited. In a moment, the door rolled up and he drove inside. Two men with pump shotguns flanked the doorway. Inside, crates and bales were stacked almost to the rafters. Three others sat at a table in a far corner, beer bottles, cards, and penny ante cash between them.

"Not a word," Sonny said to Mike. He prodded the back of Buzz's neck with the revolver. "That goes for you too. Step out slowly and walk in front of me."

Buzz climbed out of the car. Sonny gestured with his chin. "Up the stairs. No tricks."

Sonny gave Mike a hard look that told him to keep his mouth shut. The men at the card table sat still, instinctively sensing that something was wrong. Buzz and Sonny climbed the rough planks of the stairs to an office overlooking the warehouse floor. Its blinds were drawn, but light showed between the slats.

"Knock." When Buzz hesitated, Sonny poked him in the kidney with the pistol. "Knock."

Buzz knocked, and a voice from the other side of the door said, "Come in."

Marty Holbein looked totally out of place in the shabby office. His tuxedo and starched white dress shirt contrasted the scarred office desk and the beat up swivel chair where he sat, leaning back with his hands on the arms. A vicuna overcoat and top hat for an evening on the town hung from a coat tree that listed to port on a broken leg. Two men in rumpled suits slouched against the walls.

No one spoke for a moment. Marty noticed Sonny's hand in his pocket. So did his gunmen, who slipped their hands under their coats. "Tell me about it."

Sonny set his tool bag on the desk. "The money's in there. Eight grand, just like you said. We left the rest, but Buzz and I had a little disagreement about it."

Holbein's eyes shifted to Buzz. He didn't say a word, just stared into the thug's eyes and drummed his fingers on the arms of the chair, waiting for Buzz to start talking.

"Marty, I didn't take anything extra. I mean, it was there, piles of cash, but Sonny said no, and I listened to him."

Holbein shifted his gaze to Sonny.

"After I pointed a gun at his head."

"No, that's not true. This little weasel's lying."

Sonny set Buzz's pistol on Holbein's desk. "That's his. I wouldn't have it if I didn't have to take it from him."

Holbein's lower lip pushed upward into a frown. With the back of his forefinger, he brushed at one side of his mustache then the other like a cat would its whiskers. He picked up Buzz's revolver.

Downstairs, the men at the card table sat in silence, waiting to see what was going to happen. A shot boomed from upstairs. The thud of a body. In a moment, the door opened above, and Sonny stepped out. Someone had to die for the sake of Holbein's discipline, but Sonny was too useful to kill; he'd live another day.

"Miles, I'm in trouble." Jim Devane leaned inward over his plate to speak in hushed tones. All around them, the luncheon crowd at Chez Gerard chattered and laughed, their silverware clinking on the restaurant's china. Devane's baby face was drawn up in tight lines that made Bilvane

Machine's executive vice-president look twice his age.

Doctor Miles Murdock set down his knife and fork. When Devane had called him and asked to meet over lunch, he sounded troubled, but in person, he looked as if he might collapse at any moment. Apparently, he hadn't slept in days. Murdock laid his palms flat on the white linen tablecloth and looked straight into Devane's eyes, an exercise in sympathetic bedside manner, cultivated over years of medical practice. Full attention, no questions. Let Jim say what vexed him in his own time.

Devane fidgeted, silent, for a full minute then the words tumbled out. "Eight thousand dollars is missing from payroll. I'm the only person with the combination to the safe except for Jed Billings, my partner, and he's been in Europe for three weeks. He thinks I embezzled the money." He stared across the table at Murdock, who still said nothing. "I didn't," he blurted. "I–I didn't."

Miles took a sip of his coffee and carefully set the cup in the saucer. Around them, white-jacketed waiters scurried filling water glasses and balancing trays. Jim Devane's life was caving in around him, and the rest of the world went on, oblivious. "Of course you didn't, Jim. You're no more a thief than I. You mentioned the safe. Was eight thousand dollars all that was in it?"

"No. There was nearly twenty thousand in cash in there to meet the payroll. Twelve thousand dollars was still there, untouched."

"Have you talked to the police?"

Devane shook his head. "Jed said he wanted to avoid a scandal, and that he understood that a man can make a mistake. He said if I'd just return the money, we'd put the whole thing behind us. But, Miles, I don't have it to give. Marcia's medical bills have eaten up every dime of my savings, and he thinks that's why I took the money."

Murdock didn't know Billings as well as he did Devane, but he'd met him on different occasions, charity events and such. "Jed seems like a reasonable man. I realize you can't prove a negative, but surely Billings knows you wouldn't steal from him."

"It's not Jed so much; we have two big government contracts going right now, and if we lose them, the company will fail. And the shareholders; if they hear about this, I'm finished. They'll scream for an audit and demand I surrender my shares to offset the missing money. They'll call in the police. It'll be all over the papers. I'll be ruined, the company will be ruined, and it will poison what little time Marcia has left."

"It is odd. If someone opened the safe, why take eight thousand and not the other twelve? It makes no sense."

Devane's voice broke. "All I know is I'm being ruined, and I did nothing wrong."

"I can lend you some of the money, and I – "

Devane put up a hand in a halting gesture. "That's not why I came to you, Miles. I could borrow the money and give it to the company; hell, I could sell my house for the cash, but that would be the same as admitting that I stole it. I won't do that. I don't want money; I want a fresh perspective on all this."

"Let me speak – in confidence – to a friend of mine about this business. No names. He has good insight and may have some ideas to offer."

"Is he a private detective?"

"No. No, Jim, he's not."

Murdock's mind was already racing, sorting facts, running scenarios, forming theories. If anyone could clear Jim Devane, it would be the Purple Scar.

Miles stayed at the table for a while after Devane left, lingering over another cup of coffee. To steal eight thousand dollars and leave twelve made no sense at all. The logical place to start was the issue of the safe's combination. Devane had it and Billings had it. Had someone else found it somewhere in either of the partners' papers? Maybe a secretary or junior executive with access to the office, or even a janitor or char woman had found the combination and succumbed to temptation.

But why steal only eight grand and not the whole pile? Ten years for grand theft went with eight thousand dollars the same as it did for twenty. The key to the whole business had to be the amount. For as long as Miles had known Devane, he had been honest and trustworthy, and Miles' first impression was that Devane was giving him a straight story.

Could Billings have given someone the combination to steal the money while he was conveniently out of the country to pin the theft on Devane? It was possible, but unless he was in financial trouble, why would he do it? The whole business was a riddle.

Miles looked at his watch. Time to return to the Down Street Clinic. He finished the last swallow of his coffee and pulled a twenty from his money clip for the check and the tip. The waiter had been attentive enough to keep their water glasses filled but discreet enough to keep his distance when he saw that an earnest conversation was going on. He deserved to keep the change. Miles pushed back his chair and as he stood, he looked around him. Every diner in the restaurant wrapped up in his or her own life, each a separate and complex drama, but none to compare to his.

Miles Murdock led a dual life. By day he was a respected plastic surgeon with a lucrative private practice that funded his Down Street Clinic in the heart of Akelton City's slums where no man, woman, or child was turned away. By night, Miles Murdock donned the twisted mask of The Purple Scar, crime-fighter and nemesis of the city's criminals.

The mask was the likeness of Miles Murdock's brother John, a policeman murdered by gunmen who then poured acid on his handsome face. From that day, Miles Murdock devoted his life, his luck, and his resources to avenging his brother's death by fighting crime and criminals beyond the constraints of the law under the guise of The Purple Scar.

Miles walked across Broad Street, the Maginot Line between the safe, civilized part of Akelton City and the North Shore, a human jungle of crime and peril. Murdock walked the streets day or night unafraid, not only because he could defend himself against the city's most vicious killers but because everyone in the slums knew who he was, the relief he brought to the neighborhood's suffering, and what terrible retribution would land at the hands of Down Street's denizens on anyone who harmed the Good Doctor.

Miles stepped into the foyer of the white building and found a full complement of patients waiting to be seen. The poor, the deprived, the dispossessed deserved as much attention as the rich and privileged – more in Miles' estimation – for theirs was a lot of privation, poor nutrition, squalid living conditions, and constant danger. His fees for plastic surgery were high, some would say exorbitant, but the wealthy were willing to pay them for the quality of his work. At times, he saw himself as a modern-day Robin Hood, taking from the rich to benefit the poor, and to bankroll his crime fighting as The Purple Scar.

A door opened, and a pretty, red-haired nurse came out with a clipboard cradled in her arm. At the sight of Miles, she gave a broad smile, and her green eyes flashed a look that was unmistakably affection. Dale Jordan was Miles' head nurse both in the Down Street Clinic and in his private plastic surgery practice. She had come to anticipate his every need in surgery, and was an invaluable aid to his work.

She waved him over. "Hello, Miles." He gave her a smile that she recognized as tinged with worry. "Something wrong?"

He nodded. "But nothing that will interfere with today's agenda. What have we got?"

As Dale read off the roster of the day's patients, Jim Devane's anxious face kept swimming into the back of Miles' mind. The puzzle nagged at him, and it would take all his concentration to put it aside until his work at the clinic was through.

Jed Billings sat behind his desk in his Bilvane Machine office. Jim Devane sat across from him in a visitor chair, feeling like a kid in front of the principal. Billings, four years his senior, had begun to grey at his temples and had a perpetual crease between his eyebrows from looking askance at the world in general. He took off his spectacles and polished them with a pocket silk.

"I wanted you to know, Jim, to spare you any embarrassment, that I've had the locksmith in. The combination to the safe has been changed."

"Save me embarrassment? I suppose that means you have no intention of giving the new combination to me." An angry flush began climbing from Devane's collar to his cheeks.

"Look at it from my point of view, Jim. What would you do if the roles were reversed?"

"Considering how many years we've worked together building this company, I'd at least give you the benefit of the doubt until things are proven one way or the other. Why in God's name would I steal eight thousand dollars?"

"I asked myself the same question. Then this was brought to my attention." Billings opened the middle drawer of his desk and pulled out a sheet of paper.

Devane took it from him and read it. "Where did you get this? I've never seen it before."

"Really? Then why was it in your desk?"

The letterhead read Katzmier Clinic, Troy, New York. The letter was addressed to James Devane, and said simply that after reviewing Marcia's records, they could offer a new experimental treatment at a cost of eight thousand dollars.

"I don't know how this got in my desk; I've never heard of this place."

"They've heard of you, Jim. I spoke to Doctor Katzmier on the telephone today. He told me you contacted him and forwarded a complete set of Marcia's treatment records."

"So now you're snooping in my life?" Devane's voice rose in volume and pitch.

"Maybe you ought to take a few days off, Jim, think this through."

"You can't believe I'd steal from the company, Jed. All the years we've worked together to build –"

Jed stood and raised his hand. "Jim, I have a duty to the stockholders to look at this from all sides."

Devane's lip curled away from his teeth. "So that's what it's all about, huh? You're worried that if this comes out, and you look like you're the least bit sympathetic to me, it'll be your head on the block beside mine. Is that it?"

Billings shook his head slowly. "No, Jim. That's not it at all. You've been under a lot of strain lately, and if it were my wife who needed treatment, I don't know what I'd do."

"Maybe you don't, but I know what I'd do. I'd believe you and I'd back you all the way." Devane leaped to his feet. The chair clattered on the polished floor. "I'm not backing down, Jed. You'll see I'm innocent." Devane pointed a finger at Billings. "You'll see." He stormed out of the office and slammed the door hard enough for it to be heard in the parking lot.

Devane slumped behind the wheel of his car, his chest heaving with angry breaths. Miles. He had to talk with Miles. Maybe the mysterious friend could help him.

"And that's the story," Miles said. He poured another cup of coffee for himself and refilled Dale's. He offered to top off Tommy Pedlar's but the little man put his hand over his cup. "No more for me, Doc. I'll be awake half the night as it is."

"I agree with you, Miles, it seems strange that anyone robbing a safe would leave almost double the amount taken."

"Unless –" Miles paused as if choosing one word at a time. "Unless Jim was being set up."

"Yeah, I thought that too," Tommy said. "But by who? His partner?"

"That's a possibility, if Billings wanted to get control of the company, to put Jim under suspicion so that he'd have to resign, but if that's the game, it was a bad gamble. Jim's adamant that he won't knuckle under."

"What if it isn't Billings?" Dale said.

"Then who?"

"One of the shareholders? Maybe somebody wants Jim's stock in the company."

"You may have something there, Dale," Miles said. "The problem is finding out who it might be and proving it."

The phone rang, and Miles crossed the room to pick up the handset. "Miles Murdock."

"Miles." He recognized Jim Devane's voice.

"Yes," he replied mouthing Devane's name to Dale and Tommy. "What's going on?"

"Things have gotten worse." Jim recounted his meeting with Billings, and as he did, thoughts coalesced in Murdock's brain.

"You've never had any contact with this Doctor Katzmier?" He gestured for Dale to jot down the name.

"Never heard of him, but he's got Marcia's hospital records. I never sent them to him, but he knows all about her situation."

"Sit tight, Jim. I want you to come to my home tomorrow, say eleven o'clock. We need to talk about this in person. If Billings has hired an investigator, there may be a tap on your phone."

They hung up, and Miles said, "Well, the screws have just tightened a turn. I'm more convinced now than ever that someone has made Jim Devane a fall guy. I just don't know why – yet."

Tommy nodded. "But I'll bet a fin you do before this is over."

"Only a sucker would take that bet," Dale said with a laugh.

Miles set his jaw. "Consider it a done deal."

Jim Devane put the earpiece on the hook and within a minute, the phone rang again.

"This Devane?" The voice was deep and muffled, as if the speaker held a handkerchief over the mouthpiece.

"Yes. This is James Devane."

"I unnerstan' you're having a little trouble at work."

"What's going on?"

"Who is this?"

"Someone who can put an end to it. In'erested?"

"What do you mean? What do you know about it?"

"More'n you do. I'll be in touch." The line went dead.

Devane stared at the earpiece as if he expected it to curl into a pair of black lips and stick out its tongue. From the next room, Marcia said, "Jim? Who was that on the phone?" She'd been asleep only minutes before when he called Miles.

Devane stepped through the doorway where he saw Marcia in the raised hospital bed, sleepy-eyed, the magazine she'd been reading splayed on her chest. "Wrong number, dear," he lied. "Sorry it woke you. I'll leave it off the hook." He brushed aside a strand of her auburn hair and kissed her forehead.

The hands and wrists that lay on her coverlet were red and swollen, symptoms of heart disease brought on by rheumatic fever. Over the past year, her condition deteriorated to the point that she was almost bedfast, and her doctors offered little hope.

Marcia smiled. "That's all right, dear. I'll be asleep again in no time."

Devane switched off the bedside lamp, wishing that he could turn off his troubles with the same ease.

As soon as Marcia's asleep, he thought, I'll call Miles. He'll know what to do.

But Miles Murdock was not at home. Wearing the grotesque mask of the Purple Scar shielded by the brim of a fedora, he slipped from the shadows to the main building of the Bilvane Machine factory as the watchman rounded the corner. The Scar had been watching the plant for two hours and had seen the same uniformed guard, Detex drum on one hip and a long-barreled .38 on the other, making the night watch rounds. He appeared to be alone.

Scaling the wall around the plant was an easy task for the Scar's gym-tuned body. The lock on a side door was child's play for the masked vigilante, and in a moment, he was stealing down the corridor to the payroll office. That door had a better lock and took a few minutes for the Scar to work his picks and rake to open it.

In the glow of the electric torch, he saw the Kenzler safe, a monolith in its niche in the wall. He drew a small vial of talcum powder from the pocket of his trench coat and poured a small mound into his gloved palm.

On one hand, it seemed futile dusting for prints; it had been several days since the theft was discovered, and in the interim, Devane had opened the safe, and his prints would be on it. If anyone else had opened it to steal the money, they would have wiped the surfaces clean. And if the purpose was to frame Devane, they'd be sure to wipe down the safe, leaving only his prints for the police to find. But experience taught the Scar that thoroughness often paid big dividends.

He blew a small cloud of the talc over the face of the door around the dial and the toggle. There were several smudged prints, and a few clear ones. He lifted these with a strip of cellophane tape and attached it to a playing card rectangle of thin glass. He noted the number on the dial under the ring: 72. Some people simply spun the dial to clear the tumblers, others returned it to zero. Some reset it to a specific number to know if another's hand had tried the dial. He pulled a stethoscope from his pocket, pressed the bell against the safe, and went to work opening it.

The thought crossed the Purple Scar's mind many times that he was often as adept as the criminals he pursued, or perhaps more so at the ways of their trade, but to catch a thief ... In a moment, the tumblers clicked into place, and the door swung open. The safe held files, a petty cash box, some rolled up diagrams and blueprints, and other odd papers. But that wasn't why the Scar wanted the door open. He dusted the door again, this time on the inside, the stair step ledges opposite the hinges. Sometimes in the heat of a crime, the criminal gets careless.

In the light of his torch, the Scar found two partials and a whole print where someone had clamped his hand over the door. Maybe they were Jim Devane's; maybe they belonged to whoever was trying to frame him. Time would tell.

The Scar wiped the traces of his sleuthing from the vault door and quietly closed it. He returned the dial to 72 and stopped to listen at the payroll office door. Silence. He slipped into the hall and started toward his exit when he heard the thump of a closing door. Footsteps on the floor above, heading for the stairs. The watchman was still on his rounds. Someone else was in the building.

Thinking fast, the Scar jumped in the air and caught the top of the ornamental cornice over the door frame and pulled himself upward. He got his feet on it and straightened his limbs to reach overhead to press his fingers against the hallway ceiling. The shadows hid him and unless someone turned on a light, he couldn't be seen. The footsteps reached the top of the stairs. Two people, heavy steps. Two men.

"Well, if you find out anything – anything at all, call me at once."

"Yes, sir, Mister Billings," the other voice said. "My partner and I have a close watch on him, everywhere he goes, everyone he sees."

The voices faded along with the footsteps, ending with the closing of the outer door. The Scar dropped catlike to the floor and headed for the side door he'd used for entry. He was right; Billings had a private eye on the case. That made it probable that he wasn't involved in the frame, because the detective would uncover that as easily as anyone else.

The Purple Scar had no access to the police fingerprint files, but he had an ally in the police department who did, Captain Dan Griffin. Miles Murdock had met Griffin when the homicide detective brought him in to identify his brother John in the City Morgue. While Griffin could not publicly condone vigilante violence, he applauded the Purple Scar in his heart.

Griffin knew the Purple Scar's identity, but would never reveal it. He understood the crime fighter's motivation, and found cooperating with him expedient. When a message would come over the telephone in a voice like Death itself or through the mail in an unknown hand, telling him where he might find a wanted criminal bound and gagged and waiting to be arrested, or information needed to solve a difficult case, Griffin took it in stride and made the most of his provident ally. The Scar had no doubt that Griffin would cooperate with him this time as he had in the past.

In fifteen minutes, The Purple Scar had returned to the Swank Street mansion, removed his dreaded crime fighter's mask, and once again become Miles Murdock. He poured a snifter of brandy and sat at the desk in his study.

He laid the cellophane strips with the lifted fingerprints in front of him. A powerful magnifying glass made the prints stand out vividly against the green of the desk blotter. The prints from the inside of the door were distinctly different from those on its face around the dial. With nothing to compare them to, Murdock had reached a dead end for the moment. He took the print strips to the floor below where he maintained the plastic surgery clinic that financed his public and his not so public operations.

In the consulting room, he had a high quality Graflex camera used to photograph patients during various stages of facial reconstruction. The lens was ground for high-detailed, close-up photography, and the Purple Scar often found it useful in investigations.

Miles mounted the strips of tape on a dark background and took several shots of the prints, then took them to the darkroom to develop them. Satisfied with the pictures, he put one set in a manila envelope. He'd deliver it himself to Dan Griffin in the morning. That should start the ball rolling. Griffin's cooperation would point Miles in a useful direction.

The Purple Scar was able to open the Kenzler without the combination, and so could a handful of pros. He was convinced more than ever that Jim Devane was innocent and the robbery was solely intended to frame him. The motive was the puzzle. Who would want Devane pushed out of Bilvane Machine, and why?

The phone rang. No one called with good news at three a.m. Miles picked it up on the second ring. "Miles Murdock."

"Miles." He recognized the voice as Jim Devane's. "Something's happened." Devane recounted the phone call he'd had earlier. "He said he'd be in touch. What do I do if he calls back? Or worse, shows up in person? He called me at home. He knows where I live. I have a gun; I'm not afraid for myself, but I'm afraid for Marcia."

"I have an idea." Miles said, "Stay home tomorrow in case the mystery man calls back. I'll come over and bring my nurse Dale Jordan with me. You can tell Marcia you wanted another opinion on her condition. I'll suggest leaving Dale with her overnight to monitor her readings, and she can contact me immediately if anything happens. I've spoken to my friend, and he's aware of your situation. He thinks he can help."

"Thank heaven for that. What should I do now?"

"Now? I know you're probably not going to sleep at all tonight, but give it a try anyway. What time does your housekeeper arrive in the morning?"

"Mrs. Sullivan usually is here by seven thirty."

"Leave her a note to not wake you, in case you do fall asleep. Take the phone off the hook and tell her to leave it off so that you aren't disturbed. You shouldn't talk to anyone until Dale and I arrive. I'll be there at ten o'clock."

"I'll do what you say. What about your friend?"

"He's already on the case."

"Miles, I can't thank you enough."

"No need, Jim. That's what friends do for each other. If you can't sleep, at least try to get some rest."

Miles hung up the phone and rose from his chair. There were things to gather and things to prepare.

+++

At ten the next morning, Miles and Dale were ringing the doorbell of Jim Devane's house. Not quite a mansion, the house was still a large and dignified Tudor on a tree lined street in Akelton City's affluent Hunter's Knob. The autumn weather was crisp, and Dale wore her nurse's cape over her starched white uniform.

Miles didn't like involving her, putting her at risk in even the least way, but she eagerly accepted the role, wanting to help in any way she could. Her eyes were bright, and an excited flush colored her cheeks.

The door opened, and an imposing, grey-haired woman, nearly as wide as she was tall, filled the doorway, as if guarding the castle gate from intruders: Mrs. Sullivan. She squinted at the pair over her gold-rimmed spectacles, paying particular attention to Miles' black leather medical bag. "Yes?"

"I'm Doctor Miles Murdock, and this is my nurse Dale Jordan. We've come to see Mrs. Devane."

Mrs. Sullivan processed the information and finally gave a single nod. "All right. Come in."

She stepped back from the doorway and Miles and Dale entered the foyer. The rug was missing. "Clean" spots on the walls and empty hooks showed where pictures had been hung. Jim Devane had been selling off household items to pay for Marcia's care.

"The Missus is upstairs. Himself is not to be disturbed. He –"

"It's all right, Mrs. Sullivan," a voice came from the top of the stairs. Miles looked up and saw Jim Devane in shirtsleeves and suspenders. "I'm awake. Welcome, Miles, Miss Jordan. Thank you for coming. Come on up. Mrs. Sullivan, would you please bring a tray with coffee?"

"As you wish, sir," she said, and bustled off to the kitchen.

Miles and Dale followed Devane down the second floor hallway. It too was missing non-essential items. A niche in the wall designed to hold a small sculpture stood empty, and indentations in the carpeting showed where a pair of chairs once flanked a table.

Devane saw Miles' look. "Yes, I've been selling things a few at a time to pay the bills, particularly Mrs. Sullivan's wages. I couldn't afford to keep her on otherwise, and without her, I'd have to put Marcia in a nursing home, and she couldn't bear that." He tapped on the door. "Honey, you have visitors."

Marcia Devane lay in a white enameled hospital bed, the upper half raised. Her blue eyes were bright, and her smile was genuine. Her swollen hands held a mirror and a hair brush. "Miles, how good to see you. It's been a long time."

"Not so long, Marcia. When was it? The Veterans Hospital charity ball?

That was only a year ago." He hoped his face didn't betray his surprise and dismay at how much her condition had deteriorated. "This is my nurse, Dale Jordan."

Marcia set down her brush and Dale gently shook her hand, mindful of the swollen wrist. "You're a pretty young thing," Marcia said. "Watch out, Miles, she's liable to steal your heart."

Everyone laughed at that, and Miles took a stethoscope from his bag. "Let's see how you're doing."

As the exam proceeded, Miles realized that Marcia's ailment had advanced to a difficult level. Listening to her heart, he realized that she had damage to at least one valve, and the rash across her collarbone was an angry red. Her ankles were swollen, and when he listened to her lungs, it was obvious she was short of breath,

"I'd like to collect some data," Miles said. "I'd like Miss Jordan to stay for a day or two and take regular readings of your pulse, blood pressure, and other indicators. Would that be all right with you, Marcia?"

"Of course. It would be nice to have some company. Do you play Scrabble, Miss Jordan?"

"Not very well, I'm afraid."

"Good. Maybe I'll win a few games. I haven't beaten Jim in years." She turned to Devane. "Have Mrs. Sullivan make up a room for Miss Jordan."

"I'll get your bag from the car," Miles said, and gestured with his head for Devane to follow him. Outside, he said, "I have some equipment in Dale's suitcase. I need to attach it to a telephone extension that only you will answer."

"My study. It's upstairs across the hall from Marcia's room."

"That will do." Miles lifted the suitcase from the trunk of his car. The bag was heavy but Miles used his strength to make it seem that it contained nothing but Dale's clothing. "Don't look," he said quietly, "but that green Packard down the block was there when we pulled up. When we go back in the house, take a look and let me know if it's familiar, maybe belongs to one of your neighbors."

Devane nodded.

"Now, smile and talk about anything. Make it look normal."

Inside the house, Devane peered through the curtains of an upstairs window. "I don't recognize the car."

"It may be totally innocent, or it may be someone watching the house. Billings was snooping into your life. Maybe he's hired a private eye."

Devane's hands closed into fists. "If he has, I'll put a stop to it immediately."

"Don't. I believe you're innocent, and a detective may uncover evidence to prove that. Let it go on. Just be aware that you're likely being watched."

In Devane's study, Miles opened the suitcase. Under Dale's clothing lay a wire recorder and a set of plugs and cables, one ending in a pair of brass alligator clips. Miles unscrewed the cap from the baseboard telephone junction box, exposing a set of wires. He attached the clips to them and plugged the cable into a jack on the side of the recorder. He set the machine on the desk.

"When the phone rings, push this," Miles said, indicating a red button on the side of the machine. "It will record the conversation. Push the black button to stop it."

"Then what?"

"Tell Dale, and she'll pass the information along to me." He set the recorder inside a desk drawer and closed it, hiding the machine from view.

"What about your friend? How does he fit into all of this?"

"He'll be ready when the time comes. I need one more thing from you." Miles took a small leather case from Dale's bag. "I need your fingerprints."

"For what?"

"My friend asked for them. He'll explain later."

Miles took a set of Devane's prints, transferring them to a standard card, which he slipped into his inside suit pocket. "I have to get to the clinic now, but Dale will be staying with you. I know it's foolish for me to tell you to act normally, but if you stay home, you'll be okay."

Devane nodded biting his lip.

"It'll be over soon. I promise."

Miles backed his sedan out of Devane's driveway and fish hooked into the street. As he drove past the green Packard, he took note of the license number in the rear view mirror. One more item for Dan Griffin's attention.

When Miles Murdock walked into Dan Griffin's office, Dan was at his desk, sleeves rolled up, tie pulled down, and a cigarette dangling from his lower lip. He was poring over a file and jotting notes on a pad.

"Hello, Dan."

"Miles," he said with a smile. "Haven't seen you in a while. How have you been?"

"Busy," said Miles with a raised eyebrow. "I thought maybe you could help me with something."

Griffin looked over Miles' shoulder. "Kick the door shut."

Miles did and sat in a chair in front of Griffin's desk. Without speaking, he handed the photo of the prints from the safe to the detective.

"Where did you get these?"

"Unofficially?"

Griffin nodded. "Of course."

"They're from the safe in the Billvane Machine Company's payroll office."

"Billvane? I didn't hear anything about a robbery."

"You won't. It's all part of some plot to implicate one of their executives."

"And these prints?"

"They may point to the people responsible. One set of prints belongs to James Devane, one of the partners. He's the person I believe is being framed. It's the other prints I want to know about."

"What's your interest in this?"

"A friend is involved." Miles gave a thumbnail sketch of the case and his plan to snare the culprits.

Griffin squinted at the photograph. His eyes widened. "Hold on a second." He rose from his desk and went out into the hall. In a moment, he came back with a file folder. The detective opened the file and pulled out a fingerprint card. He set it beside the photograph and studied the two carefully. "I'll be damned."

"What do you see?"

"An odd little crescent scar on the left index finger is a dead match, if you'll pardon the pun, to a body found in an alley in North Shore, a thug named Walter 'Buzz' Miller."

"I've heard the name."

"He's got a rap sheet like a roll of john paper. Armed robbery, assault, burglary, one of just about everything."

"When was he found?"

"Eight days ago. According to the coroner, he'd been dead a day and a half, give or take, before he was found."

"That jibes with my timetable on the safe job. Was he a cracker?"

Griffin shook his head. "He was dumb side of beef, an ex pug who took too many to the head. I'd bet he had to keep his shoes tied and shove his feet in them with a shoehorn."

"Any known associates?"

"Half of Akelton City's underworld. Word is lately he'd been muscle for a hood named Marty Holbein."

"Another familiar name."

"Does this mean what I think it does?"

Miles nodded. "It does."

"Look, Miles, this is a murder investigation. I can't just stand by and–" He stopped in mid sentence, recognizing the look on Miles' face; the tightened features highlighting the tiny spade shape that looked like a scar but was really a slight paralysis, the result of a football injury years before. Griffin knew the look meant that Murdock was unyielding in his request.

"Dan, if you send a squad of cops into Billvane, you'll scare the bad guys away, or at least drive them underground. I may never catch my crook, and you may never catch your killer. I suspect they're one and the same. Give me a day."

"You mean give you a night." Griffin took in a deep breath and let it out. "All right, I'll be generous; thirty-six hours, and then you hand it all over to me."

Miles hesitated. "Fair enough. I almost forgot." He handed Griffin a slip of paper. "This license number. Can you run it for me?"

"You want me to run that too?" He rolled his eyes. "Shall I check the oil and put air in your tires?"

"You have my number if you come up with anything."

"And you have mine. Share and share alike?"

"Share and share alike."

Jim Devane sat in his study staring at the telephone as if it were a coiled snake ready to strike. He'd been waiting most of the day for the dreaded call, ready to push the red button on the recorder. Across the hall, he could hear Marcia and Dale laughing over a shared joke. Marcia was having a good day, ignorant of the turmoil he was in, and he wanted to keep it that way.

"Can I bring you anything, Mister Devane?" Mrs. Sullivan stood in the doorway holding a tray with a tea service.

"No, thank you. Nothing right now." She turned to leave and he said, "But if you would, please bring my supper up here tonight."

She nodded. "As you wish, sir."

Devane went back to staring at the telephone. That saying about watched pots, he thought, must apply to watched phones as well.

+++

Miles pulled the Medical Association Directory from the shelf in his office. He thumbed through the pages to the Ks and found a listing for Rudolph Katzmier, M.D., Ph.D. Emigrated to the U.S. in 1932, opened a cardiac clinic in Troy, New York in 1936. He dialed the operator and called the number.

"Katzmier Clinic. How may I direct your call?" The voice at the other end was a middle aged woman with a heavy German accent.

"My name is Doctor Miles Murdock. I am calling for Doctor Katzmier."

Miles listened to the clicks and buzzes on the line as the operator plugged and unplugged cables. Must be a pretty big establishment, Miles thought as he hung up the phone, to have a switchboard and an operator. In a moment, another woman, this one younger and with no accent, came on the line. "Doctor Katzmier's office."

"My name is Doctor Miles Murdock. I am calling regarding my patient Marcia Devane."

"Doctor Katzmier is making his rounds right now. Did you say you are calling about Marcia Devane?"

"Yes." Miles spelled the name. "She lives in Akelton City."

"If you'll please give me your telephone number, Doctor Murdock, I'll have him return your call." There was a pause. "One moment, sir. He just walked in." Miles heard a brief exchange muffled by the secretary's hand over the mouthpiece. In less than a moment, Miles heard a click and a heavily accented voice came on the line.

"Doctor Murdock? This is Doctor Katzmier. How may I help you?"

"I am the personal physician of Marcia Devane. I understand you are reviewing her case."

"Nothing formal, Doctor Murdock. Her husband made some enquiries concerning an experimental treatment I am developing."

"You have reviewed her records?"

"Yes. I do not recall seeing your name as her physician."

"I was brought in only this week to provide another opinion."

"I see. Mister Devane is very concerned about his wife's health."

"Yes, he is. Is there any likelihood that she may be admitted for treatment

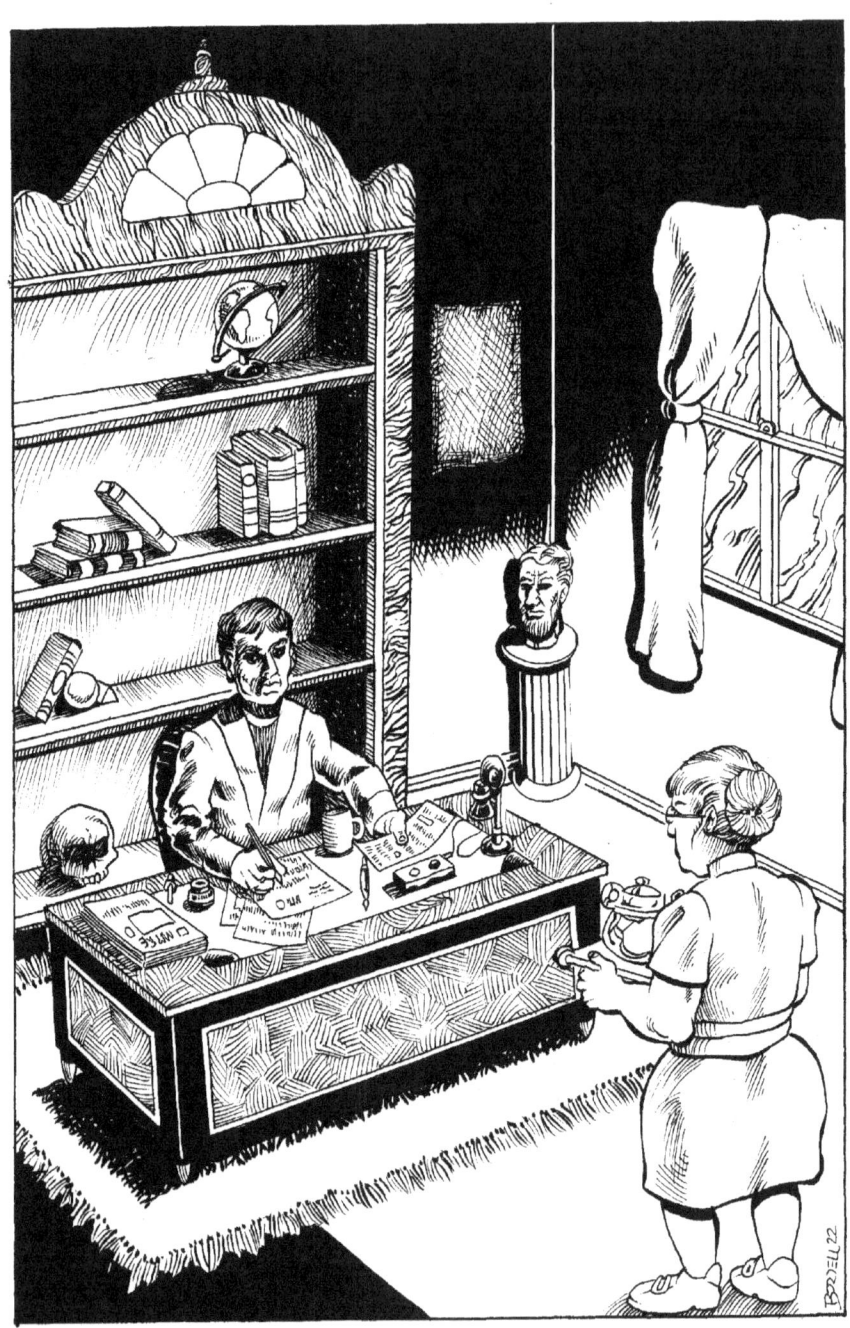

"Can I bring you anything, Mr. Devane?"

any time soon?"

"As I told Mister Devane, the treatment is intense and consequently very costly. He said he would gather the appropriate funds and contact me when he was ready."

"I understand that the details of the treatment are proprietary, but I would appreciate being apprised of Mrs. Devane's progress."

"Of course, Doctor Murdock. If you would be so kind as to write a formal request and send it to me at the clinic, I will be happy to keep you informed.

"Thank you, Doctor Katzmier. I will do that."

As he hung up the phone, Miles decided that Katzmier was an unknowing patsy in the scheme. Someone was going to great lengths to frame Jim Devane.

Tommy arrived a few minutes later, and joined Miles in the study. He sat in one of the armchairs and put his porkpie hat on his knee. The former second-story man known to the underworld as the Sticky Fingers Kid joined the Purple Scar's team after Miles saved his daughter's life. Tommy leaned back in the chair and gave Miles his lopsided grin. "What's up?"

"Tell me about Buzz Miller."

"Miller? He's wrapped up in this business?"

"Was. He's dead. He left a print on the door of the Billvane safe."

"No, kidding?" Tommy shook his head. "Never figured him for a cracker."

"It's not likely. I'd guess he was hired muscle in case something went wrong."

"That sounds about right. So he's dead, huh?"

"And it fits the timetable around this whole caper. Now tell me about Marty Holbein."

"Him too?" Tommy whistled. "There's a cold one. He'd kill anyone for any reason or none at all. You think he's behind this?"

"His main trade is hijacking trucks, but maybe he's branching out."

The phone rang.

"Miles?" He recognized the voice as Dan Griffin.

"Yes."

"The plate belongs to Jimmy Connors, the private eye."

"Confirms my suspicions. Thanks, Dan. I'll keep you posted."

"Do that. Remember, thirty-six hours."

"It may be sooner."

"Be careful, Miles. Holbein's a dangerous character."

"So I've been told. Thanks, Dan."

Devane watched the sunset through his study window. The green Packard was gone. The call had not come, and every hour that passed frayed his nerves a little more, which, he decided was the point. Across the hall, Mrs. Sullivan was taking Marcia's tray from supper. His own sat untouched on his desk. His stomach twitched at the thought of eating.

"Mister Devane." Mrs. Sullivan stood in the doorway holding the tray. "You've not touched your meal. Would you like me to heat it up for you?"

Devane hesitated then said, "Yes, if you would. I'd appreciate that."

She set Devane's tray on top of Marcia's. "And I'll brew a fresh pot of coffee for you."

The housekeeper bustled out of the room, and Devane crossed the hall where Dale was taking Marcia's temperature and writing numbers on a clipboard chart. Marcia smiled at him around the thermometer.

"How is she doing, Miss Jordan?"

"Her vital signs are consistent, and her appetite is good. I'd say she is doing very well under the circumstances. And please, call me Dale." She took the thermometer from Marcia's mouth and read the temperature.

"Is there anything that you need?"

"No, Mister Devane, nothing. We're all set here, right, Marcia?"

Marcia laughed. "I could get used to this, Jim. Better get her out of here before I get spoiled."

Devane smiled sadly. "If anyone ever deserved spoiling, darling, you're the one." He bent over her and kissed her forehead.

"I'm going to get Marcia ready for bed now," Dale said.

"That's redundant," Marcia said, "I'm already in bed," and she gave a laugh that broke up into coughing.

Devane slipped out of the room as Dale gave Marcia a drink of water. He crossed to his study and went back to staring at the telephone.

+++

On the street outside, the green Packard had been switched for a red Pontiac roadster. Inside it, a man in a rumpled suit and a grey fedora lit a cigarette. The flare of the match showed his features for a few seconds. Heavy brows, a lantern jaw, and a blunt nose: Jimmy Connors.

The Purple Scar also noted that the lock button on Connors' door was up. He crouched beside the car and on his haunches, came to the driver's side of the Buick. His gloved hand closed on the handle, and he pulled.

What happened next was almost too fast to follow. The Scar yanked the door open with one hand and caught Connors by his collar and threw him to the ground with the other. A short punch to the private eye's jaw made his cigarette explode into a shower of orange sparks. A second punch put him out cold. The Scar put Connors behind the wheel, pulled the brim of his hat over his eyes, and quietly closed the door.

Lights were on in both floors of Devane's house, no movement in the windows. No word from Dale, so Devane hadn't gotten his follow-up call. It would come. He crossed the street, staying in the shadows, and slipped around the rear of the house where a rose trellis afforded an easy access to a second floor window.

+++

Devane sat in an armchair in his study, head in his hands. The supper tray was still untouched. He was bone weary; his eyes felt as if he'd rubbed ground glass into them, and his head ached. Mrs. Sullivan was gone for the night, and no sound came from Marcia's room.

He'd poured himself a stiff scotch and debated the wisdom of drinking it. Yes finally won the argument. He reached for the glass when a low rasping voice said, "Better not. You'll need a clear head."

Devane turned to see a face from a nightmare; features twisted and burned into a mass of violet tissue that humped and bulged like a granite crag. He opened his mouth to cry out, but the Purple Scar's hand shot out and clamped it shut. "I was sent by Miles Murdock," he said in a hoarse stage whisper. "Don't cry out. No one else can know I'm here. Do you understand?"

Devane nodded and the Scar took his hand away. "Do you know who I am?"

"Yes. I've heard of you. When Miles said he'd send his friend, I didn't expect the Purple Scar."

"Doctor Murdock and I have been a mutual benefit to each other from time to time. Have you gotten your second call?"

Devane shook his head. "No. Not yet."

"I have no doubt it will come. When it does, record it. As soon as you hang up, tell Nurse Jordan, and she'll report to me. Do you want to clear yourself?"

Devane gave one curt nod. "Of course I do."

"You'll have to help me."

"Whatever it takes."

"I hope you mean that. These are dangerous people you're dealing with, and it may put you at some risk."

"What do I have to do?"

"Whatever the caller asks, play along, cooperate."

"All right. I'll do what you say, but I won't put Marcia in any danger."

"Nurse Jordan is quite capable and will be with her every minute. Even though you may not see me, I'll have your back. My word on it. You have a gun," a statement, not a question.

"Yes." Devane patted his trouser pocket.

"Keep it handy." The Purple Scar listened at the door for a moment, opened it, and slipped into the hallway, closing it behind him.

Devane stared after him. Could things get any stranger?

Outside, the Purple Scar dropped to the grass from the trellis and carefully picked his way across the darkened garden to crouch behind a thick arbor vitae that concealed him but also afforded a view of the rear of Devane's house.

The downstairs was dark and only a few dim lights showed from the second floor. Nothing to do now but wait.

The phone rang, waking Devane from his doze in the chair. He caught the call on the second ring and hoped it didn't wake Marcia. "This is Devane."

There was a long silence and then the caller spoke. "Good evening, Jimmy Boy. I hope you t'ought about what I said last night."

"I haven't thought about anything else." Devane suddenly realized he hadn't pushed the button to record the call. He thought fast and said,

"Hold on. I have to shut the door." He set down the phone and pushed the red button on the recorder. He picked up the phone again. "Like I said, I haven't thought about much else but your offer, if it is an offer."

"Could be. But it ain't sometin' to gab about on the squawk box, if you get my drift. Somebody wants to meet you eyeball to eyeball. Then maybe an offer will be fortcomin'."

"When do you want to meet?"

"Now."

"Well, I can't leave my wife alone. She's very ill."

A muffled laugh. "Come on, Jimmy, don't try to snow me. I know that pretty young nurse is there tonight. Unless she flew up the chimney when we weren't looking. Put on your coat and walk out your front door in ten minutes."

"All right. Ten minutes."

"And in case you got ideas about calling anybody – "

The line went dead. Devane rattled the hook a dozen times. No dial tone. The line had been cut.

He crossed the hall to Marcia's room where Dale was waiting with a small leather case in her lap. She put a finger to her lips and tilted her head toward Marcia, who was snoring softly. She gestured toward the hall, and she and Devane tiptoed from the room and into his study.

Dale unzipped the case and pulled out a small metal box with a telescoping antenna and a pair of dials. She reached behind the desk and pushed the button to stop the recorder. Another button rewound the wire. While it did, Dale turned one of the dials and a low hum came from the device. "PS-1," she said softly into a small grille at the bottom. "This is PS-2. Do you read? Over."

"I read you, PS-2. Over." Devane recognized the rasping voice as the Purple Scar.

"Dale pressed the playback button and held the transmitter beside the speaker. When the playback was finished, the Purple Scar said, "Tell Devane to comply. Over and out." Soft static replaced the voice. Dale looked at Devane and shrugged.

"I guess I'd better get my coat."

+++

Below, the Purple Scar removed his earpiece and tucked the short wave radio into his pocket. Time to move. He circled to the front of the house, staying in the shadows of the trees and shrubs, finally crouching behind a hedgerow. The front door opened, framing Devane's silhouette in pale light. He stepped outside and closed the door behind him. Almost immediately, headlights flashed down the block. A dark Buick sedan rolled up to the curb. Its front and back doors opened simultaneously and a pair of men stepped out. The Purple Scar tried to read the license number but the light over the plate was either burned out or blacked out. No matter; he had a good idea where it was headed.

One of them, the tall one in the front, waved for Devane, who hesitated for a second, then moved down the sidewalk to get into the waiting car. The big man patted Devane down and took his revolver. He said something the Scar couldn't hear and held out his hand. Devane hesitated, shaking his head, and the short man put his pistol behind Devane's ear and cocked the hammer. The Scar was ready to leap from his cover and intervene, but Devane nodded and dropped something into the tall man's hand. The short one took Devane by the elbow and steered him into the back of the Buick.

The Scar raised the muzzle of a small compressed air pistol and aimed carefully, timing his shot to cover the sound with the closing of the door, he squeezed the trigger and fired a wax pellet filled with white paint to mark the car for certain identification. The pellet struck the car just below its right tail light, leaving a small spatter like the droppings of a bird.

Instead of getting in himself, the tall man stood by as the Buick rolled away. He took a last drag on his cigarette and blew a lungful of smoke into the night air, then started up the sidewalk. His job was to watch the wife – leverage, the boss always called it. Maybe he'd have some fun with that pretty young nurse while he was waiting. He turned the key in the front door lock and the door swung inward. He stepped into the foyer and closed the door behind him.

A radio was playing upstairs; a torch singer was breathlessly crooning "Someone to Watch Over Me." He dropped his cigarette on the floor and crushed it under his heel. He climbed the stairs without worry. The music would cover a creaking board or a heel tap. On the second floor, he saw the rectangle of light from an open door, the sickroom. There was still carpet on this hallway, so his steps made no sound as he approached the light.

He entered the doorway and saw Marcia, her head turned into the pillow, snoring softly. The nurse was sitting in an armchair reading a magazine. He stepped into the room and said with a wolfish grin, "Hello, there, beautiful."

"Hello, there, yourself." The nurse smiled and dropped the magazine, and the tall man saw the muzzle of a .38 pointed at his nose. His hand darted for his own piece but a steel grip stopped him. A gravelly voice hissed in his ear. "Move and you're dead." The hand spun him around, and he found himself staring into a twisted nightmare of a face.

The Purple Scar kicked the thug's feet from under him and he thudded to the floor. The Scar sat on his chest, pinning the thug's arms with his legs.

Dale was out of her chair holding her pistol on the intruder, but he didn't notice. His eyes were fixed on the hideous face hovering over him.

"Now," the Purple Scar rumbled, "First things first. I know you. You're Vince Cataldo. You work for Marty Holbein, don't you?"

Vince sneered. "I ain't telling you a thing." It was pure bravado; The Purple Scar could hear the tremor in his voice and feel his muscles twitching.

"And I'll bet you know who I am, don't you?" The Scar said. No answer. "And you will tell me what I want to know." He reached into his coat and pulled out a small brown glass bottle. He pulled the cork with his teeth and spat it away. He poured a few drops into his palm. Then he produced a second bottle, and poured a little onto the first liquid.

The solution bubbled, fizzed and foamed. "Nasty stuff." The Scar poured the first bottle over Vince's face.

"My eyes! It burns! You bastard!"

"Not like it'll burn when I pour the second bottle on you. It'll boil your face right off and leave it looking like mine when it's done, unless you start talking."

The Scar tipped the second bottle and the few drops that escaped fell on Vince's cheek and began to sputter and fizz. He poured a line across the crook's forehead.

"Aaugh! All right! I'll talk!" Vince began sobbing.

"Where are your friends taking Devane?"

"To the warehouse."

"What warehouse?"

"Central Shipping. By the docks."

"And it's Marty Holbein behind this."

"Yes, yes," Cataldo sobbed. "Please don't burn me no more."

"We'll just put you out of your misery."

Before Vince could move, Dale plunged a hypodermic needle into the hollow of his collarbone, his eyes rolled back, and he went limp.

The Purple Scar stood up and tossed the second bottle aside. He turned to the horrified Marcia. "The first bottle was vinegar extract." he said. "It stung just enough to be convincing. The second bottle was a solution including enough capsicum pepper to make it sting and bicarbonate of soda to make it bubble and foam."

The Purple Scar rolled Vince onto his stomach and tied his hands and feet. "I'm going now."

"Should I call the police?" Dale said.

"Wait." His voice told the women there was no arguing the point.

Dale pulled the miniature radio from the pocket of her uniform. "If anything else happens, I'll call you."

"Keep the frequency open. If I hadn't called to warn you about him," the Scar prodded Vince with his toe of his shoe, "who knows what might have happened." Without another word, he slipped out the door, down the stairs, and into the street, heading for his car.

In the back of the Buick, Devane rode between the short man and a heavy set thug who wore a waist-length jacket and a newsboy hat. He uncrossed his arms to reveal an automatic pointed at Devane's midsection. His crooked jaw grinned at Devane, a gap toothed smile that belied his dead, cold eyes. He said through his grin, his mouth barely moving, "I t'ought you'd be taller."

"It was you on the phone?"

"Inna flesh, Jimmy Boy."

"What's your name?"

"Otto," he said with a chuckle. "As in Otto-matic."

Mike and the other hood, whose name was Marco laughed at the joke. Devane tried to laugh with them, but it didn't work.

They haven't blindfolded me or put a hood over my head, Devane thought. They don't care if I see their faces or if I know where they're taking me. Does that mean they're going to kill me when this is over? A cold bead of sweat ran down his temple into his collar.

Mike, Holbein's wheel man, turned on the radio. It hummed and crackled as it warmed up, and the thug turned the tuner dial to a station playing big band. Bing Crosby crooned "Lady Be Good," and Devane recalled dancing to the song with Marcia on one of the last occasions she was well enough to go out. Now he was dancing with the Devil, and he prayed that the Purple Scar was good for his word.

The Buick pulled up to the warehouse and Mike flashed the code with its headlights. The hoods were making no secret of anything they did. The short man tugged at the door handle. "Out." Otto prodded Devane in the ribs with his pistol. Devane stepped out of the car and followed Marco through the open door of the building, Otto close behind.

The warehouse was dimly lit by floodlights in the open trusses overhead. Crates and bales were stacked in rows three and four high, leaving narrow paths between them barely wide enough for a hand cart to pass through. At the end opposite the entrance, Devane saw a flight of stairs leading up to a closed-in office tucked into a corner of the ceiling. At the top of the stairs, Marco knocked at the door. In a moment it swung inward.

Marty Holbein sat at his desk, palms flat on its scarred surface in a pinstriped suit this time. His lip was pulled back around a thin cheroot, the glimpse of teeth giving him a sneering look. He eyed Devane up and down then said around his cigar, "Get Mister Devane a chair." Marco roughly rolled a wheeled desk chair into the backs of Devane's knees and Devane sat in it awkwardly. Marco rolled the chair forward so that Devane's knees banged into the front of the desk.

"My name is Marty Holbein," the gangster said. "Ever heard of me?"

Devane nodded. "I've seen the name in the papers."

"Then you have an idea what I do but nobody can prove." He chuckled. "Well, Mister Devane, I bet you're wondering why you're here."

Outside the warehouse, the Purple Scar crept behind the Buick. He shielded the glare from his pocket torch and flashed a thin beam on the rear fender. The spatter of white paint identified the car. The driver was sitting behind the wheel smoking a cigarette. The window was down and his elbow rested on the sill. Music drifted through the open window.

The Purple Scar pulled a blackjack from his coat pocket and eased along

"…Marty Holstein. Ever heard of me?"

the driver's side of the sedan until he was just behind the driver's door. When he was within reach, he drew his right arm across his chest for a backhand swing. He clamped a hard grip on Mike's elbow and yanked him halfway through the window. Before he could cry out, the Scar sapped him between his eyes and he slumped back into the car. The Purple Scar reached inside and took Mike's watch, his wallet and a revolver from his holster. If Holbein's people found him, he'd look like the careless victim of a mugger.

The doors to the warehouse were closed and surely locked, so the Purple Scar slipped through the shadows around the side where a standpipe rose to the roof. Climbing it was an easy task, and soon, the Scar found himself peering down through a grimy skylight into Marty Holbein's office. The gangster was leaning forward in his chair, his fingertips steepled under his chin.

Jim Devane was alive, and looked as if he were still in control of himself. The Scar could hear a little of the conversation, enough to understand what was going on, and what they wanted Devane to do. He could drop through the skylight at that moment and take Holbein and his cronies down, but Devane could die in the fight. Too many bullets, too small a space. Instead, he took a stethoscope from his pocket and pressed the bell to the glass.

"The man on the phone said you could help me with my 'problem.'"

"That's right. You do have a little dilemma at the office, don't you, Jimbo? It so happens that I can make that little problem go away."

Beads of sweat ran down Devane's spine. "You can? How?"

"A word in the right ear, a few bucks in the right pocket, and the cops will conveniently find the missing eight grand in the mattress of a member of the local – shall we say – criminal community. A few safecracker tools in his closet, and case closed," he took the cigar from his teeth and poked it toward Devane as if he were throwing a dart, "and you, my friend, will be in the clear."

No matter how frightened he was, Devane knew he had to brazen it out. "And for this to happen, what would I have to do?"

"'Would?' Not 'will have to' do?" Holbein's eyes went as flat as a cobra's. "You're talking as if you have a choice. People say no to me once. There's no second chance. Billvane just landed a Navy contract, or did I hear wrong? Some kind of fancy guidance system for torpedoes?"

Devane blinked. "How did you find out about that?"

Holbein waved his hand in a dismissive gesture. "Top Secret don't mean a thing to a man with money." Holbein tapped an ash into the ashtray beside him as if he were discussing the weather. He studied the tip of his cigar. "You have the plans for the prototype. I meet all kinds of people on the docks. I figure I'll find some folks who'll pay plenty for them."

Devane's eyes widened. "You mean sell them to some foreign power?"

"Bright boy. Don't matter who buys them. There's war brewing in Europe. Somebody'll pay good money. But that doesn't make any difference to you, now does it? You do your part for me, and I do my part for you. You get me the plans, and wifey'll get that special treatment at the clinic in Troy. That Doc up there is all set to roll her in. Just waiting for the cash."

"You contacted Doctor Katzmier?"

Holbein ignored the question. He put his cigar in the ashtray. "So, the plans. I figure they're stashed somewhere in your office, or Billings'."

"They're in the payroll vault and my partner changed the combination. I don't know what the new one is."

"They weren't in the payroll vault when my boys were there before, and I figure you must have another safe or some other kind of hidey hole in your building for the top secret stuff."

The Purple Scar said to play along. Devane's mind raced. "Unless Billings moved them, I know where the plans were."

"Oh, not in the vault, huh?" Holbein grinned like a fox at a rabbit. "You really need to be straight up with me, Jimmy boy."

Devane shook his head. "No, not in the vault. In Billings' office there's a panel behind his desk that slides away and there's a smaller safe in there for company papers. But if Billings changed the combination to one safe, I'm sure he's changed them both."

"Opening the safe isn't a problem. We just need you to take us to it."

Devane loked at his shoes, counted silently to three, and said, "All right. I'll show you where it is. When do you expect me to do this?"

"No better time than now."

Overhead the Purple Scar could hear most of the conversation. Below him, the office door opened and a small man with rimless glasses stepped into the office. The Scar strained his ears and heard the name Sonny.

The little man stood beside Devane's chair.

Holbein grinned. "Jimmy Boy, meet the key to every lock." The gangster pushed the telephone across his desk. "And you, Jimmy boy. You phone home."

The Purple Scar pulled the transmitter from his pocket and called Dale.

She answered immediately. "Devane's calling the house right now. Answer and say this to him..."

+++

Devane blinked. "What?"

Holbein's grin flattened like a magic trick. "I said call your house."

"Why?"

"You'll understand in a minute. Just do it."

Devane dialed his home number, his finger slipping on the dial the first try and having to start again. The phone buzzed in his ear as it rang in his study. Six times, seven. A click as the handset lifted from the cradle. Silence.

"Hello? Hello?" Devane said. "Is anyone there?" A pause. His eyes widened. "Who are you? What are you doing in my house?"

Devane listened, his mouth working but no words coming out. He took the handset away from his ear and stared at it as if it were a live snake. He stared at Holbein. "You're holding Marcia hostage."

Holbein's grin returned. "A little insurance policy. Now, Jimbo, tell Sonny here about that hidden safe."

This was the chance the Purple Scar needed. An automatic in either hand, he crashed through the skylight, showering the men below with a cascade of broken glass. He fired while he was still falling, hitting Marco and Otto, a bullet each. Both fell to the floor. Neither got up.

He landed on the gangster's desk and rolled to the floor beside Sonny. He grabbed the safecracker around the waist and threw him into Devane's lap shouting, "Hold him!" hoping Marmont would shield Devane from any gunfire.

Holbein pulled a revolver and snapped off two shots. One went through the Scar's shoulder with a blaze of pain. Behind him, someone cried out, but he couldn't look to see who it was. He grabbed the edge of the heavy desk and flipped it upward, knocking Holbein backward in his chair and pinning him to the floor. Holbein fired blindly in his rage and wasted his last bullets.

Footsteps thundered up the stairs. "Boss! Boss! Are you all right?"

"Help me!" Holbein shouted.

The doorknob rattled. It was locked. A shoulder thumped against the door.

The Purple Scar wasted no time. His automatic boomed as he fired three shots in a triangle through the office door and heard a scream and a body tumbling down the stairs.

Under the desk, Holbein wriggled desperately trying to free himself. There was an automatic in the desk drawer, but it was pressed tight against his chest and wouldn't open. Then he turned his head and saw Otto's pistol on the floor among the shards of the broken skylight. His fingers closed on the grips as the Purple Scar rounded the desk. Holbein swung the pistol to fire at him, but before he could pull the trigger, a single shot from the Purple Scar's automatic put a hole through his forehead.

Devane looked as if he might faint any second as Sonny's blood ran down his trouser leg. The little safecracker's head slumped forward on his chest. His breathing was shallow. The Scar yanked the safecracker from Devane's lap and threw him to the floor.

Sudden silence. Smoke from the gunfire drifted upward through the broken skylight. The Purple Scar picked up the telephone that had spilled from the upset desk and handed it to Devane.

"Call the police. And an ambulance for him." He started for the office door. "I can't be here when they arrive."

"What do I tell them?"

"That you were abducted by Holbein's men and brought here. Tell them about the blackmail plot, and say in the middle of it all, I broke in and these men were killed in the gunfight. Don't mention my involvement with you."

"I'll do what you say, but I—"

The Purple Scar raised his pistol. "Sorry to do this." He pulled the trigger. The bullet grazed Devane's arm, and he felt blood seeping through the sleeve of his shirt. He bent double in the chair, clutching his wounded arm. When he looked up, the Purple Scar was gone.

Dan Griffin arrived on the heels of a wagon full of uniforms. In the office, they found four dead men and two wounded. One of them lay on the floor. The other sat in a chair, his shirt sleeve torn off and wrapped around his upper arm in a form of crude triage performed by one of the officers.

"Who is he?" Griffin asked one of the uniforms.

The officer pulled his notebook from his pocket and flipped a page or two, "Name's James Devane."

"Why am I not surprised?" Griffin crouched in front of the injured man, who looked him in the eye. "I'm Captain Griffin. I'll bet you've got quite a story to tell me," Griffin said.

Devane, teetering on the edge of shock, nodded. "Yes. But first I have to call my wife and let her know that I'm all right." He nodded to the two uniforms who were first on the scene. "They wouldn't let me."

Griffin nodded. "Let him have the phone." One of the cops handed Devane the telephone. He dialed his number, and in a moment, Dale's voice came over the line. "Hello?"

"It's Jim," he said. "Is Marcia all right?"

"Yes, she's fine," Dale reassured him. "You played your part well." When he had called home, The Purple Scar had already told her what to say to Devane, that the threat to Marcia was neutralized and to pretend he was frightened. Devane didn't have to pretend. "I'll take the phone in to her."

Devane waited and he heard the rustle as the phone was handed to someone else. The rough voice chilled his blood. "Do as I told you and all will be well." Another rustle, and Marcia said, "Jim, are you all right?"

"Yes, honey, I'm okay. A little banged up, but I'll be fine."

Griffin gave him a stern look that said, "Okay, that's enough. Hang up the phone."

"I'll be home in a few hours. Love you too." He put the hand set in the cradle. "Thank you, Captain."

Griffin opened his leather bound notebook and licked the tip of his pencil. "Now, Mister Devane, from the beginning . . . ."

Dale carried the telephone back to the study where Miles sat in a chair stripped to the waist holding a gauze pad to his shoulder. He removed it and looked to his wound. His mask lay beside him on Devane's desk.

"You're lucky, Miles. An inch lower and it would have probably broken your collarbone. This whole episode may have turned out differently."

"If you'll tape a fresh pad on for me, I'll get dressed and take our friend Vince somewhere the police will find him. How is he?"

"Still asleep, and when he wakes up, he won't remember anything about last night."

"Or the last two or three days. The dose you gave him was a hefty one."

"I washed his face clean, and there's not a mark on him."

"Whatever story he tells the police won't make any sense."

"When will Jim come home? Marcia is anxious."

"Soon, I'm sure. Griffin has no reason to hold him."

When Devane was finished, Griffin had filled a dozen pages with details of theft, blackmail, and abduction at the hands of the Holbein gang and rescue at the hands of the Purple Scar, who had apparently been following Holbein's machinations closely and broke in at an opportune moment.

"Who shot you, Mister Devane?"

Devane shrugged."Captain Griffin, there were so many guns going off from so many directions, I don't know."

"But you definitely saw the Purple Scar."

Devane nodded. "One of Holbein's men shouted, 'Holy Hell, it's the Purple Scar,' so I suppose that's who it was. He had a face right out of a horror movie."

Griffin took in a long breath and let it out. He was sure there were things that Devane wasn't telling him, but he'd let it go for now. "All right, Mister Devane, that will do for now, but you will have to come to the station to sign a formal statement later. One of the officers will drive you to the Emergency Room to see to your wound now then take you home."

"Captain?"

"Yeah?"

"I'm lucky, aren't I?"

"Very. My guess is that once Holbein had what he wanted, you'd be a loose end, and you'd be a dead one. You're lucky the Purple Scar came along when he did."

Devane looked as if he might have one more thing to say, but if so, he didn't say it.

The next afternoon, Miles went to the Precinct. Two men in suits were leaving Dan Griffin's office as he came down the hall. Miles' practiced eye noted that both were carrying under their coats. He rapped at the door frame of Griffin's office. The Captain was poring over his notes from Devane's testimony. He said without looking up, "I figured you'd be here soon. Come in and shut the door."

Miles closed the door behind him and took a seat in one of the chairs facing Griffin's desk.

Griffin stared at Miles for a good minute before speaking. He threw a pair of handcuffs on the desk blotter. "Give me a good reason to not put those on you right now. Or for that matter, on James Devane for complicity."

Miles' stare never wavered. "Justice."

Griffin's lip curled back. "That's rich."

"So Holbein was innocent? I heard he was blackmailing Devane to steal military secrets."

"Who told you that?" Griffin said, his voice dripping with sarcasm. "The Purple Scar?"

Miles shook his head. "Jim Devane told me. I was at his house this morning. I'm treating his wife."

"And then there's the little matter of Vince Cataldo, one of Holbein's torpedoes. He was found wandering around in a daze down by the docks babbling about being disfigured by – guess who – and there's not a mark on him. What happened to share and share alike, Miles? When were you going to tell me about all this?"

Miles shrugged and winced at the pain in his shoulder. "My thirty-six hours weren't up."

Griffin rolled his eyes.

"Dan, the Purple Scar was following a lead, and that's where it took him."

Griffin was obviously counting to ten. "If getting rid of Holbein didn't constitute a public service . . . ."

"There's more to it, isn't there, Dan?"

Griffin snorted. "You saw those two vests who were leaving when you came?"

Miles nodded.

"FBI. They're on their way to see Devane right now. We're all being sworn to secrecy about the incident; National Security and all that claptrap. So, I couldn't use those..." he pointed to the cuffs – "if I wanted to. Might as well put them on myself."

"The good guys won, Dan. Devane is exonerated. You're rid of Holbein, his crew, and that safecracker, Sonny Marmont you've been angling to nab for a long time."

"About him; Marmont's likely going to pull through. He'll do some time for sure, but if he cooperates with us, maybe he won't do so much. Trouble is his daughter Julia; she has polio. Seems Marmont spent most of the cash he stole on her care and treatment. The wife's dead, so the kid'll probably become a ward of the state, go into an orphanage, and there goes her care. Who knows what will happen to her."

"Maybe I can help. After all, I have a clinic, I have connections in the medical world, and I have money."

Griffin picked up the cuffs, threw them in his desk drawer, and nudged it shut. "And that's the reason I needed."

Miles left the Precinct Building and drove across town to Hunter's Knob. He stood on Devane's porch shivering in the cold. The weight of his topcoat made his shoulder ache, and he was beginning to wonder which was worse.

Mrs. Sullivan answered the door, as imperious as ever. "Oh, it's you, the doctor," she said, and stepped aside to let him enter. "Himself is occupied at the moment, but I'll tell him you're here." She ponderously huffed up the staircase, her backside swaying with the effort.

Dale came from the kitchen with a tray of sandwiches and a carafe of coffee. She smiled when she saw Miles.

"Shouldn't Mrs. Sullivan be doing that?"

"She was about to take the tray up when you rang the bell." Dale lowered her voice. "Two men with badges came a little while ago, and they're in Jim's study with him. I heard one of them say they were from the FBI."

Miles nodded. "They're making the rounds today."

A door opened upstairs and Miles heard voices. In a moment, Devane and the two agents Miles has seen earlier came to the top of the stairs.

"We may need to speak with you again, Mister Devane," one of them said.

"I'll be happy to cooperate with you gentlemen."

They descended the stairs and one of the agents eyed Miles. "Who is this man?"

"This is Doctor Miles Murdock, my wife's physician, and this is Miss Dale Jordan, her nurse."

Miles extended his hand to shake with the agent, but it was ignored. The man continued to study Miles' face. "I've seen you, and recently. I just can't say where."

"Don't mind Evans," the other agent said, shaking Miles' hand. "I'm agent Burns." He turned to Devane, "We'll be in touch with you." The men put on their hats, crossed the foyer, and left.

Devane heaved a sigh of relief. "Am I glad that's over. They want to depose me in detail about the abduction and the blackmail. But for the moment, they made me sign a paper that said under penalty of law, I was forbidden to discuss anything that happened last night."

"And you did sign, of course."

He nodded. "They said I'll be hearing from Naval Intelligence as well. I hope Billvane doesn't lose the contract."

"I hope so too. How is Marcia today?"

"Actually, she's pretty good," Dale said. "I think the excitement perked her up a little. Jim explained the situation to her, but she seemed to have figured most of it out on her own."

"And I have other news." Devane smiled a little. "Jed Billings called a while ago. He was very apologetic. Apparently the FBI men visited him early this morning and told him the story. There's one thing I still don't get."

"What's that?" Miles said.

"Why did the Purple Scar shoot me?"

"When he told me the story, I asked him the same question, Jim. He said that with all those bullets flying around, if you were the only person who didn't get hit, it would have looked fishy. This way, you were a casualty along with everyone else."

"I see." He rubbed his arm with a rueful expression. "But it still hurts like hell."

Not as much as my shoulder, Miles thought. "I'll take a look at it if you like."

"Not necessary. Dale changed the dressing for me a few hours ago. Go on up. Marcia's waiting for you. I'll be along in a minute." He headed for the kitchen.

Upstairs, Devane joined them at Marcia's bedside. Miles was putting away his stethoscope. "I have some news myself. I spoke with Doctor Katzmier this morning, and I've persuaded him to admit Marcia to his clinic as an experimental patient at no cost to you."

"Oh, Miles," Marcia said. "That's unbelievable."

"Believe it," Dale said. "Sometimes Doctor Murdock works miracles." Especially where money is involved, she thought.

"Miles, I don't know what to say," Devane stammered.

"Say yes."

The men left the room, and Marcia called Dale to her bedside. "It's him isn't it?"

Dale blinked. "What?"

"I wasn't really asleep last night when that awful man – Vince? was that his name? – came in here. I saw the look you gave the Purple Scar; it was the same one you gave Miles earlier."

"I –"

"Don't worry, dear." Marcia patted her hand and smiled coyly. "We girls all have our secrets, and yours is safe with me." She made an X over her heart with her forefinger, closed her eyes, and promptly went to sleep.

As they drove away, Miles said, "I really wasn't happy putting you at risk, Dale, but I knew you'd come through. Did you enjoy your little adventure?"

"I liked it a lot, Miles. Maybe now you won't be so hesitant to use me next time."

"Next time?"

She smiled and took his hand in hers. "Yes. Next time."

THE END

THE FUN OF ANTHOLOGIES

My introduction to The Purple Scar was a request from Ron to proofread an anthology of Purple Scar stories for Airship 27. I found that the old-time pulp crime fighter was being treated very well by several contemporary writers.

Part of the fun of reading a multi-author anthology is the shading of difference between one author's concept of a character and another's. Unlike contemporary canonical Sherlock Holmes stories in which the authors strain to leave not one button undone on the character, the Purple Scar's scriveners let us see the character from a variety of angles, as H.G. Wells said of the Time Traveler, to see "all around him."

I thought it would be interesting to let the Purple Scar use his skills, his wits, and his contacts to do something a little more personal than the public good. Too many superheroes and secret sleuths live in a kind of bubble on the page. Those with a Clark Kent identity never seem to have friends or even acquaintances outside their small crime fighting circle.

With that in mind, I gave Miles Murdock a friend with a problem; two actually. The result is "The Blackmail Heist" in which Miles uses both his medical persona and that of the Purple Scar to help a friend in distress and along the way, catch a few crooks and keep America safe for Democracy.

It's always fun to participate in one of Airship 27's anthologies and then when it's published, read it and compare notes with what my fellow contributors have done. I'm looking forward to this anthology, and I'm sure I won't be disappointed.

Visit my website: http://drphreddee.com

FRED ADAMS, JR. is a retired Penn State University English Professor who spends his days writing pulp fiction and his nights working as a singer-songwriter. His Sam Dunne novel *Dead Man's Melody* was nominated as Pulp Novel of the Year in 2017's Pulp Factory Awards, and his Smith Brothers novel *The Eye of Quang-Chi* was nominated for the same award in 2018. His titles include *Hitwolf* 1 and 2, *Six Gun Terrors* vols. 1, 2, and

3, and *C.O. Jones: Mobsters and Monsters, Skinners,* and *The Damned and the Doomed*. His original Sherlock Holmes anthology *The Affair of the Chronic Argonaut* was recently published by Pro Se Press. Forthcoming titles from Airship 27 include *C.O. Jones: Home Front, Six Gun Terrors 4: The Town Killers*, a Sam Dunne Mystery, *Blood is the New Black*, and *Holster Full of Death*, a Dead Sheriff novel. He lives in Mount Pleasant, Pennsylvania in "perpetual terror of boredom."

Visit Fred's website at http://drphreddee.com/author